"Momma!"

The baby reached out and grabbed Allison's sleeve.

Allison stopped. The kid had an iron grip on her shirt, and if she kept moving, she was liable to pull the poor little thing right out of the shopping cart. "Momma," the child cooed again.

Unable to resist, Allie slid her hands under the baby's arms. She didn't lift, though, and the little one frowned.

"No, honey, I'm not your mommy." Allie turned apologetically to the father. He probably wouldn't appreciate a stranger touching his child.

"I'm sorry," the father said. "She does that with every woman who looks the least bit like her mother did."

"Did?" Allie repeated.

He touched the child's head tenderly. "Her mother was my twin sister. Now it's just the kid and me. We're going to make it, though, right, Laurel?" He smiled sadly at Allie as he turned to go.

"Good luck," Allie said softly. Laurel stared up at her, tiny chin quivering. But she didn't cry as her uncle pushed the cart away, leaving Allie standing alone, unaware of the large tear that rolled slowly down her cheek.

Dear Reader,

Four more fabulous WOMEN WHO DARE are heading your way!

In May, you'll thrill to the time-travel tale Lynn Erickson spins in *Paradox*. When loan executive Emily Jacoby is catapulted back in time during a train wreck, she is thoroughly unnerved by the fate that awaits her. In 1893, Colorado is a harsh and rugged land. Women's rights have yet to be invented, and Will Dutcher, Emily's reluctant host, is making her question her desire to return to her own time.

In June, you'll be reminded that courage can strike at any age. Our heroine in Peg Sutherland's *Late Bloomer* discovers unplumbed depths at the age of forty. After a lifetime of living for others, she realizes that she wants something for herself—college, a career, a *life*. But when a mysterious stranger drifts into town, she discovers to her shock that she also wants *him!*

Sharon Brondos introduces us to spunky Allison Ford in our July WOMEN WHO DARE title, *The Marriage Ticket*. Allison stands up for what she believes in. And she believes in playing fair. Unfortunately, some of her community's leaders don't have the same scruples, and going head-to-head with them lands her in serious trouble.

You'll never forget Leah Temple, the heroine of August's *Another Woman*, by Margot Dalton. This riveting tale of a wife with her husband's murder on her mind will hold you spellbound...and surprised! Don't miss it!

Some of your favorite Superromance authors have also contributed to our spring and summer lineup. Look for books by Pamela Bauer, Debbi Bedford, Dawn Stewardson, Jane Silverwood, Sally Garrett, Bobby Hutchinson and Judith Arnold ... to name just a few! Some wonderful Superromance reading awaits you!

Marsha Zinberg
Senior Editor

P.S. Don't forget that you can write to your favorite author

       c/oHarlequin Reader Service,
       P.O. Box 1297
       Buffalo, New York
       14240 U.S.A.

Sharon
Brondos

THE MARRIAGE TICKET

Harlequin Books

TORONTO • NEW YORK • LONDON
AMSTERDAM • PARIS • SYDNEY • HAMBURG
STOCKHOLM • ATHENS • TOKYO • MILAN
MADRID • WARSAW • BUDAPEST • AUCKLAND

Published July 1993

ISBN 0-373-70554-9

THE MARRIAGE TICKET

ABOUT THE AUTHOR

Sharon Brondos has written eleven Superromance novels and has a loyal readership that looks for the wit, humor and down-to-earth stories that have become the Wyoming author's trademark. In *The Marriage Ticket*, she explores the options available to a single mother with a penchant for good deeds and a household consisting of twin children and a passel of pets.

Readers might also like to know that by the time this book comes out, Sharon will have been to Washington to celebrate the inauguration of the new president. Should be wonderful grist for the writer's mill.

Books by Sharon Brondos

HARLEQUIN SUPERROMANCE

266—SEARCH FOR THE RAINBOW
328—SPECIAL TOUCHES
353—SPECIAL TREASURES
459—A PLACE TO LAND
505—EAST OF THE MOON
527—SOUTHERN REASON, WESTERN RHYME

HARLEQUIN CRYSTAL CREEK

4—WHITE LIGHTNING

Dedicated as a birthday present and a promise
to Nick Murdock:
friend and fellow lover of a good book.
Nick, you are also the best Storyteller,
in the ancient tradition, I've ever known.
Thanks for the inspriation for M.J. Nichols!

CHAPTER ONE

ALLISON FORD slowed her shopping cart to a crawl, matching the snail's pace of the cart in front of her. Safeway wasn't crowded this early in the day. It was summertime and housewife shoppers weren't trying to work around school hours. She could have quite easily moved faster. She smiled at her unusual behavior.

Ordinarily, she raced through the grocery store, attempting each time to beat her record from the previous time. She hated grocery shopping with the kind of passion only those who had done it with regular, unavoidable, mind-numbing regularity could appreciate. It was a necessary, but boring part of life. Today, however, she found herself intrigued by the man and child using the cart ahead of her. They were quite a pair.

The child was just a baby, really. Barely two, Allie figured. A blond-haired, blue-eyed Kewpie of a kid. Hard to tell what sex. The clothing offered no clues. The outfit, completely mismatched, had obviously been selected without any eye to style. The kid looked as if she/he'd been dressed in whatever had come to hand. The little round face and chubby arms reminded Allie of Sally and Sam at that age. Though, of course, this was only one child, and at that age, her twins had seemed like seven or eight of them all at once.

Allie sighed, her mind hearing the peaceful, lonely silence in her house that would last for another two months—the rest of June, all of July and most of August, while the ten-year-old twins spent their summer vacation with their grandparents in Montana. Lonely, lovely silence...

The kid in the grocery cart was *not* being silent. Allie remembered that kind of behavior only too well. How, when the twins were small, she would push the cart through the aisles, back stiff, shoulders squared, pretending everything was normal, gathering up the food for the week, while her offspring yowled and howled. People had stared then, even as they were staring now at the lone squaller. Sally and Sam had dueted, but even together they'd made less noise than the blond banshee yodeling displeasure at his or her father this morning. From what Allie could tell, the man was taking it all with the patience of a saint. She studied him from behind.

He wasn't dressed like a local. Guys in Linville Springs, Wyoming, rarely wore outfits that made them look like extras in grade-C African safari movies. He was in desert khaki from head to toe. Short-sleeve shirt, tan trousers with a bunch of pockets. Short-topped, desert-style boots, rather than the more familiar cowboy ones. His hat, also not a cowboy-style, more like an Australian outbacker's, was crushed to damp shapelessness in his kid's hands. He had dark blond hair, slightly wavy and just long enough to curl over the collar of his shirt. It looked styled, not just cut. Like the man was maintaining an image of some kind. Odd. And interesting.

Allie couldn't be certain, since she was behind him, but something about the way he carried himself made her think he was probably handsome. There was a confidence and pride in his carriage that was at serious odds with his undignified circumstances.

Or maybe it was the way the women shoppers coming the other way all gave him a double take. At first, she thought the reason for their stares was the screaming kid. Now, she decided it might be the result of a combination of factors, including masculine good looks.

She smiled again as she watched him walk. Some woman was sure lucky to have a husband like that. Not only did he take the kid to the store, but he had a good body and excellent moves. Yeah, some women were lucky in the husband game, she guessed.

Not that it should matter to her. Once in the husband game as a loser, she was out of it for all time. She had sense enough now to know what she was good at and what she wasn't. As a mom, she was apparently okay. The twins were growing up all right. As a wife... well, she'd never had much of a chance with that. Nor was she interested in taking a chance again.

Allie reached for a box of cereal and had put it in her cart before she remembered she needed no cold cereal this week. Without the twin food-vacuums, she could make a box last for a month. Maybe more. Breakfast was not exactly a big meal for her. She'd spent too many years eating it on the run after making certain the children had plenty and were set for daycare or school.

So the cereal wasn't necessary. Bread was. She wouldn't be eating lunch out with clients seeking her financial advice much during the summer months. Soup and a sandwich in front of the computer was her standard fare when she ate at home in her office. She started to move around the man and his child to get to the bread aisle. The baby reached out and grabbed her sleeve. "Mmmaaamma!" she/he screamed.

Allie stopped. The kid had an iron grip on her shirt, and if Allie kept on moving, she was liable to pull the poor little thing right out of the cart. She didn't look at the father, who had also stopped, but at the baby, whose face was suddenly sunny and smiley. "Momma," the child cooed. The other tiny hand grasped her arm, pinching her skin. "Momma!"

Unable to resist, Allie slid her hands under the baby's arms. She didn't lift, though, and the little one frowned. "No, honey," Allie said. "I'm not your momma." She smiled and the child stopped frowning and grinned happily. The small hands released her sleeve. They reached for her embrace. Allie turned a rueful look and an apologetic smile on the father. He probably wouldn't appreciate a stranger touching his child. "Sorry, I..." she began to say, pulling away from the baby. Then the words faded.

The man looked as if he was in the grip of some strong, deep emotion. *Sorrow,* it was sorrow, she realized with a sudden sick feeling that startled her. He cleared his throat and lifted the child in his arms. He handled his burden carefully, but awkwardly. The baby instantly started screaming again.

"No need to apologize," he said, his voice loud enough for her to hear its huskiness over the shrieking. Huskiness and an odd sort of accent. One Allie couldn't place. "She does that with every woman who looks the least bit like her mother did. You've got the same length blond hair, and she's partial to blondes." He patted the little head that was now buried in his shoulder. "Drove me crazy at first. But I'm used to it, now." He kissed the child's fair hair and spoke soothingly to her.

Allie swallowed. She'd apparently stumbled onto a tragedy that was a mirror image of her own. Past tense. The little girl's mother, this man's wife, was dead. Tears stung Allie's eyes. "Would you mind if I did hold her?" she asked, hoping she wasn't intruding on his grief. "Maybe she'd calm down."

The man handed the child over, relief transforming his features. "Thanks," he said. "At this point, I'm willing to try anything. This is our first big grocery outing together. We've been getting along so well, I didn't expect her to act up. She's tolerated the quick trips with no problem, so I figured she'd be fine on a longer one. Maybe a little fussy, but I can deal with that. Never thought it would be like this."

Allie cuddled the baby, who immediately wrapped her arms tightly around Allie's neck. Memory flooded her at the sensation. It had been like that with Sally and Sam. So much need for love! So much she wanted to give... Only, she'd never been able to hold one without the other clamoring for equal attention. She remembered the constant state of exhaustion she had lived in while they were small. She'd had no one to help her. Still, it had been so wonderful to be so needed. She shut her eyes, not caring if the man saw the tears she felt falling down her cheeks.

"I know something of how you must feel," she said. "I lost my husband even before my kids were born."

Her words clearly took him by surprise, and he didn't seem to know how to respond. He smiled, frowned, then smiled again. Sympathy shone in his brown eyes, and the smile was a sad one. "I can't quite trade on your pain, ma'am," he said. "I didn't lose a wife, you see." He touched the baby's hair. "I lost my sister. Laurel's my niece."

"Oh?" Allie felt something stirring in her mind. A vague memory. Some bit of knowledge hovered just out of view.

"Her mother was my sister," the man repeated. "My twin, actually, but now it's just the kid and I. We'll make it, though, won't we, Laurel?"

Laurel turned around in Allie's arms and reached for her uncle. He took her, hugged her for a second, then placed her back in the cart. "Thanks," he said. "I think she's got the crying out of her system now," he added. "I'd better get going while she's in a good mood."

"Good luck," Allie said. Laurel stared up at her, tiny chin quivering. But she didn't cry as her uncle pushed the cart away, leaving Allie standing alone.

She took a deep breath. Only now did it register on her that the man was, indeed, good-looking. Maybe not exactly classically handsome, but definitely interesting. Square chin, firm jawline, smooth tanned skin. Warm brown eyes. Character lines etched lightly in that skin... Odd that she'd noticed all that. She had been so absorbed in emotions, she hadn't even tried to get his name. She knew something about this man, however, she was sure. But she just couldn't remember...

"I see you met our local celebrity, Allie."

The voice startled her. But she recovered her composure almost immediately. June Watson had brought the front of her shopping cart within inches of Allie's heels, and Allie hadn't heard a thing until the woman spoke. "Celebrity?" Allie asked, turning and looking at June.

"Uh-huh." June nodded, waiting. She wasn't a fat woman exactly, but she had a hefty look about her that made her seem oversized. Long ago, Allie decided that came from all the gossip June absorbed. It bloated her like a balloon. She devoured it like candy.

But didn't everyone need a bit of candy, now and then?

"All right, June," she said. "You've got me. I haven't a clue who he is."

June giggled. Her painted-on black eyebrows rose a good inch. She eased closer, lowering her voice. "Not a clue? Well, let me fill you in on..." Her slide into informational mode was cut off by a crash and a yell, followed by a bawl. It was a series of sounds that Allie recognized only too well.

"Whoever he is," she said, "it sounds like he's in trouble. I'll be right back," she added. June seemed rooted to the spot, her mouth forming an O.

The scene that met Allie's gaze when she rounded the corner of the next aisle was no surprise. How many times had she been the one standing guiltily next to a pile of cans or cartons that one or both kids had managed to pull down. Unfortunately for Laurel's uncle, the child had gone for the big-time in grocery disaster. The display she had destroyed was made—*had been made*—of glass jars. Jelly jars.

Laurel's uncle's hat lay in the middle of the glass and goo. The man was staring at the floor, apparently unable to believe what had just happened.

Allie walked up to him and touched his arm. "Don't get upset," she said, when he looked at her. "It happens all the time. Did to me, anyway."

He stared at her now. "I...I just turned away for a second. How could she...?" Behind him, Laurel cooed and giggled. She had jelly smeared on one cheek. "I...I let her have a little taste of the jelly I was buying," he said. "She liked it. I guess she wanted more."

"I guess so." Out of the corner of her eye, Allie saw the store manager approaching. "Look, let me take her while you settle this with Tim."

"Tim?" The man ran his hand over his hair, leaving a smear of jelly in the blond strands. Laurel whooped with laughter.

"Tim Swenson's the store manager," Allie said, lifting the child from the cart. Laurel wrapped her arms tightly around Allie. She felt stickiness on the back of her neck. Laurel wiggled, jamming her knees into Allie's midsection. She gasped and shifted the child's position. "Don't worry," she added. "He's a reasonable guy."

Laurel's uncle looked at her. "You," he said, "are either crazy or a saint, coming to my rescue like this. Thanks, from the bottom of my heart, friend." He smiled and really looked at her, and she realized he was actually seeing her for the first time.

And she was really seeing him. He was not just handsome; he was gorgeous! The smile did it. The gaze that he directed right into her eyes transformed him. For a fraction of a second, she felt a little dizzy.

"Um, excuse me." Tim circled the mess on the floor. "Um, hi, Allie. This guy a friend of yours?"

"It was an accident," Allie said, recovering herself. "Tim, you know you shouldn't put those breakable displays where kids can get their hands on them." Laurel cooed and slapped her little hands on Allie's shoulder, bouncing her knees at the same time. The fabric of her blouse stuck to the child's palms for a second.

"I know." Tim eyed the mess ruefully. "We've got a new display person. He thinks he's some kind of artist."

"I'll pay for this," Laurel's uncle said, reaching for his wallet. "It was my fault for not watching Laurel close enough." He opened the wallet. "How much?"

Allie nearly gasped aloud. He had a wad of bills in his hand, and from the denominations she could see, it was close to a thousand dollars. For grocery shopping? What would he do if he were really on a spending spree?

Tim's brown eyebrows jumped up into his receding hair line. "Put your money away, mister," he said, dropping his voice and looking around to see if anyone else had seen the wad of bills.

"But...?" The man seemed confused.

"I don't want you to pay for the jelly," Tim said. "I was just making sure no one was hurt."

Allie watched the money disappear. The man had a puzzled look on his face. "I ruined all that stuff, and you won't take payment?" he asked, glancing over at her and the baby, then back to Tim. "Why?"

Tim looked uncomfortable. "Store policy. The display was set up wrong."

"But I should have kept my kid under closer control."

"You don't know how," Allie said, unable to keep from blurting out the unvarnished truth. "The two of you were a disaster looking for a place to happen. I could have predicted this. It's just lucky she wasn't hurt."

The man said nothing. He just looked at her. The child said, "Momma," again and gave her a hug. Then she turned and reached for her uncle. "Daddy!" she cried out, smiling.

He took her from Allie. "Look," he said, his tone suddenly chilly. "Thanks to you both, but I can manage on my own. I don't need help, and I don't need my mistakes excused. They're mine, and I'm quite aware of them without having them pointed out to me."

He fumbled in his pocket and pulled out two wadded bills. Pressing them into Tim's hand, he said, "Take this for the jelly and as a down payment for any other disasters we may cause in the future. Don't argue."

He handed Allie another bill. When she started to protest, he said, "This is for dry-cleaning your clothes. Please, let me do this." He gave her a look that ranged somewhere between angry, proud and sorrowful. Then he hefted Laurel onto his lean hip, bent over to pick up his hat from the jelly puddle and maneuvered his cart down the aisle.

No way, Allie thought, could she refuse the money. It would be a direct attack on his dignity. Bad enough she'd shot her mouth off and criticized him. "Okay," she said, mostly to herself, but including Tim. "I can take a hint. He's on his own. I'll stick to my business and keep out of his." She brushed at the back of her blouse. Jelly stains in the form of little handprints dotted the area of her shoulders. "I'm too busy for this, anyway. Now, I've got to run home and change clothes."

Tim laughed, sounding nervous and self-conscious. "I guess you will," he said. "It looks like the kid got a good half jar of jelly on you."

Allie tried to look at her back. "Reminds me of old times," she said. "This blouse is cotton. I don't need to have it dry-cleaned, but I'll have to get some strong stain remover for the wash. It's been a long while since I needed that. At least for my own clothes."

Tim looked down at the money in his hand. "Go ahead and pick up whatever you need. It's on the house." He showed her the hundred dollar bill the stranger had given him.

Allie looked at her bill and gasped, horrified that she, too, held a "century" in her hand. She'd have to figure out some way to give it back, she decided. This was too much money! "I guess it is. You ought to give him grocery credit for at least one of those bills. He didn't break two hundred dollars worth of jelly, for goodness sake."

"I should. But I'm kind of afraid to. You know, a guy like that. You don't want to go around offending him. Think I'll give the money to the Boy Scouts or something. Donate it in his sister's name or something. Maybe the Girl Scouts . . ."

"A guy like what? You know who he is?" Allie felt her curiosity growing. Tim seemed somewhat intimidated by the man. Why? Ordinarily, he'd have joked about the mess. "June indicated he was a celebrity, but I don't recognize him."

"That's because you never buy the gossip tabloids at the checkout counter."

"He's not a movie star, is he?" She was fairly sure of that. Allie went to the movies regularly. It was one way of bringing adventure and romance into her life without any of the risks. Plunk a few dollars down and escape from reality for a while. Her reality. A reality that was simple and clean, uncluttered with dreams like those on the silver screen.

"Nope. He's not an actor. Just one of those guys who go to places nobody in their right mind would think of going." Tim managed to grin and look macho and sheepish at the same time, seemingly proud to be of the same sex as the stranger. "You know, tough guys. Actual, not pretend. Real-life stuff. Risks his life for a living.. He's some kind of professional adventurer."

Allie thought of the emotion he'd shown when he'd mentioned his twin sister and the tender way he had handled his niece. Some tough guy, all right. "Oh," she said.

"He was the guy who pulled off the rescue of that entire movie company a year or so ago. Remember, the bunch of actors and folks that got kidnapped down in South America?"

"No."

"Well, it made the news, let me tell you. The bigwigs at the studio hired him to rescue their people, 'cause the government wouldn't or couldn't. He found 'em all in the middle of the jungle and saved every single person. Since then, he's been a real celebrity out in Hollywood. He's dated a lot of that flashy movie star kind of woman," Tim explained. "That's how come he's been in the tabloids. I guess you don't even look at them when you're waiting in the checkout line." He signaled for a boy with a mop, a bucket and metal dustpan to start cleaning up the jelly mess. "Most folks do," he added.

Allie had no reply for that. She usually spent her time in the line figuring out how her clients could best invest their dollars or, lately, how her own political ambitions could be fulfilled, not reading headlines about Elvis sightings or aliens. But, then, she reasoned, it took all kinds of people to keep a grocery store in business.

"How's your campaign going?" Tim asked, changing the subject. "If you want to put some posters up here, you know you're welcome to do it. Come in and campaign some, talk to folks if you want, too. A lot of us are real happy you're taking on the big politicos. You know that. My wife thinks you're the next best thing to sliced bread, on account of your taking on women's issues specially. She's helped me understand how it'll help all of us for you to be down in Cheyenne next year."

"Thanks. I'm glad to hear that. Campaigning is new for me, so I'm not at all sure how I stand right now." Allie felt grateful the topic had turned back to something she was familiar with.

"But I guess it's going all right," she continued. "Actually, I've got to go back to my office and call my campaign manager. I had a message that he needed to speak to me. So, I'd better get cracking. Thanks for the offer. I'll probably take you up on it, come fall. At least I know enough to realize I'll have to hit it hard closer to election time."

Tim nodded. "Remember, though. I mean it," he said. He was watching the cleanup process with a careful eye. Allie left him, thinking she really ought to hurry on and not give in to her natural tendency to visit with folks. Even handsome, adventurous, mysterious strange folks...

Speaking of which...

June appeared around the corner, her shopping cart filled to the brim. When she saw Allie, her expression turned gleeful. Clearly, she wanted to continue their conversation and find out what had happened with the celebrity and the jelly jars. She also would undoubtedly be more than willing to fill in any gaps in Allie's knowledge file about that particular celebrity. Was it worth it?

No. Allie decided that satisfying her curiosity was not worth the time she would have to spend listening to everything else June had to offer. It could go on for a good while. A while she couldn't afford today.

So, she waved, smiled brightly, then turned tail and ran for the check-out line. Laurel's uncle had stirred her interest, but not all that much. Besides, she'd rubbed him the wrong way with her comments about his inability to care for the little girl. She felt badly about that. She should have known better. As she set her purchases up on the counter at the express lane, she thought back.

How well she remembered resenting even well-meaning criticism. Hadn't she reacted in exactly the same way as Laurel's uncle to helpful comments from friends years ago? You had to respect a person's privacy in grief, *and* their right to make their own mistakes, she believed.

When she got out to the parking lot with the two small bags of groceries, however, she saw he was still there and in trouble. Or rather, in the middle of a new muddle.

Laurel was yelling at the top of her lungs again, and Allie didn't much blame her. He had her strapped into a strange wooden contraption in the back seat of a truly battered old Jeep. Roll bar, but no top. Laurel looked safe enough—the makeshift car seat was likely to withstand an accident better than the vehicle, but the child was not happy about it. Allie knew she ought to pass by without saying a word, but her car was parked right next to his. She couldn't avoid him if she tried.

The man looked up as she came near. "I know what you're thinking about this," he said, his tone sour. "This is just a temporary thing. I'm going to get her a regular car seat," he explained, his tone and expression defensive. "I know her parents had one, but I can't find it."

Allie eyed Laurel. "She looks safe."

"Safe, but not happy."

"Well, isn't that the way it is sometimes for all of us?" Allie tried to sound unconcerned, but the child's cries were tugging hard at her. "Sooner she learns that, the better, isn't it?"

He seemed to be considering that wisdom for a moment. "I'm sorry I snapped at you in there," he said, not looking at her. "I had no right to do that." He patted Laurel's head. She was no longer wailing, but was sobbing softly. "You were just trying to help," he added. "God knows I probably looked like I needed it."

He sounded contrite, unhappy and at a real loss. Allie thought about it all for less than a second. "Get in your Jeep and follow me," she said, setting her groceries on the back seat of her car. She slid onto the driver's seat. "What's your name? I can't go on calling you 'Laurel's uncle,' now can I?"

"Huh?"

She shut the door and leaned out the open window. "I'm going to take you to a store for kiddie gear. If you don't have a decent car seat, it's a good bet you're missing some other things, as well. Come on. We can use some of the hundred you shoved at me for dry cleaning. It was far too much."

"Keep the money, please. I have enough of that. And I don't really need your help. I've made do." He looked angry and defensive again. "Laurel and I, we've gotten by."

"I see." Allie tapped her fingers on the car door. "And is she taking John Wayne lessons, too? I mean, a girl can't be too tough these days, ya know," she added, in exaggerated imitation of the classic style.

He looked even angrier for a moment. Then, he laughed. "Okay," he said, extending his hand to her. "I should accept your offer. I will admit I need some advice. I don't even know where there's a store that carries the kind of stuff she needs. My name's Matt. Matt Glass."

Allie shook his hand. His name meant nothing to her, not even coupled with the information Tim had provided. So why, she wondered, were little bells of recognition still going off in her head? Why did he trigger some mental path that wouldn't quite connect? "And I'm Allison Ford," she said. His handshake was gentle, but the skin on his palm was so hard, it was like touching warm wood. Warm oak with a kind of electric current running through it ...

"Hi, Allison." He smiled, and she saw a glimmer of interest in his eyes. Then Laurel announced her displeasure by crying again. Whimpering tiredly, she squirmed in her seat. "Um," he said, releasing Allie's hand and turning back to the baby. "Maybe I'd better take a rain check. She's really cranky this afternoon."

"When does she nap?"

"Nap?" He looked back at Allie, his expression blank. "Oh, I don't know. Whenever. She usually just falls asleep wherever she is while I ..."

"You don't have her on a schedule?"

"No." He looked worried. "I didn't know I was supposed to."

"First helpful hint of the day—schedules keep things from getting out of hand." She started her car. "Trust me, I know." She glanced at him and saw from his face that he was still doubtful. "Come on, I'm not trying to butt in. I'm just trying to help."

He stuck his hands in his pockets and regarded her. "Why? Why would you want to help me? I'm a complete stranger to you, aren't I?"

"Sort of."

He frowned.

"I've been informed by a reliable source that you've shown up on the front pages of the supermarket tabloids, but aside from that, I don't know you from the next stranger. As to why I want to help? I actually have no idea. Maybe it's just the way I was raised. Maybe I feel an affinity for your situation. Maybe, I..."

"Maybe you could just tell me where the store is," he said, his expression remote again. "If I can find it, I can get what I need." He paused. Then added, "I'm sure you have other things to do."

"As a matter of fact, I do." She set her hands on the wheel and remembered Ned's call. She needed to get in touch with her campaign manager soon. So, best to just give this man directions and let him go on his way. "The place to start is at the Target store up in the mall." She pointed up the hill toward the one big shopping mall Linville Springs had to offer. The East Mountain Mall complex sprawled over the top of a bluff overlooking the Safeway parking lot and much of the city below. "Go now before it gets crowded with afternoon shoppers. You won't want to stand in the line with her so tired and crabby."

Matt Glass squinted against the late-morning sun and looked up the hill. "I honestly never even noticed that place," he said, his tone bewildered. He rubbed his face. "What the hell kind of fog have I been in, anyway?" he asked, speaking to himself, not to her.

Allie said nothing. She knew exactly what he was talking about. It was the fog of grief and disbelief that had enveloped him. She knew it only too well.

Laurel, who had been dozing, suddenly came awake with a yowl. "Mmmaaamma!" she cried. "Daaaddyyyy."

Matt turned away from Allie and reached to comfort his niece. "Hush, honey," he said, softly. "I'm right here. We're going home now." He looked back over his shoulder. "Thanks for the information, Allison," he said. "I'll get to it when I can."

"Okay. Glad to help." She let off the brake and eased out of the parking place. He might be in over his head, but he really didn't want help, she decided. Whoever he was, he was used to doing things by himself. She could relate to that and respect it in someone else.

Besides, if she gave up the time to go shopping with an attractive, appealing stranger, she might as well hang up her political hat. Time was more valuable than money to her right now. She had to be selfish these days if she was going to succeed.

Hadn't she been told that a time or two?

Yeah, she had been. So, do it! she scolded herself. She drove away without looking back.

MATT GLASS SAT in the driver's seat of his Jeep and watched the woman's car as it disappeared up the hill. Why had he been so brusque with her? She had only been trying to help. He looked at Laurel who was asleep again. The baby's skin was sweaty. That wasn't good. He was an idiot to turn away from an honest, concerned offer. He could sure use a woman who knew about kids right now...

Besides, she was the prettiest woman he'd seen in this town and she wasn't married. *Forget it.* He smiled at himself, wryly. Old habits died hard. *Get it out of your head, Glass.* He was a family man, a father now, in fact if not in name. A man with responsibilities and an obligation to set a good example to a small girl. It wouldn't do to go chasing after a strange, though attractive woman as he would have in the past. No, indeed.

His tomcatting days were over. He set the Jeep in gear and checked Laurel once more before pulling out of the lot. She was still sound asleep. Innocent as a lamb, with jelly smeared all over her hands and sweaty face. Matt felt a rush of that strange emotion he'd come to recognize as parental love for this little bit of humanity.

What a surprise, he thought, heading toward home. He, Matt Glass, of all people. Turning down time with a beautiful woman. Driving home alone with a little kid. Still grieving about his dead sister, for sure. Still angry about the accident that had claimed her life. But somehow happier than he'd been in a long time... Confused as all hell, but happy! Maybe even... content?

What a surprise...

CHAPTER TWO

FROM THE GARAGE Allie pushed open the kitchen door with her hip, grocery bags in her arms. Immediately, Fred, her little poodle came dashing to greet her. Behind Fred wandered Tom, Dick and Harry, the cats. Their sedate pace belied the fact that they were immensely relieved as usual that she was back to referee their ongoing conflict with Fred. She set the bags down on the table and knelt to administer love.

Fred rolled over to have her tummy scratched. The cats strolled by, one at a time, for an ear rub. Allie cooed and greeted. All were female, despite their names. And, in typical cat style, once assured of her return and continued affection, they left her alone. Not so Fred, who remained to see what kind of goodies were in the sacks.

"Nothing for you today, girl," Allie said. "You have plenty of biscuits. I know, because I checked. I'll take you for a walk later, and we can do a deal for a treat if you do your duty. Understand?"

Fred did. She wagged her tail and went over to lie down in a patch of sunlight.

Allie unloaded the food, put it away and went downstairs to the laundry room. She stripped off the sticky, dirty blouse and stuck it in the machine. Sorting through a pile of clean clothes, she found an old, comfortable T-shirt and slipped it on. Then, moving past the washer and dryer, she entered the section of the utility room that was her private, personal space...

And her office. Her *real* office.

The office where she greeted and dealt with her financial planning clients was upstairs in a small converted bedroom. But the heavy-duty work, she did down here, in the depths of her home where there was no window, no view, no distraction to take her mind away from the task at hand. She flicked on the overhead lights and went to her desk.

ALLISON FORD FOR HOUSE. The poster lay on a pile of papers, and her own face smiled up at her from the black-and-white photograph topping the statement. Allie touched it and smiled back at herself. She was probably out of her mind to try running for the legislature, but she would be as crazy not to, she had decided. The traditional political parties and mostly male candidates weren't helping very much with issues that concerned her friends and clients. It was time for an independent like herself to make an impact. There were nine legislative slots to fill this election from her county, and she intended to get one of them. She had the fire, the intense desire to run, win and serve, and the twins were old enough to deal with her being gone from home some of the time. She picked up the poster and set it aside. Time to work.

She dialed her manager's office number, curious to know what it was that Ned thought was so important. He wasn't in, so she left her name on his answering machine. That was strange, she thought. This was the second time today she'd tried to reach him. He'd sounded extremely anxious early this morning when she had found a message from him on her own machine. Since she routinely rose at sunrise and jogged a few blocks, anyone calling before seven in the morning had to talk to the mechanical secretary.

She sorted mail, noting with some satisfaction that she was already receiving letters of encouragement. Money had trickled in, as well. Not much, but enough to give her hope. Even a small campaign these days was a great expense, if you had to do it out-of-pocket. If she didn't get more support, though, she would be in some trouble.

Her personal budget was run on a tightrope at all times, especially as the twins got older and needed more things. They ate as if there was never going to be another bite of food for them, and they outgrew their clothes at an alarming rate. She could take the risk of dipping into the special funds she had set aside for the kids' education and for emergencies, but she was extremely reluctant to do that. Only as a last resort, she had promised herself when she decided to run.

But it was, after all, still early. Few folks thought about the November elections in June. Particularly in an election year when there wasn't a presidential race. The crunch would start in August, increase in September, reach a fever pitch in October . . .

And all be over, one way or another, in November.

Her computer was already turned on—she had been at work earlier that day, so she took a few minutes to log in the checks and file them in an envelope to give to Ned for her campaign fund. Meticulous record-keeping was a deeply ingrained habit that came from having to survive a financial disaster ten years earlier. She turned her thoughts away from that and ran a budget program. Her own, this time.

It wasn't comforting. If she didn't get more support for her campaign soon, she was going to have to dip into personal funds beyond the point where she felt safe. Allie frowned and pushed back from the desk. She needed some help and advice. There must be something she could do to generate contributions now. Ned should be calling her back. Maybe, he had some good news. She could use it.

She got up and went upstairs, forcing herself to remain calm. Her palms were sweaty and her stomach churned—her usual response to money problems. She couldn't help her reaction, but she could control it. "Hey, Fred," she called. "Want to take a walk?" The little gray dog came scampering, wiggling with joy at the prospect.

The long walk calmed her. Fred did her business dutifully, then spent the rest of the excursion exploring the delights of nature along the path they took. The day wasn't too hot, though the sun was almost uncomfortably warm on Allie's skin. Real summer heat wouldn't set in until later in the month. Even then, it would cool off pleasantly at night. Wyoming's high desert climate was harsh during the winter months, but lovely most of the summer. She felt much better when they returned home.

Until she played back her telephone messages.

MATT GLASS SAT backward in the kitchen chair while he fed Laurel dinner that evening. Or, rather, while he supervised thirty minutes of a food fight that outdid any slapstick comedy version of that sport. It was dramatic and extremely messy. Laurel loved it. Actually, he had come to the point where he was sort of enjoying it himself.

Providing he remembered to wear the proper armor—old sweats and a shower cap. Otherwise, he ended up having to bathe himself three times a days as well as rinse off the little angel. This evening, however, the angel was relatively neat.

"Maybe," Matt commented as he scraped some mashed sweet potatoes off the edge of the high chair, "you got it all out of your system in the store. Trashing the jelly was certainly enough accomplishment for one day, babe."

"Jelly!" crowed Laurel. "Mmmaaamma."

Matt didn't reply. Bad enough Laurel had made a solid connection between that pretty blond woman and her own mother. He knew it would make matters worse if he tried to correct the child. He took the washcloth and wiped her face gently.

"Mmmaaamma," Laurel repeated, her tiny eyebrows drawing together.

Matt forced himself to smile. "Okay. Eat your peas, sweetheart. All gone. Then, you get a cookie. Okay?"

His niece looked at him. He could almost see the little wheels turning behind her blue eyes. "No peas," she stated, scowling. "Cookie!"

He sighed, picked up a spoon and started shoveling. The food fight became a war. There had to be an easier way, he thought. Just had to be! Women wouldn't have done this for millennia without having figured out an easier way. Would they? Too bad he didn't know an experienced one he could ask.

He sighed again, wearily. He'd forged rivers, crossed deserts and climbed mountains that were less of a challenge than this little person.

Both Matt Glass and Laurel Essex were sound asleep before the sun was fully gone from the Wyoming sky that evening. It was a toss-up as to which one of them was more tired.

"I CAN'T BELIEVE he did this to me!" Allie wailed. She ignored her mug of beer and put her head down on her arms, which rested on the dark wood table. "Cannot believe it."

They sat and drank their beers silently for a while. The bar was a neighborhood watering hole, quiet and clean. Dark enough for privacy and conversation. When Allie had heard on her answering machine tape that her manager had not only deserted her, but had actually gone over to her primary rival, Rita Morely, she had called M.J. who had suggested she needed more than a sympathetic ear to listen to her troubles. She needed an attitude adjustment, he advised, and had invited her to meet him at Shady's Spot.

"Believe it, darlin'." Her cousin, M. J. Nichols, patted her hand consolingly and lifted his own mug. He took a hearty drink. "The man's a snake. To desert you like that. Showed his true colors. He always was Rita's man, or at least a regular party man. You're better off without him since you're determined to run as an independent."

"Maybe so." Allie sat up. "But with Ned's departure comes a host of trouble, and you know it or you wouldn't have suggested I go out drinking with you, you sweet-talking jerk! You want me to forget my problems for a while, don't you."

"Don't insult me, cousin." M.J. smiled. The expression affected all the muscles in his round, pleasantly handsome face. He ran a hand over his thinning, dark hair. "I'm one of the few counselors you have you can really trust."

"Hell with you," she replied, but with a bit more cheer in her tone. "So, what's your counsel, Counselor?"

M.J. sobered. "You do have a problem, Allie. I won't fool around with that. Most candidates have thrown their hats in the ring and acquired their managers by now, even if they haven't been loud about it. There aren't too many folks left out who have any experience."

"And Ned went over to the enemy camp." She groaned again. "What in the world was wrong with me that he did that? Is Rita such a sure winner? Should I bow out now before I get in debt up to my eyeballs."

M.J. regarded her. She was his only relative here in Linville Springs, and they were close as brother and sister. They had shared confidences for years. Helped each other through good times and bad. But tonight he didn't know what to say. "I'd take your show on myself—" he began.

"No. We've been over this before, M.J. You're a trial lawyer, not a PR man. I've got to find someone who knows the political ropes and is willing to work for nothing but future hope. Rita Morely's gonna kill me, otherwise. I'm not a good sport about this. I'll mind losing terribly, but I will *hate* to lose by a wide margin."

"Don't talk of losing. Rita's got the brains of a ground squirrel. The county needs you in the House, not her. She may have the party backing, but she's not the person we need. She's just doing it because it's traditional for a Morely to be in public office."

"She could run for dogcatcher."

"Be nice, Allie."

Allie pulled a face and then changed the subject. "I ran into an interesting guy today," she said, changing the subject. "At the grocery store. He was not your average homeparent type. And he was very good-looking.'' She paused, wondering if she should go on and recite the interesting gossip she'd heard about the stranger. But M.J. wasn't paying much attention to her chatter. He was apparently thinking about her problem.

"Have you thought about Josh?" he asked, changing the subject back.

"Josh?" Allie grinned. "For what?"

"For the job. Josh Henderson isn't the brightest guy in the city, but he's done some serious campaign management in his time. He doesn't need the money, so he might be content to work for the promise of a staff job if you make it big eventually."

"I considered him first when I started looking. He's done two sheriffs' races in a row and lost them both. I just don't much feel like hitching up with a known loser. It's not good precedent. Besides, he's not likely to want to help an independent, either. He's always worked for a party candidate, hasn't he?"

"You're right. But you might have to modify your standards, you know." M.J. moved his beer mug on the table, creating small, wet rings. "There is this guy from California I heard about. A colleague of mine who's dealing with some estate work for him mentioned in passing that he'd had some experience in political campaign management. I guess she said it because she knew I'm related to you. He's supposed to be pretty good."

"He won't want to work for nothing, if he's used to pay. Which he probably is, if he's from there. Anyway, I don't want to hire out-of-state. You know how that goes over in this kind of economic environment. Everybody who hires from outside gets a black mark against their name."

"I said he's *from* California. Apparently, he lives here now. At least the estate is here, as I recall."

"Oh."

"Don't know much else. But it wouldn't hurt to call him and talk."

"I guess not."

M.J. took a napkin and scribbled some notes on it. "Here's his name. And Josh's and a few others. Give 'em all a try, Allie."

"Thanks." She took the napkin and stuck it in her purse. "I really appreciate this. And the beer, too."

"Kids okay?"

"Sure. They love it up at the ranch. I think sometimes I was crazy not to go back. Sticking it out on my own here alone? I should have my head examined."

"Nice words for a woman who's done some serious overcoming. Come on. Is this you talking? The woman who can leap tall financial columns with a single bound? Give up and go home to Mom and Dad?"

"Sometime, M.J., even us superwomen get real darn tired of overcoming." Allie sighed. "How have men managed to do it all these years without cracking up?" She grinned. "Maybe I need a wife."

"Funny. Funny." M.J. drained his beer. "I don't have one, either, and I get along just fine. You sound cheered up enough. And I've got court tomorrow. You going to stay?" He put down money for the drinks and included a generous tip.

"No," she replied. "I think I'll mosey home, as well. Fred will need to go out, anyway."

"You treat that damn dog like she was a kid."

"Better than I would a kid. She doesn't have to grow up and face the cold cruel world. Fred and the cats, I can spoil. Sally and Sam, I don't dare. For their sakes."

M.J. stood up. "You're a wise woman, Al. You'll find a new manager, and you'll win this race. You'll kick Morely's aristocratic behind." He gave her a hug. "And someday, I'll be cousin to the governor of the great state of Wyoming."

"In your dreams, M.J.! In your dreams!"

THE NEXT MORNING, Allie woke up early, jogged, showered, ministered to her pets, ate breakfast and then went downstairs to deal with her main problem.

Her dream.

She had teased M.J. for dreaming about being related to the future governor of the state, but she was dead serious about her own ambitions to try for the state's highest office someday. She did have an agenda, and the governor's office would be the best place to execute that agenda.

Someday. For now, she simply had to get a manager. No way could she continue her business, take care of her kids, run for the legislature *and* manage her own campaign. She was only human. She needed to hire a new manager.

She made phone calls for an hour before she gave up on her own list. All the people she spoke to were sympathetic to her problem, but unwilling to pick up responsibility for her political race. She was a virtual unknown outside the city limits. Although she'd served on the school board for three years and finished a term for an ill member of the city council, that didn't give her the name recognition necessary for a county election to a state office, one former politician told her bluntly. She ought to just stick to running her business and raising her kids, he said. Allie hung up the phone, her face burning with anger, her mind filled with frustration.

So, she called Josh Henderson.

"Well, Mrs. Ford," he said, slowly. "I don't know. I...I'll have to give it some thought, you understand."

"Sure, Josh," she said. "I know this is short notice. I'd counted on Ned to carry me through November, but..."

"Well, Mrs. Ford, you know Ned is interested in his own political life. Moving to Mrs. Morely's campaign does make sense."

"It does not make me think much of his integrity."

"Well, that may be, but..."

"Look, Josh. Why don't you think about my offer and let me know your decision by, say, this evening. I really do need to get things back on track right away."

"That's true." A pause. "All right. I'll think on it and call you tonight."

Allie thanked him and hung up, again. Josh was a nice guy, she thought. Nice and polite. But no intensity. He had money from his family and a degree in geology that he'd used to open a small consulting business. It was rumored he worked only when he absolutely had to. She believed he was intelligent enough, but lazy at heart, and she worried about his potential commitment to her political career. He might help, but he'd never light any fires.

And, she needed a bonfire! Maybe...

She picked up the napkin M.J. had scribbled on the night before. Hard to read his writing, especially the name of that California guy. Glore. Blane. Gla...

Glass. She opened up the telephone directory. Scanning the residential section, she found two numbers with that surname. She called. At one home, no one answered. At the other, the wife did, and she said her husband was an auto mechanic. Not at all interested in politics. Allie hung up and sat back.

Who the heck had M.J. meant?

Then, it hit her.

Matt Glass. Of course! He was the guy from the grocery store. Well, there was one person she knew could supply the necessary information she needed now. She dialed June Watson's number from memory. June would have read those tabloids and would know all!

MATT MANAGED to grab Laurel and the telephone at the same time. She had been on her way to exploring, by way of overturning, a full pitcher of lemonade, and he had barely stopped her agile little hands in time to prevent total disaster. Frustrated in her purpose, she squalled lustily while she dangled from his arm. He bumped his temple with the receiver. "Yeah? What do you want?" he snarled into the mouthpiece.

"Mr. Glass?"

Matt struggled while Laurel wriggled and howled. "Yeah. This is Glass. Listen, speak up, please. I can't hear you." He sat down on the floor, trying to hold and soothe the child and talk at the same time. The voice on the phone was female and softly modulated. Kind of sexy, too.

"I can't imagine why," the voice said, dryly. "Is Laurel okay?" No, not sexy...sarcastic.

"She's fine. Just yelling. Who is this? If this isn't important, mind calling back? I've got kind of a crisis here."

"Okay. This is Allison Ford. We met at Safeway yesterday. Over the jelly jars. I'm in the book. Give me a call back when you can."

"Safeway?" Ah, the grocery store...

"I'm the lady with the jelly on her blouse. I'd like to talk to you about managing a political campaign for me. I need help. Please call me back. Allison Ford. Okay?" She hung up.

Matt stared at the receiver. Yeah, he did remember. She was a difficult woman to forget. He reached for a pencil and a notepad and jotted down the name. Allison...Ford. Like the car. He regarded the name, thinking about what she had said. Slipping into a reverie was a big mistake.

He allowed Laurel to crawl out of his grasp while he reflected. Moments later, the pitcher of cold, sweet, sticky lemonade cascaded down on his head and shoulders. Matt roared with surprise, then collapsed in helpless laughter. Laurel, giggling happily, crawled back onto his lap. He wrapped his wet arms around her. "I give up," he declared. "Ready for another bath, sweetheart?" he asked. "I should invest in soap futures, I think."

"Daddy," Laurel crooned. And Matt lost his heart for the hundredth time that crazy day.

ALLIE STOOD at the front door and eyed the doorbell. He'd called and asked her to come over about thirty minutes ago. Matt Glass lived in the house that had belonged to Laurel's parents, Martha and John Essex. It was a mansion, really. Huge wood-and-stone thing. John Essex had been wildly successful in the minerals market in Wyoming and when prices took a nosedive, had invested his money well to cushion his family against hard times. But that cushion hadn't saved him and his wife from perishing in a private plane wreck several months ago.

She remembered it all, now. With June's prompting, it had all come back to her. She realized why Matt had triggered some memory tingle in her. It wasn't really the man, it was the child. She remembered hearing of the Essex tragedy and aching for the little one left behind. She knew only too well what it was like to be alone when you felt lost and afraid. And she'd been an adult when it had happened to her... She could only imagine the pain, confusion and suffering that small child was going through!

Well, Laurel Essex wasn't alone, now, clearly. Though to judge from what she'd heard on the phone an hour before, the little girl was living in chaotic conditions. Allie rang the bell.

Matt Glass opened the door almost immediately. "Hi," he said, smiling broadly. "Come on in. Uh, Ms. Ford, right? Glad to see you. Keep it down, if you don't mind. She's asleep, finally. We had a bit of an accident."

"Is she okay?"

"Laurel is indestructible." He shut the big front door. "I can't say the same for myself or the house."

Allie noted his hair. It was damp, as if he'd just got out of the shower. "Keeping you hopping, is she?"

"That's an understatement. Come on in the den. Want some coffee? I keep a pot up on top of the refrigerator. That way, I . . ."

"Can get it when you need it, but she can't." Allie laughed. "I remember what it was like!"

"And you had two of them." He regarded her with awe. "And you're still walking around sane."

"It can be done." She moved past him into the den. It was a room that matched the general comfortable grandeur of the house. Wood paneling that gleamed softly. Leather upholstery on the chairs and couch. A large oak desk. English hunt prints on the walls. Allie selected a chair and sat. "You just have to know your subject."

"I guess." Matt Glass rubbed the back of his neck and took the other chair. "And I guess I don't know the subject of kiddie care yet." He rubbed his eyes. It was only three in the afternoon, and he was already exhausted.

"But you have had experience running political campaigns."

"Yes. Limited."

Allie studied him. It looked as if he'd been reduced to the last of his wardrobe. One pocket on the wrinkled shirt was torn and a button was missing. The pants looked as if they'd been taken right from the dryer. His feet were bare, and he hadn't shaved.

With the damp hair, the dirty-blond stubble and the old, go-to-hell clothes, he looked far more like the adventurer he was rumored to be than a father-in-training or a political advisor. She looked away and tried to visualize him in a three-piece suit. Running a civilized political campaign . . .

Impossible.

"I was given your name by a friend," she said, opening a legal pad folder. "This person understood you had managed a few campaigns out in California."

"For friends. The offices were minor ones. County level only. I . . . I don't pretend to be a professional manager."

"But your people won."

"They did." He rested his ankle on his knee, apparently oblivious of his bare foot. He folded his hands together and placed them against his chin.

And he stared directly at her.

"You're being too modest, Mr. Glass. I checked." Allie looked down at her notes. His gaze was making her a little nervous. "According to my sources, your candidate for sheriff won against an incumbent and in a district where her political party was seriously on the outs. Your..."

"What sources?" He had steepled his two index fingers together and was covering his lips with them. Body language of caution.

"Will you work for me?"

"No. I can't."

"Then, I can't tell you who told me." She stood up. "I must say, I'm not really surprised at your refusal. You're new here. You have a handful with Laurel, and..."

"Sit down." He pointed to the chair with both fingers still steepled. "Please."

Allie sat.

"You're a very attractive woman, Ms. Ford," he said, relaxing back into his chair. "You're obviously intelligent and quick to make decisions. You'd be a breeze to manage, if you can follow instructions as well as you seem to do everything else."

Allie felt herself blushing. But she said nothing.

"I can't take your job, and I regret it. But I'd do you more harm than good, if I did. As you say, I don't know the lay of the land around here. And I honestly don't know how long Laurel and I will stay. You see..."

"You're leaving?" She felt unaccountably disappointed. "Well, I guess this isn't your home. I suppose you..."

"It's Laurel's home. I have a house and a business in California. I own an adventure-tour company, Glass Attacks, Ltd. Specialty stuff that caters to the kind of vacationer who wants a taste of danger in their recreation. I've delegated work to my staff, of course. I had no idea what I'd find when I came here. How long I'd have to stay. But that's where I live. Laurel will move there with me, when I think she's ready." He lingered over the last words, clearly giving them emphasis for himself as well as for her.

"How is she doing?" Allie leaned forward. "I know she's young, but it must be strange for her to suddenly... I mean... you know..."

"I know." Matt stood up. He walked over to the desk. "She had everything here, and it was taken away in an instant." His fist hit the top of the desk. "An accident! Why?"

"No answers for that."

His shoulders slumped. "No, there's not. You should know, since you lost your husband. Was his death accidental, too?"

Allie hesitated. "I... I don't know."

He turned around. Looked at her. But he didn't ask any questions. "I wish I could help you," was all he said. It could have meant a number of things.

"It's okay. I talked to a local guy before I called you. He's no great shakes, but I think he'll take me on."

"Well, then..." He made a gesture of dismissal with his hands.

She stood up. "Don't get the wrong idea. I didn't come here already knowing I had the job filled."

"I didn't mean..."

She held up a hand. "Josh Henderson isn't my ideal choice. I wanted to hear what you might say. I have. Thanks for your time. Sorry to bother you."

"It's no..."

"I'd better get on back home. Josh said he'd call this evening with his answer. I don't want to miss the call. Good luck, Mr. Glass." She closed her folder and gathered her purse under her arm.

"Thanks, I..." He took a step toward her. "Call me Matt, for goodness sake. Not even my father's called *Mr.* Glass."

"I'm Allie." She laughed, hearing the sound as nervous and awkward. " 'Ms. Ford' makes me sound like a new line of car."

He grinned. "Well, you don't look anything like one."

"Thanks, I think." She felt completely at a loss for something to say. She had to leave. She wanted to stay. And all he was doing was standing there, watching her, not making it any easier for her. "Um, did you get a car seat?" she asked.

"Found hers. It was out in the garage."

"Oh. Good."

"But thanks for telling me about the store. I'll get up there by and by."

She made herself glance at her watch. "I'd better go."

"I'll see you to the door."

"This is a beautiful house," she said as they walked back to the front hall. "I understand your sister's husband built it."

"He did. But I'll try to sell it once Laurel and I move back to California. I feel uncomfortable surrounded by their things. Like I'm still just a guest. Anyway, it's far too big for just two people."

"I suppose it is. If I had that kind of money, I might even consider buying it from you." She paused by the door and smiled at him. "My place is fine for just me, but with the twins growing like weeds, it seems small when they're home. And then, there's the rest of the family."

"Who...?"

"I have a dog and some cats. They're family, too." She reached for the doorknob. "Thanks again, Matt. Good luck with the parenting. See you around." She opened the door and was gone.

Only after the big door closed behind her and he heard the sound of her car moving out of the driveway did Matt realize she had left before he had even gotten around to giving her the coffee he'd promised.

You jerk, he thought. He looked in the direction of Laurel's room. Was this what having a kid did to a guy? Make him lose his mind entirely?

Or was this special? Would he have acted as stupidly, regardless? Because he found Ms. Allison Ford extremely appealing, and he knew he could do absolutely nothing about that. There was no reason for him to seek her out, or for her to get in touch with him, now that he'd rejected her offer of a job. No reason for them to get together and see if his admiration for her might be returned . . .

Or, was there? Hey, his life wasn't over. He looked around his sister's big house. Right now, his energy might have to be devoted to Laurel's needs but that was no reason he couldn't enjoy himself anymore. Was it? Hell, no! Matt smiled.

Furthermore, she did seem to know about kids. So he had two motives going for him.

CHAPTER THREE

"WE'VE GOT to stop meeting like this. People will begin to talk, Allison Ford."

Allie looked behind her. Her heart did a little leap of pleasure, which surprised her. A smiling Matt Glass, his shopping cart filled with food, and no fussy kid on board, was right on her tail. "Hi, Matt," she said, casually. "Where's Laurel?"

"Home." His smile faded, and he looked glum. "I'm trying out sitter number...let's see. I think this is the tenth or eleventh this week.

"You're kidding?"

"No, I wish I were. Either the sitters are more interested in watching television than my kid, or Laurel takes an instant dislike to them, or they want... something more..." He looked extremely uncomfortable for a moment. Then, "The woman who was taking care of her when my sister died won't come anywhere near us. I think she's superstitious. It's like we have a curse on us or something. You don't happen to know anyone who cleans houses, do you? A reliable, steady kind of woman. Someone I can trust will behave herself and do a decent job."

Allie looked at him for a moment. He was asking honestly for help. "Come on out of the line of traffic," she said, pulling her cart to the side. "I think I understand your problem."

"You do?" He pulled over next to her, rested his forearms on the cart and regarded her with an expression of hope on his face. He was dressed neatly today. Almost in a normal Linville Saturday fashion with a navy blue polo shirt and tan slacks. Jeans would have been more the local style, but the pants were acceptable. Only the sandals were unusual. They looked handmade. Foreign... Exotic...

"I do," she said. "You're the nearest thing to a celebrity this town has seen for a while. Just how have you gone about getting help?"

"Well. I advertised in the paper..."

"And?"

"The results have been less than satisfactory."

Allie smiled. She could just imagine. Most of the job applicants had probably come on to him, rather than shown interest in his kid or his house. "What you need," she said, "is personal reference. You need to have people you trust recommend a sitter or a housekeeper they trust. Ones they know. Advertising is the last resort around here. Word-of-mouth is the way to go. People believe one another, here."

"Oh."

He looked forlorn and confused. Impulsively, she reached up and patted his cheek. "I'll see what I can do, okay, Laurel's uncle?" She started to move away. "I'll give you a call, if I think of someone."

"Wait." His hand settled on her arm. She felt warmth and reserved power in his grasp. Exciting warmth and strength... "Are you busy now?" he asked.

"I'm shopping, Matt."

"I mean after. How about lunch somewhere?" He grinned somewhat sheepishly. "I think I owe you at least a cup of coffee. The other day, I let you get out of the house without any. And I'd made the offer. Not very polite of me. Let me make it up to you.''

Allie considered. This was a social move. Nothing more, nothing less. He didn't owe her a cup of coffee or anything else, for that matter. He wanted her company.

Hmm.

But...

''I can't,'' she said, feeling regret. ''Josh Henderson is coming over this afternoon for some serious campaign battle strategy. I've already lost time I can't afford.''

''So, your friend did take the job.''

''He's not exactly a friend.'' They both wheeled out into the aisle and continued down the row while they talked. ''But I've sort of known him a long time. I guess you'd have to call us acquaintances, rather than friends. We've both lived here a while, and it's a small town, really, so you know folks. And, yes, he did take the job.''

''I'm glad. For you.''

''Thanks. I'd better get back to my shopping.''

''Me, too.'' He wheeled out behind her.

They didn't speak after that. Too many other people around.

But Allie felt him right behind her. Felt him watching her. Felt an unaccustomed warmth on her face... An odd set of sensations... She was rarely this self-conscious.

When she was finished shopping, she said goodbye over her shoulder, and he just smiled at her. Going through the checkout alone was a relief. It wasn't that she was unaccustomed to having a man look at her with interest. It was just that this one surprised her with his attention. She couldn't quite figure him out. Allie was not particularly comfortable with surprises. She'd had one too many bad ones in her adult life.

Out in the parking lot, she got another one. Summer brought out the party spirit in some of the younger, rowdier residents of Linville Springs, and right next to the Safeway was a large, discount liquor store where many stocked up on liquid refreshment. It was a favorite stop for groups on their way out to the big recreational grounds southwest of the city. Not all members of those groups were willing to wait until they reached the park before sampling the goodies in their beer coolers.

"Heeyyyy, baby! Wanna party?" This from a boy in the back of a pickup truck. He was one of about half-a-dozen crammed in the back, and his buddies encouraged him by whistling and hooting at her.

Allie didn't bother to look. The truck was over by the liquor store, and the last thing she wanted to do was get into a verbal fracas with some drunk kids. So she ignored them. She unlocked the trunk and set the groceries down.

"Heeyyyy. I'm talking to *you,* sweetcheeks!"

A beer can bounced off the roof of her car. Another hit her on the hip. Allie turned and glared. She could ignore their yelling but she would not stand for their tossing cans at her. She singled out the guilty individual by the wide grin on his young face.

And she almost grinned, herself. He was the teenage son of one of her clients. She knew him, and that meant he was doomed. Never, ever, she had always warned her own kids, fool around in Linville Springs.

Someone, somewhere, somehow will know you and tell on you! Small towns, small cities are like that.

"Do your momma and daddy know where you are and what you're doing, Kevin Warren?" she asked. The boy, red in the face from drinking and sunburn, blanched. His leering grin faded away entirely. "And does the manager of the liquor store there know you're way under age?" she added. The boy turned even grayer, looked close to tears. He had no reply. But someone else did.

The driver of the truck leaned out the window. He was older and had a tough, mean face. He wore no shirt, and his arms were thick with muscles and bronzed with suntan.

"Listen, bitch," he snarled. "Mind your own business, okay? And if you tell on the kid, you're gonna regret it, understand me?"

Allie was about to react angrily, when she noted Matt strolling toward the truck. He had on dark glasses, so she couldn't see his expression. In the crook of his left arm, he carried a small grocery bag. His other hand was stuck in his pocket. She hoped he wasn't about to interfere, but it looked as if he was only heading for the liquor store. Maybe he hadn't heard the nasty exchange.

But he could hardly have helped it. Half the parking lot was watching the little drama, she realized, glancing quickly around. Now what was she supposed to do?

Exactly what she ought to do!

"Kevin's not old enough to drink legally," she replied loudly, directing her words to the driver, but really addressing the boy. Kevin had to see that she wouldn't be bullied by his companion with the muscles and the mouth. "He should know that his folks would be really disappointed if they..."

"You want disappointment?" The driver started to open the door of the truck. He grasped a tire iron in one meaty hand. Kevin, obviously frightened and aware he was in deep trouble, leaned over and spoke urgently to him. "Hell, no!" the driver said. "She asked for it, and I'm just the one to give her what she wants..."

"What did the lady ask for?" Matt had come up around the front of the truck while the driver's attention was on Kevin. He still held the groceries under his left arm. His right hand and arm were free. "Seems to me, she was just trying to help." His mouth was smiling. His eyes were hidden behind the dark glasses. The muscles in his neck and shoulders were tense, however. Allie could see that. She doubted the smile was in his eyes. A chill feeling settled over her and froze her in place for the moment. Long enough for Matt to act.

Allie saw the next part in slow motion. The liquor store manager, alert to trouble, had apparently notified the police of impending problems. A squad car slowly entered the parking lot from the east. She saw another one coming in from the southwest entrance. No one else seemed to notice the cops. They were all watching the two men. The driver of the truck looked at Matt, swore and swung open the door, his left fist balled and ready for battle, his right hand holding the tire iron aloft.

He didn't get out of the driver's seat. Matt stepped by the door, dropped his grocery sack and bent down to pick it up. Then, he stood. At the same time, his shoulder slammed into the door, trapping the driver's arms between frame and door. The man howled in rage and pain. The weapon clattered to the pavement. The ugly, metallic sound echoed in the hot summer air.

Matt straightened. Allie saw him remove his sunglasses, stare at the driver and speak. Their faces were inches apart. She couldn't hear the words, but their effect was plain to one and all.

The driver seemed to shrink where he sat. Matt opened the door and released his arms. The man bent over and hugged himself in obvious pain. Matt spoke again. The other man nodded. He didn't look at Matt.

The cops were now parked and getting out of their cars. Allie continued to watch. She recognized at least two of the officers. Matt slid on his glasses, tucked the grocery sack back under his arm and strolled away from the truck. Toward her. He was smiling and ignoring the police.

And they paid no attention to him. They surrounded the pickup, and she saw Kevin break into tears. The other youngsters in the back looked terrified. The driver, still hunched over in the front seat, didn't move until one of the officers helped him out of the vehicle. He stumbled and hid his face in his big hands.

Matt stopped in front of her. "You okay?" he asked, lifting his glasses and looking at her. "You look a bit upset." His brown eyes showed absolutely no emotion except mild concern.

"I'm fine." She put a hand over her eyes to shade them. Her fingers trembled. "That was real slick," she said, trying to sound casual.

"Thank you. I didn't want to make a scene."

"But you handled a troublemaker before he was able to get started good. I admit I'm impressed." She put her hand down. "You've done things like that before."

Matt just shrugged.

"Why did you do it? You could have been hurt, you know."

"I didn't see that as much of a likelihood." He put his glasses back on. "Believe me, I wouldn't have done anything to provoke real violence. I'm a peace-loving man."

Allie looked at him and raised one eyebrow. "Right," she said, remembering what Tim had told her about his rescuing those film people. Surely, there had to have been some violence associated with such an event. "'All's well that end's well?'" she quoted.

He nodded, ignoring or not noticing her sarcasm. "Is the kid you know liable to get in much trouble?"

"Yes." She glanced over at the scene. The cops were taking names, but nothing more. "Not from the police, but his folks will be called and he might as well kiss freedom goodbye. He'll be grounded until he's on social security. They're going to be pretty upset with him."

"Too bad. He was only acting stupid. The older guy's the one to blame." A muscle tightened in the corner of his jaw. "Not only was he leading the kids astray, but he was looking for a fight. If you hadn't come along, he'd have picked on someone else. He was trying to scare you and was enjoying the hell out of it."

"He succeeded," she admitted. "A big, mean guy with a tire iron in his hands has that effect on me. He didn't have to try very hard." She placed her hand on his arm. "Thanks. You saved me some serious embarrassment, at the very least. I owe you."

"Lunch?"

She laughed. "You're persistent, I'll give you that. No, I still can't do lunch. How about dinner?"

Matt looked interested, but before he could answer, one of the policemen came over. She smiled at him. He was a friend who went to the same church she attended. Touching the brim of his hat, the young cop nodded to Allie.

"Hi, Allie," he said. "You know this guy?" He looked at Matt.

"Yes. Walt, this is Mr. Glass. Matt Glass. Matt, Officer Walt Resner. Is there a problem, Walt?"

"Nope. Not unless Mr. Glass wants to make it one. He could press charges. Some folks might say Teddie Baker was out to bash him with that tire iron." He regarded Matt closely.

Matt shook his head. "Didn't seem like that to me. I just passed by, dropped some stuff and accidently hit the door when I stood up. Sorry if I bruised Mr. Baker any."

"Oh, he's bruised, all right," Walt said, clearly having difficulty hiding a grin. "Claims both his arms are broke. They ain't. But I think he's real mad 'cause you made him cry in front of the kids."

"I did?" Matt looked theatrically stunned. "Why, I had no such intention. I just suggested he might try improving his manners. That's all. I didn't mean to scare him."

"Right. Sure, you didn't." Now, Walt did grin. "But old Teddie ain't used to being taken down so quick and clean. Did his pride some serious harm."

"Sorry to hear that."

Walt studied him for a moment. "No, you ain't. No reason to be. Teddie's known for starting trouble. Usually, he manages to finish it before we can get on the scene. I admire what you did, Mr. Glass. As a matter of fact, you probably kept a situation from getting real nasty. But I got to warn you to watch yourself.''

"You mean, he's likely to have trouble from that man?" Allie asked. "Surely, Walt, you aren't criticizing what he did?"

"No. I mean, yes. I ain't criticizing, and yes, I'm warning him. You keep a lookout in your rearview mirror, Mr. Glass. For a while, anyways.''

"Thanks.'' Matt didn't look worried. "I appreciate the advice.''

After Walt left, Allie leaned back against her car. Her heart was beating too fast, and she realized for the first time that she had actually been frightened and not simply upset. Matt Glass had saved her from more than mere embarrassment.

"Did it all just hit you?" he asked, his voice soft and soothing. "You look kind of pale.''

"Yes. I...I mean, no. I'm really fine. Nothing happened, thanks to you.'' She started to turn away.

"How about that dinner invitation?''

"Oh. Yes. Um. I'll call you and...''

"No, I'll pick you up about eight. Is that all right?''

"Eight? It's fine.'' Allie gave him her address.

"Good. I'll see you then.'' He touched his temple with his finger in a salute. Then, he turned away and sauntered back to his decrepit Jeep.

Allie got into her car and sat for a moment, thinking. While she was no longer overly upset at what had just happened, she was still stirred up inside. Her emotions were whirling. How did she feel about the incident? How did she really feel about the way Matt had handled it? And how did she feel about his taking her place in the confrontation with the driver of the pickup truck?

Because that was what he had done. In the heroic male tradition, he'd taken her place on the firing line. Easily, naturally. And she hadn't uttered so much as a squeak of protest. Like it or not, she had just been rescued by a man she hardly knew. It would have been silly and ungrateful to have complained, she believed. She thought of the mean look on Teddie's face and the size of his muscles. The tire iron... The smooth, confident way Matt had stepped in and defused the situation...

She ran the rest of her errands with only part of her mind on business and arrived home just as Josh Henderson pulled up in front of her house. She looked at him as he got out of his car—a shiny new model that made Matt Glass's Jeep look like a piece of trash. Handsome and groomed as always, Josh was wearing a suit, even though it was Saturday and the meeting with her was an informal one.

She wondered if Matt even owned a suit.

She wondered how Josh would have handled the situation in the parking lot. Or how most of the men she knew would have behaved. Some of them certainly would have tried heroics, but she wondered if any would have been so smoothly successful as Matt Glass.

Matt was unusual, no doubt about it. Too bad she couldn't count on him for anything more than some interesting moments in her life. He was, she had seen for herself, a competent man. Sure of himself and capable of meeting life head-on.

MATT FELT totally out of control. The situation had gone rapidly from bad to worse, and he had no idea what to do. "Laurel," he said, staring at the smiling, angelic face of his niece. "What am I going to do with you?"

Laurel giggled.

Matt sighed. "I can't take you out to dinner," he said. "I think you might be a hazard to romance, my dear. You're sure a hazard to everything else around here."

She giggled again, then toddled off in search of some more fun. Matt sat on the floor of his bedroom and stared at the small hill made of his clothing. Every scrap he'd owned had been dragged from drawers and the closet. And nothing was clean any longer. Laurel had carefully doused the garments with water and soap. Lots of soap. "Washing for Daddy," she had cheerfully explained in her own charming way.

The sitter had claimed Laurel wasn't out of her sight more than two minutes. Matt put his head in his hands. It had taken considerably more than two minutes for even such a talent to accomplish this much mayhem. One more sitter scratched from the list. He heard the faint sound of childish laughter. Then, a crash.

"Laurel!" He rose to his feet and ran in the direction of the noise. "Oh, Laurel. No!"

THAT EVENING, he confessed. "I'm out of my depth," Matt said. He handed Allie a glass of wine. He had called and tried to cancel the dinner date until she realized what his problem was and volunteered to come over to his place. "I admit it. She's got me with my tail between my legs, and I'm running. What am I going to do? I need help."

Allie sipped. The wine was white, smooth, cold and refreshing. They were sitting in the living room.

"You're only confronting the normal sorts of problems faced by every parent of a two-year-old," she replied. "In your case, it's worse, though, because Laurel hasn't had two years to train you."

"What?" He laughed. "Don't you mean *I* haven't had two years to train *her?*"

Resisting the urge to explain how, in her own experience, children and pets seemed to do the training of their personal adults, Allie looked beyond him to the view out of the big picture window. Although it was nearly nine in the evening, sunlight still struck the tops of the tall pine trees and glowed off the mountain in the distance.

"Either way," she said, "you're just not used to the pattern of her life, Matt. And she's probably doing some acting-out because she knows she's lost something very dear to her, though she's too young to know exactly what it is. I know you have trouble getting her to bed, since I watched the process tonight. Does she sleep at night without problems?"

"Not always. Sometimes she wakes up and yells and cries until I come in and talk to her for a while. Give her some comfort. Hold her until she drifts back off." He set his wine down. "You know, you are a good sport to come here for dinner instead of going out. I'm not much of a cook."

"Pizza and salad is fine with me. I understand your situation better than you might think." She took another sip. "When the twins were little, I was a hermit. No social life at all."

"And now?"

"Now? Of course, I go out when I want. But, I've got more important things to do than worry about my social life."

"How did your meeting with your manager go?"

She set her glass down. "All right, I guess."

"You guess?"

"It went fine," she replied, feeling defensive. "Josh is going to do a great job for me."

"I'm sure he will." Matt got up and refilled his wineglass. "Tell me why you're going into politics." He returned to his chair. "I'm really interested."

Allie studied him. "Because of the pain I went through when my husband deserted me." It was a simple answer and the most honest she could give.

Matt's eyes widened. He said nothing.

"Paul walked out when I was five months pregnant. Just left for the office one fine day and never showed up, never came back, never called, never wrote, never... nothing. He disappeared off the face of the earth, leaving me with all the debt he'd piled up in medical school and..."

"He was a doctor?"

"Yes. Just out of training. Just starting his practice. He had a few patients already. We not only had the education bills, he had also just bought and equipped an office. Do you have any idea how much something like that costs? And how difficult it is to unload?"

Matt shook his head.

"Well, I did unload it. Eventually. And I paid back every cent he owed, but..."

"Why? Weren't those his debts? You weren't responsible if he deserted you."

"It depended on who was doing the talking. I wasn't as assertive then as I am now. I didn't know what to do, except to pay back what we owed. It doesn't matter now. It's history. But it scarred me, and I swore I'd try to see to it that other women didn't suffer the same kind of pain. I worked in a bank when the kids were small, but now I run my own business. I advise women on finance. Exclusively female clientele. And, I concentrate on those who are married and are not the primary breadwinner. The dependent ones. They're the ones most likely to be done in by the system if they lose their husbands, one way or another.''

"I see." He covered his mouth with his hand and leaned back in the chair.

Allie smiled. "And what, you're wondering, does this have to do with my decision to get into politics?''

Matt nodded. "I assume you're out to get all the men who..."

"No. Don't misunderstand me. I'm not after men or any particular group. I'm just after fair treatment for everyone. A simple thing. I just want to see each person responsible for his or her own debts, and if one member of a team bugs out..."

"The other's not left holding the bag." He nodded. "It's a fair argument for justice."

"*Financial* justice. It goes deep into our cultural past. Women frequently got the short end of the stick when it came to money. So do children. Look at the problem of collecting child support money. Look at the incredible difficulties for women in sexual harassment cases. Lost work time, lost wages. I work now to see that doesn't happen to my clients. I'd like the opportunity to make legislative decisions that would create a fairer climate, as well. It's in process, of course, but it's not moving fast enough for me. I want to do something about that."

"I see." Matt got up again and went over to the window. Allie Ford was gorgeous, smart, articulate, motivated. All admirable qualities in a woman, especially one running for public office. But, she was basing it all on one thing—her man had run out on her. He remembered the reluctance with which she had met his offer of lunch that morning. How he'd had to practically stand on his head to get this dinner thing set up. She undoubtedly distrusted men, whether she admitted it or not.

Not the sort of woman he needed to get mixed up with.

"Have you any clue about your husband?" he asked.

"I know he's legally dead," she replied. "He's been gone long enough without word or contact. Long enough and then some. That's about it."

Matt turned around and looked at her. She was smiling, slightly. Unruffled. Calm. Not exactly a grieving wife. Of course, it had been years... "Make any attempts to find him?"

Now, she blushed and her eyes seemed to darken from sky blue to the color of midnight. "I turned the world upside down," she declared, gripping her wineglass. "I even hired private investigators after the cops gave up. But I couldn't afford to do that for long." She set the glass back down on the coffee table. "I finally gave up. If he'd wanted us, he would have found some way to let me know where he was."

"And, if he couldn't? If he was dead?"

"Then, there wasn't much point in my spending money I desperately needed for other things, was there?"

"I suppose not."

"I almost married again, once." She picked up the glass and rolled the stem between her hands. "He worked on a ranch up in Montana near my folks. But, it wouldn't have been right. I don't know if I'm free."

"Legally, you are, aren't you?"

"Sure." She shrugged. "But I just keep thinking about those stories where the husband disappears and has a good reason. Then, the wife falls in love again and marries, and then the first guy shows up and..."

Matt laughed. "That's fantasy. Look at you. I am surprised no one's talked you into making the trip to the altar. Or are you still in love with the one who left you?" he asked, seriously.

"No." She regarded him steadily. "I'm not. How about you? Ever marry?"

"No." He shook his head and sat back down. "Not me. Though I'm settled for now with Laurel in my life, I'm the original rolling stone. Just like my old man." He drained his glass. "He walked out on my mother, just like your husband walked out on you. But he didn't give her the grace of disappearing. He took me, and every so often we'd make a pass back through town to say hi to Mom. Keep her hoping, you see. Then, off we went again. She never knew where, when or for how long."

"That's awful!"

"Yes, it was. I was well into my late twenties before I realized how awful. That was when Mom died and Martha married John Essex. Now that I'm a mature man of thirty-four, I..." He let the words trail off. "I'll order the pizza now," he said. "It takes about twenty minutes for them to get here, and I'm hungry. How about you?"

"Sounds fine to me." She smiled, wryly. "We are a pair, aren't we?"

"Huh?"

"Look at us, Matt. I'm out to make my 'sisters' financially safe from the depredations of their unreliable mates, because of what happened to me. You're taking on your two-year-old niece by way of penance for what your father did and..."

"Laurel's no penance!"

"Hey, don't get angry. I just think..."

"You don't know me. I love that kid."

"Matt, I'm not denying you love her." Allie stood up and went over to him. "It's plain to see by the way you behave. Your concern for her is admirable. But..."

"But you don't think I'm competent?" He bit off the words, one by one. "I'm not fit to be her father?"

"I didn't come here to fight with you, Matt. I came to enjoy dinner in your company."

"Sorry." He looked away. "I had no call to get angry at you." He took a deep breath and blew it out. "I'm not used to feeling like this. At a loss, I mean. Over what to do with Laurel. I guess I'm lashing out."

"Has someone questioned your right to care for Laurel?"

He laughed, the sound bitter. "Would you believe her folks' lawyer? The woman as much as told me straight to my face I wasn't an appropriate guardian for the child. My sister left her affairs in order. Laurel inherits the whole kit-and-caboodle. But she neglected to name a guardian. So, I get the job, since I'm the nearest blood relative. That doesn't make the lawyer happy at all."

"Maybe you need your own lawyer. My cousin is..."

"I don't need anyone. I have a right under the law to care for my niece." He paused, and Allie thought she saw deep emotion which he quickly buried. "She's all the family I've got now," he added.

"Your father...?"

"He's not family, Allie. He belongs to everyone and no one, least of all to me." He reached out and touched her face. "You don't know how lucky you are. Maybe your husband did leave you, but you have children. *Your* children, not his. And you have your parents. You have *people*. Family."

She felt tears in her eyes. "So do you, now, Matt. Laurel's yours."

"That's right." He clenched his fist. "And God help anyone who tries to take her away from me!"

His expression was so fierce it frightened her, and Allie remembered how easily he had handled the bully in the pickup truck. How just a few words had apparently intimidated the man to the point of tears. Matt Glass, she decided, was not just a nice guy, taking over for his deceased sister. He was a complicated man with some deep and serious anger. What did she really know about him? In spite of his tenderness toward Laurel, there was a hard edge to him.

And she needed to ask herself right now if she was willing to get involved with that sort of man. Right now, before the ground under her feet started to give way.

And, looking at the passion and fire in Matt Glass's handsome face, she decided if he directed that energy into a romantic relationship, the ground could give way real fast.

CHAPTER FOUR

MATT'S EMOTIONAL MOMENT had passed quickly, and they had finally settled down in the dining area with the freshly delivered pizza and the surprisingly good salad he had made. The wine he offered was outstanding, and the conversation had remained comfortable, if impersonal. Allie was feeling pleasantly relaxed.

Not for long.

Laurel's scream was so sudden and full of terror that Allie knocked over her wineglass. Matt was already on his way down the long hall to the baby's bedroom when she caught up with him.

"My God," she said. "I've never heard a child cry out like that. So much fear!"

"I know." Matt opened the door completely—it had been left ajar—and turned on the light. Little Laurel sat in her crib, the sheet twisted around her legs, her face red and her cheeks streaming with tears. He reached for her, and cuddled her straining body to his, holding her tight and telling her it was all okay.

Over the child's head, he gave Allie a look of total sorrow and helplessness. This, from the man who had so easily subdued a violent bully that morning. She felt her own eyes tearing. What her heart was doing was beyond her comprehension at the moment.

Finally, the baby's shrieks subsided to sobs, then to hiccups and then to babbling talk. She pulled away from Matt's tear-and-slobber-soaked shirt and looked around at Allie. A big smile burst through the wetness on her face. "Momma!" she stated, reaching.

Allie took her. "I'm *Allie,*" she said, stroking the soft head of hair. "Auntie Allie, okay?"

"Momma."

"She's elected you for the evening," Matt said, his tone rueful. "Believe me, when she gets that tone of voice, nothing will change her mind."

Allie laughed uneasily, her insides still quivering from the feeling of turmoil that the screams of the child and the sight of Matt's helpless expression had caused. "I don't believe you said that, Matt. Boy, does she ever have you wrapped around her little finger!"

"You try dealing with her. You'll see."

"All right." She regarded him, then Laurel. "I never could resist a challenge." She hoisted the baby onto her hip. "Hey, Laurel. How about getting some pizza with Auntie Allie?"

"Pizzzzaaa. Mmmaaamma." Gurgling laughter. A whoop and hiccup of happiness.

"See?" Matt turned back to the disarrayed crib. He stripped off the tangled sheet and blanket. "She's set on it, and you can't change her mind."

"'I have not yet begun to fight.'" Allie headed for the door. "But first, Laurel, would you like to go potty?"

"Pizza. Momma. No potty."

"I warned you," Matt declared, moving past her with an armload of bedding. "She's got a bladder like a camel when she wants."

"No child this age should be trusted right after they wake up." Allie eyed the sheets, felt Laurel's pajamas. "Unless she's already wet."

Matt sniffed. "Nope. She's pretty good about it. Got great control," he added proudly.

Allie considered this. If Laurel hadn't lost her toilet training, that was an excellent sign of emotional strength in so young a child. But right now, the strength did present a slight problem, since she was sure Laurel was just being stubborn. It came with two-year-old territory, and it didn't need special trauma to bring it on. "Laurel," she said. "*I* have to go potty. Will you come with me?"

"Pizza." Laurel stuck several fingers in her mouth and banged on Allie's shoulder with the other hand.

"After I go," Allie said. She carried the child into the bathroom and shut the door in Matt's face. "Girls only," she added.

Laurel thought this shared toilet experience was hysterically funny, and bolstered Allie's eroded confidence in her mothering abilities by performing, as well. In a few minutes, they were back out at the dining room table, dealing with the pizza.

"You should get a drop cloth for the floor," she suggested, watching the process of Laurel and Matt at work, eating. "Even though it's good hardwood, it's going to stain and cost a fortune to redo when you want to sell."

Matt caught a juicy section just before it hit the floor. "I expect at this rate, I'd probably do well just to have the place demolished and sell the empty land."

"Don't be a defeatist."

Laurel's milk glass tipped, sending white rivulets across the top of the polished wood table. Matt slapped a pizza-stained towel over the mess. "Why not, may I ask?" he asked. He sounded dead-tired and discouraged.

Allie got up. "Look. She's your kid. Your responsibility, and I hate to say anything, but you are doing it all wrong." She went over to Laurel and picked the child up. Laurel whined a protest that had all the signs of becoming a full-blown wail over being thwarted. "You can't let her stay in control. Mind if I try?" Allie asked.

"Be my guest." He waved his hand, put his fingers in his ears and shut his eyes.

"Okay, Missy Essex," Allie said, her tone firm but friendly. "Let's go into your eating room." She carried her into the kitchen and pulled out the high chair.

"No!" Laurel kicked.

Allie didn't say anything. She placed the now angrily complaining baby in the chair and pulled it up next to the kitchen table. Matt came in, carrying the remnants of the pizza. He put it on the table, as she directed.

"I don't know what you're planning," he said, "but I guarantee it'll never work. When she starts like this, she gets madder than an old-line Democrat at a present-day party caucus." Clearly, he anticipated her failure. He had a sad but smug smile on his face.

Which faded as Allie went into action. She sat down and placed the pizza in front of her. As long as Laurel howled, she did not look at the child. She placed her hands on the table and kept them still. After a few minutes, Laurel quieted. Allie picked up a small square of pizza. She turned and placed it on the high chair tray. "Here you go," she said. "You may eat now."

Laurel picked up the pizza and threw it on the floor. She started yelling again. Allie looked away, ignoring the deafening shrieks. Put her hands on the table and waited. She couldn't see Matt, but she sensed his bemused gaze on her.

It got quiet. Allie picked up another piece and handed it to Laurel. She repeated her instructions. "You may eat now." This time, the child ate.

When Allie smiled up at the dumbfounded Matt, she did her best not to look as smug as he had. She doubted that she'd succeeded, however.

An hour later, Laurel was cleaned up and back in her bed, asleep. Allie smoothed the covers over her one last time and turned from the crib. Matt was standing by her side. He bent over and kissed Laurel's curly little head. He and Allie walked from the room together.

"How often does she have nightmares like that?" Allie asked. They stood in the hall outside the bedroom, whispering. She had been unwilling to bring the topic up in front of Laurel. One never knew what a small child could understand.

Matt looked unhappy again. "Too often, in my book. Once, twice a night, sometimes. Some nights, of course, not at all. Sleeps like an angel. I asked the doctor about it. He was going to give her a sedative for the rough times. I didn't like that, so I never went back."

"Who was the doctor?"

Matt told her.

"There are are others in town who will be of more help," she said. "I'll see what I can do to get you . . ."

"Allie." He stopped and put his hand on her arm. "It's not your problem, it's mine. You have enough to do in your own life without worrying about us."

"I'm not worrying." She looked at him. "I'm just trying to help."

He touched her face, tracing the line of her cheek with his fingertips. "You'd better learn how to say no now, or you're going to be in a world of trouble that you won't believe."

"Because of you?"

"No, because of politics." He dropped his hand and looked away. "I was thinking of your dreams and ambitions. Others will take advantage of you. Use you for their own purposes. A politician has to be essentially selfish, no matter what public line he or she gives out. You have to learn to dance on the waters, Allie. Dance gracefully, but not sink. I wonder, really, if you can."

That made her angry. "I can do it. And I didn't ask you for advice."

He stepped back, put his hands in his pockets. "Yeah, I know. But I was giving it, anyway, wasn't I."

"Thanks, but..."

"Just like you gave it to me about Laurel." He started back down the hall toward the living room, his step suddenly full of energy again and his fingers snapping. "I have this thought, Allie..."

She followed him, but apart from offering her a drink, he didn't say anything more until he'd settled next to her on the big sofa and was sipping brandy from a snifter. Allie had declined, realizing how tired she was the moment she sat and knowing she had yet to drive home. Then, he spoke of what he had in mind.

"We need to share our experiences and knowledge," he said. "We each know things the other needs to know."

"Are you suggesting a brain trust?"

"Exactly. You give to me—I give to you. No money changes hands. No contracts, no specific commitments. Just a sharing. What do you think?"

Allie blinked. "It sounds to me like you just want to be friends."

He stared. Then, he chuckled. Then, real laughter rolled. "By God, you are quick. Put me right back in place, just like a pro." He took a deep swallow of the brandy and leaned back. "If you'd obey a canny and competent manager, you'd be well on your way to winning your election."

"Obey?"

"Yeah." Another swallow. "You know. Follow instructions. Do what you're told. Keep out of hot water in public confrontations. Lots of matters too detailed to list here. But obedience to the manager who knows what he or she is doing is the prime directive."

"Arf, arf," she said, putting her hands up like paws and panting.

Matt regarded her. She had misunderstood him. Thought he intended her manager to be her boss. That wasn't what he meant at all. She and her manager would have to work together as a *team*. He made himself grin at her joke, though. What he was thinking right now wasn't exactly just friendly.

It was far more than that. She had touched something inside him. He *wanted* to be involved with her life and her dreams. He wanted to be involved with *her*.

He felt confused, suddenly. Confused and awkward. The damn brandy, probably. He set the snifter down. He was too tired to be drinking, his emotions too raw and close to the surface. He decided it was time to tell her some truth as he felt it. "I want to be friends with you, of course," he said, measuring his words. "But that's not all. I want more than just a casual friendship. I need you to be willing to be..."

"Involved?"

Matt sighed. "Yeah." Then, he leaned forward and kissed her lips. She didn't move away. "This surprises me somewhat," he said, softly. "How about you?" It was not just a comment. It was a sexual invitation, and they both knew it.

Allie sat very still, savoring the sensual feelings that rose in her body. It had been a long time since she'd felt this way. And it was his gentleness, his delicacy that caused it. Just touching her lips with his. Breathing on her cheek, the sweetish smell of the brandy in her nostrils. The warm sensation of his skin so near hers. The way the lamplight caught the dark gold in his hair... Allie pulled away and sat back on the sofa.

"I just can't get romantically involved right now," she said. "It wouldn't be fair to you, Matt."

He sat back, too, breathing deeply. "The hell with fair!"

"You know what I mean! You're emotionally tangled up because of Laurel. I'm in a political race. We..."

"We what? Because we have problems and difficulties, we can't explore this thing between us? Don't be ridiculous, Allie. You're the first woman in a long time who's set off my system like this, and I don't mind admitting it to you right here and now. I'm going to be honest. Maybe there's no future for us, but why can't we have the present?"

"Boy oh boy, is that a line!"

That hit him hard. "If you don't like it, I'm sorry. But, it's no line."

"Matt." Allie touched his hand. "Look at this. You're alone in a town where you have no friends, no support and you're dealing with a yardful of trouble unlike anything you've faced before. You are completely out of your depth with Laurel. I come along. I know about kids. You're looking for a friend. You see a potential lover. You're bored, socially and . . ."

"You really are cynical, aren't you." His eyes were narrowed now, regarding her coldly.

"I have reason to be." She stood up. "Thanks for dinner, but I think I ought to go."

"Allie, sit down. Please." He patted the sofa cushion. "Maybe you're right. Maybe we shouldn't get involved. But that doesn't change the fact we could stand to pool our resources, does it?"

She sat, gingerly. On the edge. Said nothing.

"Okay." He smiled wryly. "It's almost one in the morning. What with the wine and the brandy and the excitement of Laurel's bad dream, I'm a bit out of focus. I made a move I shouldn't have. But you can't tell me you didn't feel something, too, when we kissed."

She nodded. "I did."

"So . . . ?"

"So, the idea's good, I guess. Of our pooling resources. Sharing knowledge, at least. For the other, I . . ."

His hand moved toward her, and his fingers lightly touched the fine, fair hair on her bare arm. "For the other, let's just see."

Allie felt something wonderful trying to rise to the surface from deep inside. But it was strange and unfamiliar and frightened her more than a little, so she just laughed. "I'd better get home," she said, standing again. "But if you mean it about our being friends, then how about a picnic tomorrow? The three of us."

"Sounds good." Matt didn't move, but he didn't look as if he was going to protest her departure, either. He looked exhausted.

And very sexy. Allie was sorely tempted to stay with him.

Soon after, however, she was on the road home, regretting her good sense in leaving him, but confident she'd made the right decision. Quick romance and sex was not her style, and would be political death if she indulged herself like that right now. All the voters needed to know about a candidate in their town was that that candidate led a scandalous private life. Just look at what it had done to some major national contenders in the last decade. Besides, this was essentially a small town, and you couldn't hide much for very long. Nothing was secret; nothing was sacred. Like it or not, that was the way things were.

She drove slowly down the mountain road, keeping an eye on the sides for deer. The Essex home was about one third of the way up Linville Mountain, and the deer browsed the land freely, as if cars had never been invented. Allie respected their right to be there. She would have driven off the road herself in order to avoid one, if it ever came to that. Besides, in her mind, only an idiot took the twisting mountain lane at any speed.

No deer interfered in her passage tonight, though she saw many out in the lush fields. But as she hit the straightaway down to the valley and town, she noted that hers was not the only vehicle on the mountain road at this late hour. Another car was following her, and the strange thing about it was that it had no headlights. Allie slowed, hoping the driver would pass her, and see that he or she had neglected to turn on lights.

But the other car slowed, too. Annoyed, she picked up speed. So did it.

A strange sense of dread fell on her. She thought of the altercation with the man in the parking lot that morning, and suddenly she was afraid. Matt's house was fairly isolated, being one of only four or five on the road.

And hadn't Walt warned him to watch his rearview mirror? A warning from a policeman carried some weight in her mind. And that Teddie whatever his name was would connect her to Matt, wouldn't he?

Fear combined with anger. Crime in Linville Springs was a rarity, compared to large urban centers, but it did happen.

But not this time. When Allie reached the bright orange arc lights of the main highway that led around the city, the other car switched on its lights and pulled off onto a residential road. Just a late-night driver who'd been unaware of his problem, she thought. She'd been silly to have had such wild thoughts.

She did, however, make a note in her mind of the license plate. She had been too far in front to read the number, but the plate was not from Wyoming. The car itself was boxy in shape. She noted that, too.

THE NEXT MORNING, she barely managed to drag herself up in time to get ready for church. She let Fred out into the backyard, apologizing for neglecting their standard early-morning walk. "It was a late night for me, girl," she said, letting Fred back into the kitchen after the little poodle had dutifully done her business. "I'm off schedule, I know, and I'm sorry."

Fred pouted, but ate a hearty breakfast anyway. By the time Allie left for church, Fred was back asleep on the unmade bed. *Lucky dog,* Allie thought, smiling to herself. Fred's worries were limited to a few issues like morning walks and whether or not her owner had restocked the doggie treat box.

Church failed to relax and restore her. Usually, it did. But today, anticipating the upcoming picnic with Matt, she couldn't concentrate on worship. She sat, distracted, through the familiar service and didn't linger over the fellowship-coffee hour afterward. Several friends asked if she was free for Sunday dinner, but she declined, saying she had plans. That brought some smiles and raised eyebrows, but she didn't elaborate.

It was no one's business, she figured.

Back at home, she prepared hurriedly for a picnic and then called Matt's number, figuring he, at least, had been able to sleep in. Laurel ought to have given him a break that morning, since the little one had been up so late herself. Allie stood there with the phone ringing, Fred barking for a walk and the three cats winding around her ankles, whining for kitty treats for some time before she decided he wasn't home.

Or wasn't answering.

She thought again of the car that had scared her the night before. What kind had it been? A boxy vehicle. Four-wheel drive kind of thing—a Bronco or Suburban, maybe. The one good glimpse she'd had under the lights had left her with that impression. That and the out-of-state license were the only bits of information she had. She tried to remember. Had it been behind her from Matt's house, or had it picked her up farther down the road. More important, had it been following her?

She didn't know.

Suddenly, Fred's barking tone changed. Instead of heckling her, the dog was sounding a warning: territorial invasion. The doorbell rang. She hung up the phone and went to the front door. She hesitated. Then, feeling silly, she opened it.

Matt and Laurel were there, clean and dressed in jeans with smiles on their faces. Fred danced, barking to high heaven.

"Doggie!" she squealed. "Wow-wow!" She leaned out of Matt's arms and reached for Fred, who decided to back away as quickly as her legs would carry her.

"Morning," Matt said. "Get my message? I said I'd be here an hour ago. We were a little slow getting in gear. Sorry."

"Morning." She stepped back, letting him in. "No, I didn't... Oh, I guess I didn't check my machine when I got back from church. It's okay that you're late though. I'm not quite ready, either. I went right to the kitchen and fixed lunch for us. Fred, be quiet." The dog had backed down the hallway and was yapping for all she was worth.

"Doggie," demanded Laurel. Then she spotted the three cats, who were lined up by the kitchen door, watching the show. "Doggie?" she asked.

"No," Allie said, picking up the nearest feline. "This is a cat, Laurel. Meeeooow. Cat. Her name's Tom. Kitty-cat."

"Kitty." Laurel gave Tom a quick touch, then pointed back to Fred, who had settled down a little and was only barking every twenty seconds. "Doggie!"

"This is quite a menagerie," Matt said. "Could I put her down? Will the dog bite?"

"Yes. No." Allie set Tom down, and the big calico raced for parts unknown. "Fred's all right, and she won't bite. She just doesn't see many kids quite this young, and you startled her. Just a minute." She called the dog and Fred approached, silent now. Belly to the floor. Eyes pleading. When she reached Allie, she went flat and rolled over, exposing her soft tummy. Allie

picked her up. "Here, Laurel. Touch gentle, now.
Gentle." Fred seemed to tremble with terror.

Laurel complied. Entranced, she stroked Fred's
back. Fred relaxed and licked her hand. Laurel
squealed, drew back, then giggled. "Soft," she said.

"She is," Allie agreed. She stood, watching carefully, but sensing the relationship between child and
dog was all right. Harry, the most mellow of the cats,
a part-Siamese, came over voluntarily to sniff Laurel
and check her out. Amazed, Allie watched the child
stroke the cat's head, leaving the tempting long tail
alone. "Matt, she's so gentle. Like she understands the
animals are skittish. You must think about getting her
a pet."

"Just what I need." He looked impressed, however.
"She is being good, isn't she," he added, pridefully.

"She is." Allie smiled. "I'll get the picnic lunch. Just
a minute."

Matt knelt down by Laurel and Fred. "Take your
time," he said, petting the poodle. Allie watched for a
second, entranced.

They looked like a family. *Her* family. She shook her
head, ridding her brain of the image and the words.
They were strangers, friends at best. She had her own
family, the twins, and her own life. That was what
mattered.

Laurel and Fred persuaded her to let the dog go
along on the outing. Both child and canine had looked
so forlorn when she announced that Fred had to stay
home, that she relented. And, to her amazement, Fred,
who always sat on her lap when riding in a car, even
when she drove, took position immediately in the back
seat next to Laurel's car seat, remaining just close

enough for an occasional pet or two from an obviously devoted little girl.

"I think you may have lost your dog," Matt confided, settling into the passenger seat after stowing the picnic basket in the trunk. "Or gained a kid."

"Thanks, but no." Allie started the engine. "Two's plenty for me, and Fred is only using this ploy to try to make me jealous. She's a natural schemer." She pulled out of the driveway and headed down the street. The warm June air blew in the window, making her loose hair tickle her skin. It felt good, so she left the window down.

"I don't believe you." He touched her shoulder, then her cheek, making her skin tingle even more. "I think you trained her to entice Laurel so that I'd have to spend all my time with you."

Allie glanced at him, saw he was teasing and smiled. "You really are smooth, Matt. No wonder you got to date all those gorgeous movie stars."

His smile faded. "Don't believe everything you read in the tabloids."

"I don't read them."

"Then, how...?"

"Everybody else in town seems to. I got the skinny on you from one June Watson. She's the resident authority on Hollywood gossip."

He covered his mouth with his hand and swore, softly. "That was a hell of a silly period in my life," he said. "I got kind of caught up in the glamour scene before I realized how insane and shallow it was."

"Hey." She reached over and slapped his leg. "Don't take it so seriously. I certainly don't. No movie stars here. Just us folks. This is Sunday. The day of rest. We are going on a picnic. You know? Have fun? Relax before hitting the rat race again tomorrow?''

"There is no rat race in Linville Springs, Wyoming,'' he intoned. "Trust me.'' He let his head fall back against the headrest. "I've never felt so wrapped in cotton in my life. In spite of my worries about Her Majesty back there. This place should be renamed Valium City.''

"Maybe, it's just normal.''

"Do I detect defensiveness?''

"Well, I didn't make a nasty remark about your home.'' She turned the corner and headed for the highway out of town. "I'm not being defensive. Just protective.''

"Come on, Allie.'' His voice had an edge to it. "You've got to admit this is life in the stop lane compared to New York or Los Angeles. Or any world capital. I mean, if we were trying to go on a picnic in L.A., we'd have started hours ago, just to deal with the traffic.''

She laughed. "You might call that the fast lane. I call it suicidal.''

"Maybe.'' Now, *he* sounded defensive. "But that's where the opportunities are. That's where life's happening, my dear.''

"And here it's not?''

"I didn't say that.''

"No, maybe not exactly.'' She flashed him a challenging look and smiled. "But you sure implied it. Okay, Mr. Matthew Glass, I'm going to prove to you that life with a capital L is right here in Valium City, as you called it.''

"I can't wait. The anticipation is killing me."

"Good." She grinned again. This time, wickedly. "It might save me the trouble."

CHAPTER FIVE

THE LOCATION she had chosen for their picnic proved a good start to her campaign. Step one was to show him the countryside. Step two, she knew, would come later, when she introduced him to all the possibilities in Linville Springs itself: the cultural and sports events, the intellectual opportunities, and perhaps, more importantly, the quality of life that a "fast lane" city could never offer.

She smiled to herself. He had no idea! And, unlike a big city, everything was just about fifteen minutes away from your front door. No traffic to fight or hours of boring commuting.

Paradise!

They drove for a while down the I-25 and took a turnoff that led up into low mountains. The road became barely two-lane, and she noted that Matt gripped the "chicken" bar tightly from time to time as they made their way around tight hairpin turns. She was sure he'd been on worse roads in his time and decided he must not have faith in her driving skills. That, however, was his problem, not hers. She knew what she could handle.

Laurel and Fred were asleep, apparently lulled by the warmth of the day and the motion of the car. The poodle's head rested against the baby's leg. Odd, Allie thought. Fred was not a children-dog. She liked the twins well enough, but Sam and Sally went their way and Fred went hers, and she'd never cuddled with them like she was doing with Laurel.

Interesting. She drove on.

Because of the recent heavy rains and the high altitude, the wild flowers were still abundant, making the wide meadows look like the work of an impressionist who had reached for the outer limits. Blue, yellow, orange and red spangled in the sun. Even the wild grasses were multicolored, varying from deep greens to pale olives and even purples and gold. Matt regarded this rapturous scenery with no comment, but she could see the admiration in his expression.

"This is high desert country," she said. "When we get a lot of rain like we did this spring, it blooms like mad. Some years, this would all be dried grass, by now, burned brown and gold by the heat and dryness. No flowers left."

"Hard to visualize. It looks so lush."

"Trust me. This is hard country. Drought is more common than flooding. If the snowpack's not deep enough, the land just withers at the first sign of heat."

"How do things live, then?" He seemed interested at last.

"They've adapted. The antelope and deer will eat anything when they have to. I remember one year it was killing cold almost all January. I mean twenty, thirty below zero. The big herds lost all the weak animals. You'd see them just lying out in the snow. But the others survived by eating plants they wouldn't touch right now. It's amazing to observe the cycles. We're in a good one this year."

"I assume the antelope and deer are suitably grateful."

"I suppose."

He stared out the window. They drove through a wooded area by a narrow, rushing creek and small beaver ponds. She pointed out the dams and the gnawed tree stumps. "The beavers aren't out right now," she explained. "Too hot. But they'll be back at work again tonight. Chewing, mending, fixing, building and storing for the winter. They thrive if they're left alone."

"Predators?" he asked. "Natural ones?"

"A few left. Most have been killed off by men, of course. Some of that was necessary. Most of it wasn't."

"The history of our species. Tame it or kill it. Sometimes, both." His fingers tapped on the window.

"We are a pretty scary bunch. That's for sure. And you see it close up and personal out here."

"I don't know. Drive-by shootings in L.A. are pretty close up and personal. The rage factor on the freeways. Drugs."

"I though you were defending your neck of the woods. What's this?"

"Just speaking the truth. I didn't say it was safe there. I said, it was exciting. Dynamic. Central."

"Central to what?" she asked, turning off onto a dirt road that was more of a path than a drive. The spring rains hadn't done much for the dust along the trail, and it blew upward like grayish-white plumes behind them. "Armageddon?"

"Very funny." Matt held on to the door grip. "What's the purpose here? Demolition of my kidneys?"

"We're off-roading. I thought you were a great adventurer. Surely, you've been on rougher roads than this in your career."

"Not with a kid and a poodle and a picnic lunch, I haven't." He grinned, taking the sting out of his words. "And not with such a pretty driver, either. And you're good. I have to admit that."

"Thanks." She slowed and steered around a large rock in the middle of the road. "But flattering the driver won't make the journey any easier or shorter. It'll be worth it, though, believe me. I'm taking you and Laurel to a special place."

His fingers touched her cheek again, tracing the line of her jaw. "You already have," he said.

Allie shivered with pleasure and thought that, in a way, it was too bad they had the dog and child along. In other ways, it was a darn good thing!

The scenery went through another dramatic change as she neared her goal. The dirt road wound upward through the hills and rocks and past huge cliffs of white-gray stone and earth. Everywhere, the wild grass and flowers peppered the stony soil with color and life. By now, Matt had abandoned all pretense of disinterest and was staring and commenting openly on the beauty and grandeur around them.

"And this is, what, thirty or forty minutes from your front door?" he said. "And since we left the highway, we've seen no other vehicles."

"Wyoming has more cattle and sheep than people," she said. "You know we aren't even classified by the feds as a rural state. We're too sparsely populated. We're *frontier.* That's our official government status."

"I'd say it's appropriate," he said. "In California or Arizona, an area this beautiful would be overrun on the weekend. There'd be a theme park. And some New Age group would have set up a consciousness raising camp up there on the rocks. It'd be a real mess."

"Our saving grace is the climate," she admitted. "It's too harsh most of the year. Saves the beauty for those of us willing to put up with the hard times."

Matt was silent. He'd had no intention of being impressed, but she had managed to do it. This wasn't a soft, otherworldly land. In its way, he supposed, it was harsher than the urban morass he had left or some of the tropical jungles he'd explored. For all his travels and adventures, he was, essentially, a hot-weather man. A month of temperatures below zero! That was a serious hardship to contemplate!

"When it gets so cold," he said, finally, "what do you do? I mean, I'd understand outfitting an arctic expedition or an Everest climb, but regular people? Dealing with that kind of weather? How does a community keep running?"

She laughed. "Very carefully, believe me." She slowed as they crossed a tiny stream. It ran right through the dirt road. "Funny thing is it can be forty below and then just a few hours later, twenty or thirty above. The weather can change almost in a blink. When that happens, water pipes will burst. The plumbers do a landslide business then."

"Have you ever had pipes in your house go?"

She nodded. "Sure have. Right after I moved in. The kids were about Laurel's age. Maybe a little older. I was asleep. It was the middle of the night, and I woke up to the sound of a creek babbling. Only it wasn't a creek and it was babbling all over my basement. Fortunately, I hadn't started working for myself then, and there was no computer down there or..."

"What did you do? How did you cope?"

She shrugged. "I filled up everything I could find with water, including the tub, and then shut the water off. In the morning, I called a plumber. Very popular fellow that day, let me tell you. Pipes had burst all over town during the night. But he came out eventually. And after the pipes were all fixed and the mess cleaned up, I had the insulation on the house beefed up." She slowed the car to a halt. "Well, here we are. What do you think?"

Matt was silent. He wasn't sure whether to respond by saying what he thought of her or of the location.

Both were magnificent!

"It's great," he said. "Let's eat. I'm starved." He felt like a jerk after saying that and seeing the brief look of disappointment on her face, but he didn't trust himself to express his true feelings.

In fact, he wasn't even sure what they were. Just this welling up of something deep inside. Something he'd never felt before.

Allie took his casual comment as a mild criticism. He was right. She had driven them much too far so near lunchtime. Poor judgment. But the place was worth it, even so. And Laurel had slept, hadn't fussed at missing the regulation noontime feed. She did start to fuss the moment she woke up, but the sight of Fred turned her whines to giggles.

Matt helped the child out of the car seat. They were parked in a narrow valley, filled with cottonwood trees and edged on one side by high, gray rock cliffs, which sported yellow wildflowers in crannies and one brave pine tree growing sideways out of a deep crack. On the other side, the land rose more gradually, finally spreading out into a wide, flower-strewn meadow about twenty feet in elevation from the valley floor. A tiny stream sang through the lowest part of the valley, and it was toward the stream that Allie indicated they were to go. She hefted the picnic basket, giving him no chance to offer help. Matt took Laurel's hand and followed Allie. Fred danced alongside.

He spotted their destination immediately. A huge flat rock by the water made a natural picnic table. Fred, obviously familiar with the location, ran ahead, chasing after invisible tracks of local creatures. The poodle ran into the stream and lapped the fresh running water, and Laurel giggled and strained to follow.

"Don't let Laurel drink the water," Allie warned. "It's probably pure, but nowadays, you can't take the chance. Fred's doggie system can handle it, though, and we could boil it if we needed." She set the basket down and took out a cold thermos and cups. "Here, Laurel," she said, pouring liquid into a cup. "Lemonade. Yum, yum." Laurel reached for the cup and drank thirstily, letting a goodly portion trickle down her front.

"Maybe she could take a bath in the stream," Matt commented.

"Maybe all of us will," Allie responded as Laurel almost threw the cup back at her, splashing the remaining lemonade on her jeans. "But that's what it's there for. The twins and I have skinny-dipped here for years. We build a little dam with rocks, just like the beavers, and splash away to our hearts' content." She turned away, setting out sandwiches, small bowls of potato salad, slaw and Jell-O, busying herself about the domestic business of feeding a man and child.

Matt laughed, uneasily, thinking of her taking off all her clothes and splashing around in the shallow water. The gentle breeze would stir her long blond hair... Sunlight would catch the drops of water on her bare skin, turning them gold against the ivory whiteness of her body... As she bathed, her pink nipples would pucker and tighten into hard little points... He cleared his throat, trying to shake off the erotic, romantic image.

But he couldn't. It was more than sexual. The maternal image was almost stronger, since he was seeing her with her children and not with him. Eternal mother—strong, young, at ease with nature and herself...

"Momma?" Laurel had been wandering around, checking out small details like a yellow flower, a gossamer insect and anything that interested Fred.

"What?" Allie answered without thinking.

"Dis?" Laurel pointed at a shiny flake of stone.

Allie got up and went over to the little girl. She knelt down and explained to her about the rock in very simple terms.

And Matt Glass felt his heart do some very strange things.

Eventually, they ate lunch. Fred, exhausted by her frantic initial bout of exploration, dozed in the dappled sunlight. Laurel played for a while, getting messier by the moment, but eventually, she too slept on a blanket next to the dog. Birds chirped in the trees, a ground squirrel fussed and the wind sighed in the cottonwood branches. Matt also sighed.

"This has to be heaven," he said, lying back against the rock, using his shirt as a pillow. The day had grown hot, even at this altitude, and he'd taken the shirt off in order to enjoy the air and sunlight against his bare skin. "I'm relaxed as I can ever remember being."

"So nap." Allie smiled as she repacked the picnic remains. "That's what Sunday afternoons are for."

Matt closed his eyes. "Allison Ford, you live in the twilight zone. Sunday afternoons are for worrying about Monday mornings."

"Naaah. Not here."

Silver clinked, and he became aware that nothing she had brought along was disposable. Regular silverware, hard plastic plates that were meant for the dishwasher and years of reuse. Even the napkins were cloth. He approved, having seen enough ecological damage done to fragile environments to last him a lifetime. This environment, for all its toughness, was undoubtedly just as fragile as a rain forest. She was respecting the land she obviously loved. Matt thought about that . . .

And dozed.

Allie sat quietly, almost sleeping herself, and watched the man. Relaxed in sleep, he looked younger, kind of innocent and certainly more vulnerable. Most men did, she reflected, looking away. Had nothing to do with reality, just the result of relaxed muscles.

But he had something intriguing in his face that drew her attention back.

She studied him. He was undeniably handsome as all get out. Nothing plain or common about his features. They were charmingly, beautifully male with just enough ruggedness to make them interesting—make him seem a little tempting and deliciously dangerous. Now that she could see his bare upper torso, she knew the rest of him was just as appealing. She picked up a tiny pebble and tossed it into the creek. Fred's ears perked, but no one else moved.

If she and Matt did have a romance, she could keep it discreet. She'd done it before. She wasn't the kind of single mom who brought home "uncles" for the kids to deal with. The female needs she had were not driving her beyond her control and she could handle them, just as she always had. Physical drives were only as important as you let them be.

Matt sighed in his sleep and started to snore lightly. An oddly comforting sound. As if his trust in her was strong enough for him to relax completely. A large horsefly buzzed over his chest and she shooed it away, batting at it viciously as it passed over Laurel's slumbering form. Fred opened one eye. Then closed it again.

What would the twins think of Matt? Allie pondered that while keeping watch for the return of the fly. They had liked her Montana cowboy, but he was connected with the ranching life they had learned to love from her parents. Matt had no such connections. Actually, he was completely alien to all they were familiar with. *And* he came with an addition—another kid. How would that go over?

Well, it was silly to think about it right now. Nothing had happened between her and Matt other than a little kiss and some stirrings on her part. She had no idea what Matt's attitude toward her was, apart from the fact that he obviously enjoyed her company and seemed attracted to her, as well. He was probably bored in some ways, and she was a handy means of entertainment.

No, that was unfair. He was more decent than that.

But, stripped of all frills, wasn't that about it—she was convenient.

Well, so was he. Allie tossed another pebble. Watched as it tumbled in the cold, clear water. She was not in any position to be making accusations about motives. She lay down. Just to rest a minute, she told herself. Overhead, the sky was clear, brilliant blue. Not a single cloud in sight. Typical Wyoming summer sky...

She relaxed, almost dozing.

Later, Matt, Laurel and Fred were busy in the creek, playing with the water and one another. Matt had discovered Fred's penchant for chasing small, smooth rocks, retrieving them and presenting them back for another toss. As usual, the little poodle performed this task without a sound. For Fred, rock-chasing was too serious a business to involve unnecessary barking.

Allie sat up. That odd feeling of family swept over her again. Matt, who was dividing his attention between Laurel's splashing in the inch-deep water and Fred, waved and grinned. "Hello, sleepyhead," he said. "Have sweet dreams?"

"No dreams." She stood, stretching. Looked up at the sky. "Uh-oh."

"What?"

She pointed. Since she'd been asleep, threatening clouds had gathered in the sky. They hovered at the horizon now, dark as night, and while overhead it was still clear, the wind had picked up and Allie could see that the storm front was moving quickly in their direction. "Time to bail out," she said. "Storms's coming in from the north."

Matt gathered up Laurel, ignoring the child's protests. "That's bad?"

Allie scooped up Fred. "It could be. I'd rather not be caught on the dirt road when it hits. So, let's shake it."

They did. Less than five minutes later, they were traveling along the dirt path at a bone-jarring pace. This time, Matt sat in back with Fred on his lap and his arm securing Laurel in place in her car seat. He didn't totally trust the device, he explained.

Allie had a feeling he also still didn't totally trust her driving.

They were half a mile from the hard road when the rain and wind hit them. Matt, who had seen all kinds of tropical storms in his life, was astonished at the ferocity of the wind and hail and rain. "Stop!" he yelled over the almost-deafening thunder of hailstones on the roof of the car. "Find some shelter, quick!" He grabbed Fred and cradled Laurel.

"I got it!" Allie screamed. "Just about a hundred yards ahead." She bent down, peering through the gray sheeting of rain and hail. Slowing the car to a crawl, she watched for the turnoff she knew was just ahead.

"Just stop," Matt suggested, hollering over the din. "We'll be safer standing still."

"Trust me." The sudden humidity in the air from the rain had fogged the windshield on the inside, and she reached forward, swiping at the glass with her hand. "We're nearly there." She drove on, in spite of his continued objections. Fred was barking, a frantic, frightened sound, and Laurel was crying.

Allie reached the turnoff. She swung the vehicle, felt it hydroplane for a second, then the heavy tires caught in the mud and water. They moved slowly, ponderously, then freely and she drove under the shelter of a dense grove of cottonwoods. The battering of the hailstones ceased almost entirely, since the heavy branches full of summer leaves sheltered them.

"Whew." She leaned back and shut off the engine. "That was a little too much excitement for me." She turned around. "What about you guys?"

"We're all right." Matt had a lapful of upset dog and clinging child. Once the engine went off, Laurel had managed to scramble out of her seat and onto the security of his lap, sharing the space with Fred, who was shaking like a furry leaf. "Forget what I said about a Valium state of being. *I'm* wired. Especially when we almost went off the road back there."

"Nonsense. We were perfectly safe." She reached over to pet Fred, who was gradually calming down, but still pressing her little body tightly against Matt's chest. Laurel had already recovered her courage and was looking with wonder at the piles of hailstones just beyond the trees.

"Sure we were," he commented, skeptically. Then, he started to show Laurel how to draw on the misted window.

"I wonder if she remembers snow," Allie mused, resting her chin on her hand. "I wonder if she'll remember this? I hope she wasn't too scared."

Matt drew a Happy Face. Laurel giggled and poked her finger at the drawing. Fred bounced over and licked at it, her fears apparently forgotten.

"Probably not, and evidently not," he said. "She's tough and resilient, I believe. We all carry scars in this life, but we go on, anyway, don't we?" Then, he leaned forward and kissed Allie's cheek. The caress was light and quick, but there was promise behind it. "I've met a lot of people in my life," he added. "But no one quite like you. You keep surprising me. And that's good. You're some piece of work, you know that?"

"Not yet." She stared into his brown eyes. "But I'm willing to learn."

For a long moment, they gazed at each other, the sexual electricity building to an almost intolerable level, eclipsing all other sensations. Allie felt it coursing all through her body—that magical sense of closeness and desire.

Bam! Bam! A big fist hammering on the window by her head startled her out of her sensual reverie. Allie yelped. Matt shouted. Fred barked and Laurel screeched. A gruff voice hollered, "Hey, you people gonna sit out in the rain the rest of the day, or do ya wanna come inside?"

Allie rolled down her window. An old man, an old friend, actually, whom she recognized with a sense of relief, stood there, a smile on his face and a huge umbrella over his head. "Kelly McClean?" she asked. "Is that you?"

"None other, missy. You and your husband, your puppy and your kid come on inside the house, now. Lightning and such around yet. Gonna be a twister, too, 'less I miss my guess. Radio says so, anyways."

"Twister?" Allie felt her heart chill. She reached back for Fred. "Is there a warning or just a watch?"

"Warning." The old man's smile faded, and he looked deadly serious. "Best we all get inside and into the cellar."

"Is he talking about a tornado?" Matt asked, making sure Laurel was secure in his arms. "Here?"

"Just get out," Allie said. "And get inside. I'll explain once we're in the shelter."

They all bundled out, huddling under the big black umbrella and following the man into a house that Matt hadn't even noticed. It was scarcely more than a wooden shack, it seemed, hidden back in the trees. But once inside, with the door shut against the rising wind, he saw it was tight and cosy and surprisingly neat.

But he had no time to inspect the place. The old man led them to a trapdoor and down into a dark cellar. A kerosene lamp lit the small area and the smell of it, combined with the scent of earth, sent Matt back in time to a moment in his childhood when he and his father had once sought refuge in such a place.

But it was not the weather they'd hidden from then. It was from other men. Angry men who wanted to kill them for trespassing on territory forbidden to explorers. They had invaded a temple, the men had said, but Robert Glass had been certain that they had simply stumbled into a smuggler's nest. They had been in Central Asia; Matt was still in his teens. Just one of the many excursions that had led the two of them into deep trouble with local folks.

Matt held Laurel tighter. It was a wonder she still had one relative left alive, given the way he'd spent his childhood with her grandfather! For years, he'd believed being in danger was normal. Maybe that was why he found the calm pace of life around here so…different. *This* was normal, not the way he'd been raised… He let that thought wander around in his mind for a moment, then turned his attention to their host.

"It was King here let me know you was up there," the old man explained, gesturing toward a rising shape in the corner. "He musta heard you, 'cause he set up a howl until I went up to take a look. Good boy, King," he added. King, a big, rangy hound greeted them, sniffed at Fred and obviously found her acceptable.

Allie set Fred down. The two dogs exchanged canine greetings, tails awag. She turned to the old man. "Mr. McClean, I'm Allison Ford. We've met, but it's been a long, long time."

"I remember you, missy," McClean said. "You married that doctor fella that disappeared. The one was treatin' them important fellas like that politician. Dr. Paul was his name. He saw me once when I needed some doctorin' help, just like I was somebody important." He chuckled at the memory. Then he went on talking.

"I guess I've seen you a few times since, too. You was workin' at that bank in town. You had them two twin young'uns." He regarded Matt and Laurel. "This your new one?" he asked, not indicating whether he meant Matt or the little girl.

Allie didn't explain in clear detail. "This is my friend, Matt Glass, and his niece, Laurel Essex," she said. "We were picnicking up at the big flat rock and got caught by the weather. I wasn't keeping my eyes peeled."

Matt reached out and shook McClean's hand. It was like grasping leather and steel. "She was napping, sir," he said. "Laurel and I were playing with the dog, and we're kind of new to this part of the country. Tenderfeet or greenhorns, I guess you'd call us. Didn't know what the clouds could mean."

McClean nodded, as if that confession was exactly what he expected. "Name's Kelly McClean. Need to learn to read the skies out here, son," he said. "That's where the weather tells you what it's gonna do to you. Set yourselves down." He indicated a folding chair, several blankets and a bedroll. "I got a transistor radio we can listen to. Plenty of food and water if we need it. Make yourself to home."

They did. "A tornado warning is indicated when one's been seen nearby," Allie explained to Matt. "And nearby can be as much as eighty to a hundred miles away from the reporting site. A watch just means one's likely.''

"They seen one about fifty mile out in the flats," Kelly informed them. "Don't think it'll come this far into the hills, but best to be safe about it." Everyone agreed. And so, for the next hour, Matt sat cross-legged on the hardpacked dirt floor with Laurel scampering around, playing with the two dogs, and listened to the story of a life. Kelly McClean's life. It was fascinating.

Allie positioned herself on a blanket and proceeded to draw Kelly McClean out. It wasn't difficult, since the old man loved to talk about himself. She'd heard parts of the tale from others, but wanted Matt to have the opportunity of listening to it from the source.

Kelly McClean was one of the last of the old-time cowhands. Retired long since, and living off royalties from a lucky piece of real estate investment that had turned out to hold oil. Even with the prices down, he could count on a steady income, good enough to support him in the simple style he preferred. "You live close to the land all your life, son," he said, addressing Matt, "you don't want to go living in no fancy high-rise old folks home.''

"There's a senior citizens' apartment complex in town," Allie explained. "Right near shopping and theaters. But it's not for you, eh, Kelly?"

"Too damn many folks all crammed into a little space." Kelly patted King. "And they wouldn't let me keep my dog. Say he's too big for an apartment. So I stay out here."

He went on, telling about his years working in Colorado, Wyoming and Montana. Riding fence, herding cattle, breaking horses and training them. Matt realized he was hearing living history. What he wouldn't have given for a tape recorder at that moment! He also learned that the old man had known Allie's husband fairly well. That they had shared a dislike of what Kelly referred to as city-life. Allie quickly changed the subject when Kelly seemed to want to talk more about the missing doctor.

Interesting.

After a bit, Kelly slowed down and reached over to raise the volume on the radio. The announcer made some statements that Matt didn't quite get.

Both Allie and Kelly spoke at the same time. "Danger's over," they said. King barked, and Fred joined in the chorus. "Let's go see what happened," she added.

They all went up the narrow ladder to find the day sunny and bright again. Wind had blown several large branches off the cottonwoods around the little house and the top of Allie's Eagle was somewhat dented, but otherwise everything looked sparkling clean. Hailstones were piled almost a foot deep in places.

Matt breathed deeply. The air smelled earthy, and the contrast between the green summer foliage and the white hailstones made the scene look like a fantasy set for some high-budget movie. The two dogs immediately began running around, noses to wet ground, and Laurel whooped with delight when she touched a cold pile of melting hailstones.

"Wow," Matt said. "Next time I say this place is boring, you just give me a swift kick in the rear."

"All right." Allie reached over and patted his bottom. "I'll just do that," she promised.

And her eyes told him that she was interested in doing much, much more.

CHAPTER SIX

BUT AS SOON AS they returned to town, Matt noted that Allie's attitude underwent a radical change. Quiet on the drive back, once they reached her home, she became distant and distracted. As if she were consumed with disturbing thoughts. Almost as if she had become another person. He just couldn't figure out why. He wondered if the old cowboy's mentioning Paul Ford had anything to do with her mood. It didn't seem likely, since she'd been cheerful enough while they were all crammed into the little cellar. But, he filed away the idea for later inspection.

They had left Kelly McClean with effusive thanks for his hospitality and assistance and cheerful promises to return for another visit. Matt remembered that, as they said farewells, the old man had mistakenly referred to him as Allie's husband again, but he had dismissed that as a product of Kelly's age and social attitudes. A forgivable and understandable mistake on his part. She couldn't have taken offense at that. That couldn't be what she was pondering so darkly.

Could it?

She was certainly friendly enough as she helped him get Laurel's car seat back in his Jeep. "Look," she said. "We never did get much brain-trust work done this weekend. And I agree with you that it's a good idea to share our expertise on an informal basis. I'll call you, all right?''

"Sure." *Don't call us* . . .

Laurel fussed about leaving Fred for a few minutes, but once they were on their way up the mountain to home and she recognized the passing scenery, she seemed to settle down and greet reality squarely.

Just as he had to do.

Fred wasn't hers.

Allie wasn't his.

He pulled into the driveway of his late sister's home. The afternoon storm had blown through here, too, scattering leaves and small branches, but doing no real harm.

Maybe that was the way his relationship-friendship with Allison Ford was supposed to be: a little clutter on the path of his life, a little excitement, a little calm romance, but nothing significant.

He pulled into the garage. "Okay, honey," he said, turning to his niece. "We're home, now."

"Mmmaaamma," Laurel demanded. "Wow-wow! Tred!" That was what she had started calling the little poodle. And she cried loudly now when he tried to explain that the dog and Allison were at their house and he and she were here, at theirs. Cried and exclaimed she wanted them both. "Momma *and* Tred!"

Matt sighed. Nothing significant?

Right.

ALLIE GREETED the cats and let Fred out into the backyard. The poodle dashed in a wide circle, going at what seemed to be nearly the speed of light. It was one of Fred's favorite forms of letting off steam and getting exercise. A much-deserved treat after the perfect behavior the dog had exhibited during the afternoon.

"Good girl, Fred," she said, clapping her hands and encouraging the little animal to run faster. "You are a gold-star dog. Big treat in the dinner dish tonight, girl."

Fred frisked, wagging her tail, eyes dancing with glints of mischief, well aware, it seemed, that she had done her job properly for the day. Allie let her into the house, and Fred abandoned all pretense of goodness, barking and taking off after the three cats, who clearly did not care to share her high spirits. Fur flew.

Ignoring the yipping and yowling, knowing they would all four stop short of actually drawing blood, Allie went downstairs to her office and checked the answering machine. Matt's message—the one she'd missed that morning—was first.

"Hi," his message said. "Haven't heard when you want us to show up, so we'll just arrive when we're ready. Looking forward to this, I have to say. I need you...your help." He'd stumbled a bit over that last phrase.

She let the tape move on to the next message.

It was from M.J. "Darlin' cousin, I take it you've forgotten the Greek dance entirely. It's next weekend, and as a political candidate, you'd be an idiot not to show up. I'm sure Josh hasn't thought of it. It's not his sort of thing, anyway. You can still order tickets, I think..."

Allie slapped her forehead as she listened to his instructions. The Greek Church in town had this festival every summer, and it was *de riguer* for politicians and candidates to go and be seen. Spread the old name around and hope people would still remember in November.

It was also a hell of a party.

But, she needed an escort. It was not the sort of event a woman went to unescorted, not even if she was a political candidate. M.J. would have offered, ordinarily. Even though they were cousins, it would be all right to show up together. But M.J. must have a date, himself. Allie needed to find a suitable man who wouldn't raise eyebrows or make gossips' tongues wag. She needed to think of her reputation as well as her image.

Especially since she was running for office. The Greek community was large, highly political and very conservative, for the most part. Family meant everything. Respectability ran a close second. She was far more acceptable as a widow, than she would have been as a divorcée, but she still needed a man's arm to...

Matt.

She reached for the phone. Heck. It would be fun for both of them. She sort of owed him that. Her mood on the ride back home had been strangely gloomy, and she knew he'd picked up on it. She'd let the fun dribble out of the afternoon by thinking about the future. Thinking about her political hopes. Thinking about Kelly McClean mistaking her and Matt for husband and wife. Wondering if she and Matt would ever become more than friends. Worrying about a kind of tomorrow that might never come. One that involved a relationship with him that would never have any permanence.

Darn it. She was borrowing trouble and making herself unhappy for no reason. She started to punch in his number.

Then, she set the phone down.

If she did show up on Matt Glass's arm, that could be a public statement in and of itself. A statement that they had something going. True or not, it would be quickly carried along the grapevine until everyone in the county would know about her and the handsome man from California. Would *think* they knew. Was she ready or willing to do that? Allie sat down.

She sure *wanted* to. But it was a terrible idea, given her political ambitions. Matt's reputation was public knowledge. As well, he'd made no secret about intending to leave Linville Springs. To be associated with him in any sort of romantic friendship would be detrimental to her future hopes. That was for certain.

Damn.

Fred came running downstairs, her little pink tongue hanging out. She flopped on her blanket beneath Allie's desk and sighed contentedly. Apparently, the fracas with the cats had gone to her satisfaction.

"If only life could be so simple for me," Allie said, glowering at the dog. Then, she bent down and stroked Fred's back. "But if it were, it'd be a dog's life, wouldn't it. And I'm a people, last time I checked." Fred grunted and rolled over for a tummy scratching. Allie obliged for a moment. Then, she straightened and picked up the phone again. There were times when acting on feelings the way Fred did seemed the only sensible way to go.

Matt answered after the seventh ring. He sounded out of breath. "Yeah?" he asked, curtly.

"Hi," she said. "It's Allie. Sorry to bother you, but I need a date for next Saturday night. Nothing personal exactly, but it's a big local function that's important politically. And it's a church-sponsored thing, so to be proper and acceptable, I do really need an escort. Single women are okay if they're with their extended families and are too old or too young for action, but the rest of us need our own man in tow. I know it sounds like a stodgy event, but I'm sure it will be fun. Would you mind?"

Matt stared at the wall in front of him. He had grabbed the phone in the kitchen and the wall he faced was decorated with his sister's family photographs. Mostly candid shots, they showed a life he had only imagined and dreamed about as a boy and younger man. Now, he was a shadowy part of that life—kind of a guardian angel, though certainly no angel—who had stepped in when the real parents' lives were erased. For some reason, this realization plus the breezy impersonalness of Allie's invitation made him feel a little sick inside. He was a substitute for Laurel and now, a substitute for Allie. It hurt, deeply, he suddenly realized. Cut right to the center of his pride and sense of self-worth. All his instincts screamed for him to run away. But something stronger kept him on the phone.

"Sure," he said, keeping all emotion from his voice. "I'd be happy to go. I said I'd help out with your campaign, didn't I?"

"Oh, great!" She grinned down at Fred, who was observing her with one dark little eye open. "Thank you, thank you, thank you! You don't know what a relief this is!" She hesitated for a moment. "I'll be proud to be seen there with you, Matt," she added.

He had no idea what she meant by that. "It's next Saturday night you say? I'll need to line up a baby-sitter."

"Oh, let me, please. This way, we'll be helping each other out. If the sitter works well for Laurel, then you're ahead on that part of your overall problem."

Matt had to smile at that. "Then, we have to work on a housekeeper, don't we?"

"I'll start making calls in the morning. I can do it between clients. Matt, I did have a terrific time today, and I'm sorry if I seemed a little withdrawn toward the end. I have a lot on my mind."

"I understand. But I could have used some help explaining to Laurel that Fred was staying with you once we actually got here. She pitched a fit."

"Oh, dear. Maybe we ought to..."

"Allie, I just told you that because I wanted you to know you and Fred have already become very important to her. I think I know what you're about to suggest, and I don't think it would be a good idea to get her used to the idea that Fred could come visit or she could come see you whenever she wants."

She was quiet for a moment. "You're right. She's already lost too much. She needs to get attached only to those people and things that she can count on." A sad little laugh, then: "I don't much see Fred as a rent-a-dog, anyway. She's happy enough away from home as long as I'm in sight-or-smelling distance. Otherwise, she gets extremely upset. One time, the kids tried to take her up to the ranch without me and..."

She babbled on, hearing herself sounding like an idiot, chattering away, but unable to stop. Her emotions were in such conflict that she had no clear way to express her feelings. She didn't even understand them herself.

Why was she being like this? It made no sense. None at all!

Finally, after promising to call him back tomorrow or Tuesday with a baby-sitter's name and number, she hung up. Touching her forehead, she found to her absolute amazement that she'd been sweating. "Fred?" she asked, looking down at the now-sleeping little dog. "Am I really going out of my mind?" Fred just huffed softly and turned over, seeking a more comfortable position on her blanket.

Allie smiled in spite of her concerns about her strange emotions. No help from Fred when it came to talking something out. Poodles and cats were a great source of creature comfort—"warm fuzzies" and such—but they couldn't do any giving and taking when intellectual input was needed. They were always a comfort, but no help. So, she picked up the phone again and dialed for help. She dialed her friend, confidant and cousin, M. J. Nichols, Esquire.

"YOU'RE IN LOVE, cousin," M.J. said, scooping a generous helping of Mongolian beef onto her plate and an even heftier one onto his own. They had agreed to meet in The Fragrant Cooking Pot, a favorite Chinese restaurant of theirs not too far from Allie's home. "It's that simple."

"Wrong." Allie sipped her Tsing-tao beer. "I hardly know the guy. I do not love him."

"I didn't say that. I said you are *in* love. A condition I recognize easily, having been there quite often myself."

"M.J. Please make sense to me. I feel all . . . twisted up and turned around inside. I can't be *in* love, as you put it. I've barely kissed the guy."

"Makes no difference." M.J. added a scoop of rice to his plate and went to work on the meal with skillfully applied chopsticks. "Don't you remember hero worship or having a crush on someone in high school?"

"Sure, but..."

"Same thing."

"No, it can't be!" Allie slapped her hand down on the table. Several nearby diners glanced at her. She lowered her voice. "I am no high schooler with dreamy notions of romance. I thought I had real love once, and it didn't work out for me."

M.J., who had been teasing in his attitude up to now, turned serious. "I know that, Allie. And it's made you both extremely careful and extremely vulnerable. I know this may sound a bit nineteenth century, but as your nearest male relative, geographically speaking, I want to meet this Matt Glass. Frankly, he sounds like he might be dangerous to you."

"He's the sweetest man imaginable."

"I don't mean physically, honey, and you know it. I'm talking about emotions. And I have an idea. I'm taking Miranda to the Greek dance. She's a natural mixer and wouldn't mind sharing me for a while with you two. Why don't we double-date?"

"Um." Allie sat back, considering. "That's a generous offer. But, no thanks. I don't want to interfere with your love life just because I'm all messed up about mine."

"See?" Her cousin pointed at her with a chopstick. "You just pleaded guilty. You confessed you were messed up about your love life. We double-date. Final word on it. The prosecution rests."

"Damn." She grinned. "I hate arguing with a lawyer. I never win."

"Not with me, you don't." M.J. grinned back. "'Cause I'm so terrific."

"And modest!"

He preened, jokingly, mugging and brushing his hair with one hand. "Right. Don't forget modest." He sobered again. "Let's get back to your emotional life," he said. "Think about it logically."

"There's nothing logical about it. That's just the problem."

"Wrong. You're too close to see it, *that's* the problem. Look." He set down his chopsticks, and his tone became persuasive.

"You meet this guy under the most domestic of circumstances—in the grocery store with a little kid in tow. He's nice to the kid, even when the kid half destroys the store. He's attractive to you, socially and physically."

Allie frowned, trying to follow.

M.J. picked her confusion up and explained. "He behaves good, he looks good. And, there's more. The implied 'danger factor' that makes him fascinating to women. You find out by gossip and grapevine that he's some kind of adventurer-hero who's saved people's lives and who has now given up all that wild, exciting life for the sake of his orphaned little niece."

"Not just for her. What he used to do was a young man's game. He said so. And, he's getting older," Allie added.

"So are we all." M.J. swept that away with a wave of his hand. "But he hasn't quit being a hero. Not to you, anyway. Right there in front of the grocery store, he does his thing. He rescues you from an embarrassing scene with a tough-guy type, and from what I've heard about the incident, acts cool as..."

"That happened just yesterday, and you were in Denver." She shook her head. "How did you hear about it? You aren't keeping tabs on me again like you did when I was first on my own, are you? Because, much as I appreciate the thoughtfulness behind that, I do not need it anymore, and you know it." She put an edge in her tone, because she had a sudden suspicion. She remembered the car that had seemed to be following her when she'd left Matt's. Could that have been someone whom M.J. had asked to watch out for her?

However, the lawyer put her concerns to rest immediately. While he might be able to sway a jury with intellectual verbal gymnastics, he could never deal with her in any manner but honestly. She always saw right through him.

"No." He smiled, his expression full of love and respect. "I am not worried about you, and I wouldn't violate your privacy by keeping tabs, anyway. I know now that if you need help, you've sense enough to ask for it." The smile turned impish. "Like now."

"You're a sweetie," she said. "Now, where did you hear about Matt and the parking-lot cowboy?" She reached over and covered his hand with hers, a friendly gesture that was usual with them, but that caused a middle-aged couple sitting a few tables away to raise eyebrows. The woman, she noticed, was heavy and had black hair; the man thin and anxious looking. Funny, Allie thought, they seem to be watching us and listening to our conversation.

Well, no real wonder. She knew her own voice had been raised from time to time and that the topics she had mentioned were often somewhat spicy, and so she figured the pair were just interested in possible gossip. They were not, however, folks she recognized, and she put them from her mind. That was easy enough as they were relatively nondescript.

M.J. shrugged. "You know this town. Gossip gets good mileage when the story's even remotely Old West. From what I heard, it was right out of a classic bad guy-good guy scene with you as the damsel in distress. Walt and the other cop on the scene—I've forgotten his name—couldn't wait to spread the word about how smoothly your boyfriend handled..."

"He's *not* my..."

M.J. ignored her interruption. "So, then you go to his house and have a romantic dinner, alone. Then a picnic with a little more *safe* danger thrown in with the weather situation and..."

"This is ridiculous. Our dinner at his place was far from romantic. We ordered out for pizza. Laurel had a nightmare, and..."

"And don't tell me you didn't share some quiet, intimate moments. Oh, I don't mean sex, of course. Not time for that yet. But you got to know a little more about each other, felt a little more comfortable and trusting, and..." He broke off and stared at Allie. "You're white as a sheet, Al! What's wrong?"

"I think I just had a sudden news flash," she said, grabbing her beer and taking a long swallow. "I think I know why I'm tied up in knots about this guy."

"You agree with me?"

"Not exactly. See." She put down the beer and tapped her fingernail on the table. "Maybe I am terrified of what he represents to me subconsciously—a husband for me and a father for my children."

"What? I can't follow you on this." M.J. looked totally incredulous. "Allie, you really have lost it, hon."

"No. Listen. It makes perfect sense. If I was in love, as you put it, more would have to have happened between us sexually. I can't buy that at my age and level of romantic experience, I would just go gaga over a man without..."

"Road testing him?"

She laughed, then sobered. "Don't be crude. But, yes, that's right. So, see, what must be happening in my inner self is a fear that anyone I'm attracted to will turn out to be the same kind of man Paul was. A man who will make me love him, then leave me. It sounds silly, but I think it's possible that's what's eating at me, deep inside."

"I think you may be on to something there. About your feelings, at least." M.J.'s eyes narrowed. "But husband and father? That's a pretty heavy label to put on the man, isn't it? Even in the depths of your psyche?"

"He's pretending to be one. Trying to be a father to Laurel. Pretending, sort of, to be a husband to me. Oh, not consciously, of course. But, see? We have odd little meals together, tend the baby, talk and visit, but it's all rather domestic and friendly and impassive..." She broke off as another idea occurred to her.

"What? Now you look like you're on another track."

Allie shook her head. "I don't know. I'm still confused about my feelings. Maybe what I need is a real date with him. One where Laurel can't interrupt us or a storm can't drive us underground to hang out for hours with a neat old man who keeps calling Matt my husband or..."

"Or you can't use some excuse of your own making to avoid the attraction you feel for the guy." M.J.

shifted in his seat. "I'm not all that comfortable advising you about sex, Al. But maybe, you just ought to go to bed with him and get the mystery out of the way."

She rested her chin on her hand. Looked off into the distance. Saw again that the strange couple were still staring. They couldn't have overheard the last part of the conversation, though, since she had consciously kept her voice low, so she went on talking. "Maybe," she said, "I should."

M.J. regarded her. Then, he pointed at her food. "Eat, then," he said. "You're going to need all your strength."

She ate, eventually. It took a while before she could, however. She was laughing too hard.

ON SATURDAY Matt found himself wound up to a fever pitch of what he could only describe as ridiculously adolescent anticipation and excitement. He hadn't been close to Allie in nearly a week, and he was eager as a teenager to see, touch, smell and talk to her again, face-to-face. He was also just as nervous as an inexperienced youth, and that amazed him!

In so many ways, the week, including last weekend, had been a good one, thanks to her. In other ways, it had been just shy of a nightmare, but that had nothing to do with Allie Ford. The young college woman Allie had suggested as a baby-sitter had been over twice already and had proven capable of handling Laurel reasonably well. Debbie Preston was a serious person with a quiet sense of humor, a student majoring in psychology and a woman able to sympathize with Laurel's situation. She was also engaged to a young man and had absolutely no interest in seducing Matt.

Things seemed to be falling into place.

The problem was, he didn't really know what that place was or what he wanted it to be. His feelings about Allie were clear enough in many ways; unclear in others. Did he really just want her as a friend and/or temporary lover? Did he have the right to become her lover, knowing her history, the way her husband had walked out on her, knowing he would be leaving her eventually, as well? With the messy way things were going over his guardianship of Laurel and the management of the Essex estate, he wanted to get out of this place just as soon as it was all settled.

Hell, why did it have to be so complicated? He checked his image in the mirror, briefly, nodding in self-approval at the conservative look of the dark suit and white shirt, the plain red-and-navy-striped tie. A church dance, she had said this would be. So, he'd dressed for church. He vaguely remembered her mentioning a specific ethnic group's religious organization, but had forgotten whether it was Italian or Greek or whatever. That didn't matter, either. The evening would be pleasant, but hardly wild, he was sure. What mattered was that he would be spending it with her.

ALLIE WAS just about ready when she heard the doorbell ring. She stopped for a moment, listening to Fred yap and realized she had neglected to tell Matt *anything* about the evening.

Including the fact that they were doubling with M.J. and Miranda. Well, he was supposed to be an adventurer. Now was his big chance to prove it. She put the hairbrush down and went down the hall, telling Fred to be quiet. She opened the door and smiled . . .

. . . Unable to say a word.

Matt Glass looked like a real movie star or a *GQ* model—cool, suave and groomed to the nth degree. He did not look like a rough-and-ready adventurer. Further, he didn't look like a harassed single parent of a feisty two-year-old girl. A big change had occurred in a small space of time, and she approved, wholeheartedly.

Since she had last seen him—a brief encounter up in the mall two days ago when Laurel was too much of a distraction for them to have a decent conversation—he'd had his hair cut and styled, and the usual endearing but grubby shadow of blond whisker was gone from his face. He looked smooth, tanned, sophisticated and expensive. The suit was obviously tailormade.

"Uh, hi," she finally managed. "Come on in."

Matt did. Fred greeted him, enthusiastically, but as he bent down to pat the little animal, he had trouble tearing his gaze away from Fred's owner. When he'd first set eyes on Allison Ford, he remembered, he had thought that if she was fixed up properly, she could hold her own with the best of the beauties of Hollywood.

He'd been right. Tonight, she could hold her own anywhere. Her hair was curled and pulled up and back, giving her a glamourous look that enhanced her natural beauty. Makeup was minimal, but just right, and the blue silk dress was a natural match for her eyes. Whatever perfume she wore blended perfectly with her own sensual scent. He almost sighed aloud.

"I'm not quite ready," she said, still smiling in an uncharacteristically self-conscious way, as if she wasn't totally comfortable with being all dressed up. "And I forgot to tell you we're going with another couple."

"Oh?" Matt straighted. "Who?"

"My cousin, M. J. Nichols, and his date, Miranda Stamos. M.J.'s a lawyer."

Matt smiled. "I know there's a good lawyer joke in there somewhere but I just can't think of it right at the moment."

"You don't mind?"

"Of course not. In fact, I'd like to meet this lawyer cousin. If we hit it off, I might take some of my business problems over to his office. I'm beginning to think I need a personal attorney here, as well as the one I have in California. The Essex estate is getting more complicated than I thought it would be, and I'm really not at all happy with Martha's lawyer, nor, it would seem, is she with me. Of course, there's nothing I can do to change that, but..." He shrugged.

She put her hands on her hips. "Are you having trouble over the estate because your sister's lawyer doesn't *like* you?"

He held up his hands. "Let's not get into that tonight. Tonight is for relaxing and having fun." He put his hands on her bare shoulders. "And getting you political points, remember?"

She moved closer, and the temptation to kiss her became almost unbearable. But he had to resist. A kiss, an intimate touch, and he would be a lost man, he knew!

"There's something else you ought to be forewarned about tonight," she said, laughter in her tone, though her expression was serious.

"What's that?" He managed to speak normally, despite the strength of his desire.

"This town is unique in its social dress code. We are, as a group, unwilling to conform. Most events, you'll find folks dressed anywhere from a formal suit or a fancy dress to jeans. And you cannot tell who is who by what they wear. The most important person at an event could easily be one of the most casually dressed. Tonight'll be no exception.''

''Am I overdressed?''

''No, you look great. A lot of men will have on nice suits. That's not the problem.''

''What, then?''

''You're really going to regret wearing that red tie with a white shirt,'' she said, breaking into outright laughter.

CHAPTER SEVEN

SHE WAS RIGHT about the tie, of course. But Matt didn't find out why until later that night. It had nothing to do with formal or informal dress. The reason was far more entertaining...

About fifteen minutes after Matt arrived at her home, her cousin and his date showed up. Matt took an instant liking to M.J., though he also knew immediately that he was under censorious inspection by the man because of the lawyer's relationship to Allie. Clearly, M.J. cared a great deal for his cousin and watched out for her interests.

Nevertheless, Matt decided this was a guy who would be a friend one could trust with one's life. Matt's instincts for such good people rarely failed him and had kept him from disaster more than once during his years of risky living.

M.J.'s date, Miranda Stamos, who was dark-eyed and beautiful, flirted with Matt briefly when introduced, but she obviously did so out of habit rather than serious intent. All in all, Matt decided as they left Allie's house and piled into M.J.'s Saab, it was likely to be a pleasant evening, spent with pleasant people.

Miranda, M.J. and Allie chatted about local matters as M.J. drove them across the city to the only place large enough to cater for this sort of event. Allie explained to him, with occasional interruptions by M.J.,

how the Events Complex had been a political mill-
stone around the neck of the last municipal adminis-
tration until someone suggested making it more easily
available to nonprofit private events as well as public
ones. The financial problems had begun to turn around
after that, Allie said.

Then, the conversation turned to Matt.

"I know M.J. says you're from California," Miranda said. "But somehow I get the feeling we've met
somewhere before." She regarded Matt from over the
back of the front seat, her dark eyes full of frank curiosity.

Matt slid his hand over to cover Allie's. "I don't
think so," he replied, smiling. "I'd surely remember."
He gave Allie's hand a squeeze. She responded, indicating she understood his flirting with Miranda was
only out of good manners.

"No, you've got me wrong. I'm not coming on to
you," Miranda said, frowning now. "I mean, I really
do think I've seen you..."

"Miranda," M.J. interjected, laughing. "Give the
guy a break. He just..."

"You're on TV!" Miranda turned almost all the way
around in the seat belt and put her hands on the back
of the seat, gripping the headrest. "I mean, not around
here. But I've got one of those satellite dishes and I get
channels from all over. And I've seen you..."

"I have an ad for my business on a local Los Angeles station," Matt admitted. "I run an adventure-
tour company. That must be..."

"No." Miranda looked determined. "It was something else."

Allie watched and listened. Matt was uneasy and
hiding something. Why? His hand was still over hers

on the seat, and she had the urge to move away from him. But she decided to wait. To trust him a little longer.

"You might as well confess, Matt," M.J. said, glancing at them through the rearview mirror. "I neglected to explain that Miranda is not only a first-class beautiful woman who runs a first-class business, but that that business is a private detective agency. Best in the state. If you've got some deep dark secret, she'll ferret it out, make no mistake about that."

"You're a P.I.?" Matt stared at the dark-haired beauty.

Miranda grinned and nodded.

Allie made a funny sound. He couldn't tell if she was laughing or groaning.

"Okay," Matt said. "The truth is, I'm embarrassed as hell about it, but they've made a TV movie about me. That's what's clicking off the signals in your mind. It hasn't been aired yet, but they're already doing some promo material. I think it's scheduled for some time this fall. I intend to be out of the country when it happens. Far, far away! If you've been watching the L.A. channels, they've been covering the project pretty closely, since it involved important and popular people from the industry. Good press, you see."

Allie was stunned. "They did what? Made a movie? About you? Why?"

"Shoot, Allie," M.J. said. "Don't make it sound like the guy's not worth it. What did you do to deserve it, Matt?"

Before he could reply, Allie shouted out, "Oh!" Realization suddenly hit her. "That rescue thing. The movie people in the jungle. Right?"

"Right." Matt pulled at his shirt collar, clearly quite uncomfortable now. "And sometimes, I wish I'd just stayed home and left them out there in the damn jungle. They're more dangerous than half the wild animals there."

"What jungle?" Miranda was practically panting with curiosity at this point. "What movie people? What? What? What?"

As Allie listened, Matt gave a laconic, deliberately undramatic account of what had been a spectacularly dangerous and dramatic operation. Matt had rescued almost a hundred people who had been caught in the middle of a small uprising in a politically unstable country. He and a small group of specially trained men had gone into the area, created a diversion, which distracted the kidnappers, and then had led the movie people out to safety through a trackless area of jungle. An area not even the local soldiers dared to tackle. Though he glossed over the trek, she could tell it must have been a harrowing adventure. Everyone had survived and the injuries had been minimal. When Matt was done with the telling, there was silence for a few moments.

Then: "Wow," Miranda said.

"I'll second that," added M.J.

"All in favor..." Allie raised her hand.

"Allie." Matt sounded annoyed. Annoyed and concerned. "All of you, please listen. If this gets made too much of and heard by the wrong people, it could do me more harm than good. It shows an image I'm trying to live down. A man who lives for danger. What kind of father is that? I'm through with that kind of life. I want to live safely and raise Laurel in a home where she'll have the kind of security I... Where she'll be secure and know it. So, I'd really appreciate it if you'd all try to keep a lid on this TV thing.''

Allie said nothing, but she wondered just what lay beneath the surface of his insistence on safety and security and what he meant by the wrong people. Who in the world would care that he'd been a hero once, and was now ready to settle down to raising a child. It showed strong character, as far as she was concerned.

Didn't it?

M.J. turned off the highway onto the Events Center access road. ''If you hated the idea so much, why'd you contract to let them tell your story in the first place.''

''That was almost four years ago,'' Matt explained. ''I was different. My life was different. I made a mistake and had no idea I was doing it, until recently. But, no one can read the future.''

''Well.'' Miranda reached back and patted his cheek. Then she settled down into her seat. ''Don't worry about me, Matt. My business is keeping secrets.''

''And I won't talk, either,'' M.J. said. ''Don't let my much-maligned profession scare you.''

''My lips are sealed,'' Allie added. ''But once that show airs, with your name, you know you'll have to deal with the consequences.''

''By then,'' Matt said, his tone strange, ''I hope there'll be none.'' He stared out the window off into the gold light of the Wyoming summer evening.

Before Allie could pursue this, however, they had arrived at their destination. M.J. pulled into a parking space. ''Here we are, folks. But before we bail out and start partying, who's volunteering to be Designate for the Night.''

Matt raised an eyebrow and looked at Allie. "Does he mean designated driver? What for? I thought this was a church party."

After the laughter ceased, Allie explained. "It is. But it's also a total social blowout, complete with dedicated eating, drinking and dancing." She reached for the keys M.J. dangled in his hand. "I'll take the sober role tonight," she added. "Not only do I have to do some political glad-handing here, I'm heading up to the ranch on Wednesday, so I'm planning to get some work done on my real job tomorrow afternoon. Can't do that with an ouzo hangover. I'll be tired enough from all the dancing."

Matt slapped his forehead. "Ouzo! Greek! Dancing. I get it now. This is like a village festival." His grin was as wide and genuine as Allie had ever seen it. "Come on," he said, taking her hand and slipping his arm around her waist. "We are going to have one hell of a good time!" He pulled her out of the car and started sidestepping in a complex dance pattern, his free hand over his head, fingers snapping out a rhythm.

"Good grief!" Miranda watched, astonished. "He knows the steps. Like a native!" She turned to M.J. "Here moves an expert. Observe and learn, you Wasp barbarian."

"You know how to do this?" Allie stumbled and found herself pulled tightly against Matt's side. "Greek line dancing?"

"Learned it before I hit puberty," he said, releasing her with apparent reluctance. "My father and I spent winters in the Greek islands for a while. Before the Southeast Asia bug bit him, and we were off to Thailand and Singapore. Yes, I can dance quite a few standards." He gazed at her, an unreadable expression in his brown eyes. "I'm just delighted and astonished to find the opportunity here."

"In Valium City, you mean?"

He grinned. "I deserve that. And, I concede I was wrong. Let's party," he said.

And they did.

The dinner and dance were held in a large hall off to the side of the Events Complex. They were met at the door by teenagers, all dressed for the occasion. These kids, Allie explained, were the church's youth group, doing their part. The women did the organizing and special cooking, the youngsters did the decorating and manned the ticket tables. The men found and paid for the authentic band.

As they handed in their tickets, they were presented with round silver stickers declaring them Greek for a Day. The stickers were to be attached somewhere on clothing, so that party crashers would be detected.

Allie put hers on the top of her dress just below her right shoulder. "It'll stay, believe me," she said. "The stickum on these is incredible. I put one on my bathroom mirror once after one of these parties a few years ago—I was not very sober that night—and I'm still scraping little bits of it off when I clean the mirror."

Matt attached his to his tie. Allie raised her eyebrows, but said nothing. She wondered if he'd noticed how few other men were wearing ties. Even M.J., usually conservative in his dress, had on a polo shirt.

They joined the throng and mingled. Matt found that, just as Allie had described, it was composed of people of all ages, extremes ranging from Greek great-grandparents whose English was still limited and heavily accented to young children who could fly from one language to the other without missing a beat. Many

of the revellers, however, were not Greek but were local folk who came to enjoy this traditional fest with
their ethnic neighbors. And clothing was as varied as
she had predicted. Though she introduced him to everyone she spoke to, he held back, letting her domi-
nate the conversations. These were her people, not his,
and this was her night. He was only there to help her
with her political ambitions, and for no other reason.
He watched her lovely face and her sensual form as she
smiled and moved.

No other reason. No selfish motives on his part . . .

Right.

To his great relief, no one gave any indication that
they recognized him. He and Allie had already decided that he was only to be Matt Glass, my friend
from California. Some women stared at him, but no
one said anything.

During dinner, they sat with Miranda's family, a
large convivial group, all of whom accepted Matt
merely as Allie's friend. Not boyfriend or potential
suitor.

Until he made the mistake of laughing at a joke delivered by an aged uncle. The joke was delivered entirely in idiomatic Greek. Silence fell.

"You understand?" Jason Stamos, Miranda's father, a proud, handsome man asked. "You got Uncle
John's joke?" He stared at Matt, his attitude toward
the newcomer now obviously in flux. Every other Stamos at the table also stared intently.

Matt cursed himself. "I didn't mean to eavesdrop."

"No, no, no." Stamos spread out his hands. "You
misunderstand. We are impressed and pleased." He
indicated his family. "It's rare to have a . . . stranger who

can converse with us in our language, much less get a joke. How long did you live in my country?''

Matt explained briefly about his childhood. His audience, Allie noted, was rapt, hanging on every word. '':I never had trouble picking up languages,'' he said. ''We lived in so many places that I just would learn on the street what I needed to make my way.'' He shrugged, plainly uncomfortable with the topics of his skills and his childhood.

''But your poppa?'' Miranda's grandmother looked alarmed. ''Was he not with you? Keeping you from trouble on those streets. A young boy should have a poppa to watch over him. To hug him when he is good. Punish him when he is bad.''

''My . . . father was a busy man.''

''But . . .''

''Grandmomma, I think Matt has told enough about his private life.'' Miranda turned to her uncle. ''But you should also know that he can dance.''

''Ahhhh!'' The exclamation was collective.

From then on, Matt knew he'd changed status. The family was clearly fond of Allie, and now he met some strange standards of approval. In spite of Miranda and Allie's attempts to keep him off the griddle, pointed questions were fired at him concerning his past, his future and, particularly, his intentions toward Allie. With her help, he evaded as best he could. Then, he was saved. The music started.

Allie hadn't noticed the band setting up while they had been talking. She'd been too busy trying to protect Matt from the Stamos family who were most interested in him. But when the first notes of the Greek music wailed through the air, she found herself lifted out of her chair and led toward the wide, circular section set off for the dancing.

"Uh, I'm not all that familiar with the steps," she said, hesitating and pulling back. "Why don't you go on without me for a little while. It looks like mostly men out there now, anyway."

Matt paused. Holding her around the waist felt so good, he hadn't paid much attention to which dance was being played. "You're right," he said, smiling at her. "It is a men's dance. I was in too much of a hurry to get away from Great-grandmother and her questions. I'd like to do this, though. Mind?"

"Not at all." She indicated a large group of people gathering toward the back of the room. Political discussions were radiating from the bunch. "I have my work to do. You enjoy yourself."

"All right. But I won't let you work all night." He touched her face with his fingertips. "I'm sure once the men have had a chance to show off, they'll get into the village dances where everyone can join. The steps are not that hard to learn. If you've done it before, you'll remember, and I can teach you the easier ones with no trouble."

"I'm sure of that," she replied, wondering if either of them was talking about dancing now.

So, she left him, already moving to the rhythm of the music and shucking off his jacket. It was, however, difficult to tear her gaze from him, he made such a romantic picture as he moved in and joined the men in the line. His body picked up the rhythm and the step pattern immediately. The dance was elementally male without being overtly sexual at all. Showing off the men's strength... Their purposefulness... She could watch him all night...

No, she could not! Sighing, she reminded herself of her real purpose for being there. She made a quick survey of the crowd and wandered over to the far side of the room where the biggest political guns were congregating.

Most of them around Rita Morely.

After greeting some friends and a few lesser local political lights and competitors, Allison approached, nerves on edge. She hadn't seen Rita tonight before this moment and had secretly hoped the other candidate had not realized the potential of this gathering or had not managed an invitation.

But, clearly, she had done both. And her escort was one of the great silver-haired foxes of Wyoming politics, David Benning, a former U.S. senator, a man who had retired ostensibly due to a heart condition. A consummate politician and wheeler-dealer, he was also known as a clever manipulator of other things besides politics, and that's what had supposedly led to his downfall. Allie had heard rumors about dear David cutting and running before some romantic scandal caught up to his coattails, but it was purely speculation and gossip, of course. What bothered her was the fact that he still had a fair degree of political clout.

And here he was with Rita, a widow, just as she was, on his arm. Allie pasted on a smile and moved in.

Rita saw her first. "Well, hello, if it isn't Allie Ford," the older woman said. She extended a perfectly manicured hand. "How are you tonight, dear? Really didn't expect to see you here. You're so busy with your family and your little business and all."

Allie touched hands. Her own nails were short and unpainted. "Oh? Why not, Rita?" she asked, looking up a little bit. Morely was taller by several inches, and her high pompadour of graying black hair made her seem even taller. She was also thin as a rail. "I always send the kids up to my parents' ranch for the summer, and I've adjusted my work to take in the time I need for campaigning. Besides, I wouldn't miss this party for anything," Allie added.

"But your escort?" Rita looked around. "I don't see you with a date. Don't tell me you came all by your lonesome self? How dreary for you, darling."

Here, David Benning broke into the conversation. "Haw, haw, haw," he said more than laughed. "No, Rita, honey, she did not get here by herself. Our Allie here has landed herself a fine catch of a man for tonight's festivities." His bushy white eyebrows rose. "Or, at least an exciting one, so I hear. Just her speed, if you ask me." His tone had some ice in it, despite his warm words. He bent down and gave Allie an unnecessarily long kiss on the cheek. "How are you, darlin'?" he asked.

"Fine, David, I . . ."

"What exciting man?" Rita interrupted. "Don't tell me that Josh Henderson got up enough nerve to take you out. Of course, I'd hardly call him exciting. Not in politics, anyway. But I suppose you already know that."

Allie bit her lip, determined to say nothing about Rita's stealing her former campaign director, Ned, and leaving her to manage with Josh. This could deteriorate to a catty snarling match if she wasn't careful.

"No," she replied. "I didn't bring Josh. I asked another man out tonight. Just a friend. He's not from around here. You wouldn't know him, Rita."

A carefully penciled eyebrow shot up. "Oh?" Rita looked unconvinced. "I thought I knew all the single..."

"Hey, they're playing our song, Allie." A warm hand settled on her shoulder and turned her around with gentle playfulness. Matt, in all his masculine glory, stood in front of her, blond hair blazing gold in the artificial light, his handsome face glowing with sweat and exertion, his smile broad, genuinely full of life and joy.

True to her prediction, his tie was gone, and the stains on his collar from where his sweating had caused the red dye to run onto his shirt were pinkish. He saw her notice, and he smiled even wider. "You were right about the tie," he said. "Should have listened to you, as usual."

Allie started to introduce him, but he pulled her away from the group. "Come on, darlin'. Dance with me!" he said. He nodded at the other people gathered there, but his eyes never left her face. The world of Ritas and Davids receded, and Matt became the center of her universe.

A sense that all was right with the world filled her.

"Okay," Allie said. "I'll try." She took his hand. The sense of harmony increased on contact. *This* was why she'd come to the dance, she realized as soon as they touched. Heat radiated from him, including her in the sweet warmth. The chill of the encounter with Rita Morely left her as she was led toward the dancers. He pulled her into the line, and in a few minutes, she was at ease with the simpler steps and moving smoothly and rhythmically with the music and the other dancers.

Especially, though, she moved easily and harmoniously with Matt Glass. It was as if they had been made to dance together, even in this unpartnered style. As if their bodies already knew how to move smoothly in concert.

For the rest of the evening, she danced with Matt next to her in the line, his hand in her hand, or his arm across her shoulders and her arm around his waist. It was an intimacy that teased by not being quite complete. Teased, but also promised delicious and wonderful things that no words could have done more eloquently.

Things Allie began to want very much as the minutes flew by on the notes of the music.

From time to time, when the band took a break or when the tempo and pattern of the particular dance was too difficult for her, she and Matt stood outside on the terrace overlooking the city in the cooler night air. It could have been a very romantic place. Oh well, she mused, at least if it wasn't so crowded with people it gave her a chance to visit and talk politics.

The view of Linville Springs was spectacular, bringing out local pride in almost everyone who gazed on the lights of the city. Rita's little entourage, Allie noticed, never left the back of the room. Never joined the dancing. Never came outside to chat with the people enjoying the fresh air. They huddled, talking with one another and speaking with any others who wandered over, but made no effort to share in the fun.

Their loss, she figured.

The only thing that bothered her was the venom in the other woman's stare when she caught her looking directly at her. David Benning also watched her. Matt, it seemed, however, came under a more calculating scrutiny from the older politician. Allie filed that for future reference, hoping that nothing would ever come of it, but beginning to wake up to the fact that she'd better be ready for anything.

And, she decided she ought to mention her concerns to Matt. Even though he was just a friend, an innocent bystander in her political business, some of the trouble might rub off in his direction if she made too much of their relationship. Rita was obviously angry and more than willing to play dirty.

Which, Allie realized when she thought about it, was actually a good sign, because it meant Rita was worried about her as an opponent. Allie clutched Matt's hand as they danced in the line, and she threw back her head and laughed for the sheer pleasure and joy of it. At that instant, her worries disappeared like dark smoke.

Matt felt her happiness go right through him like a jolt of electricity. Through their joined hands, he could almost experience her emotions directly. Right then, he wanted to escort her from the dance floor, find a secluded place and make love for the rest of the night.

It would be a night like no other for both of them, and he knew it in every atom of his being.

And, he also knew that if he did that, he'd be the biggest scoundrel in the history of romance. She was too vulnerable, and she would place far too much stock in what happened. Think he'd fallen in love with her. Think he'd be likely to stay with her. Which, no matter how much he wanted her right now, would never happen. It would be the same experience she'd had with her husband. Love and desertion. Betrayal, for whatever reason, was still betrayal.

He couldn't do it. It was not right! But there was no denying he wanted Allie. Desperately.

Fortunately, he was no randy teen, but a man experienced enough to hide his rampaging desires reasonably well. At least in public. What would happen when they finally were alone was anybody's guess.

Allie could sense that her friend was feeling far more than merely friendly. By the time the party was over at the traditional midnight hour, he seemed almost too hot to handle. His brown eyes had depths of desire in them beyond anything she'd ever seen before, and when he fixed his hungry, heated gaze on her, she felt herself respond, eagerly. Her body seemed to melt and swell and sink and rise, all at the same time. She knew the feelings, but it had been many years since they had come on her so strongly. Many, many years.

She wanted him. Wanted this man who had such strength and grace in his body, passion in his eyes and gentleness in his hands. Who was not hers to keep, but only to enjoy for a time.

And, she determined, she could do just that! She joined M.J. and Miranda, who were both feeling very little pain, and Matt, who still seemed relatively sober, and began to figure which home she and Matt should use for their first night together. Would his baby-sitter be willing to stay for the entire night at his house? Or should they just take a chance on Laurel's interrupting them with another nightmare... It was a dilemma, but one she could deal with, eventually.

But, as they were making their way toward the exit, Rita Morely and David Benning intercepted them. Rita was all smiles. David looked as if he was smiling at something no one else could see or appreciate. Allie suppressed a shiver when she saw the strange expression on the older man's face. He looked downright spooky. But she forgot about him when Rita spoke.

"I have finally found enough people with enough information to put it all together," she said, addressing Matt directly and not looking at anyone else. "*You're* the young man who came out when Martha Essex died and is *claiming* to be her brother." She stared rudely now, looking at him as if he were a bug on a glass slide. "My, my, my. Allison, you do manage to ally yourself with the *strangest* men. First, one that ran away from you, and now this." The words hung in the air like a bad smell. She gave the entire group another smile and swept past. David Benning had the good grace to try looking embarrassed as he followed her out the door.

Allie looked at Matt. *He* looked as if he were ready to take the world apart with his bare hands!

CHAPTER EIGHT

"*CLAIMS* to be Martha's brother?" Allie put her hand on Matt's arm. "Matt, what's she blithering about?"

"Nothing." His face was stone.

"Matt, what's the deal?" She shook him, gently. "What did Rita mean?"

"It's not your worry," he said, cold as ice. "I'd better get home. You ready to drive?"

"Hey, man." M.J. moved in. "You have a problem? You're with friends, remember."

"Not here." Miranda pushed at them all. "Let's wait until we're out in the car. Alone."

But once in the Saab, all Matt would say was that he was having some trouble with Martha's lawyer, Penny Jackson. "She's beating on the fact that Martha and I weren't brought up together. That we were essentially strangers. She doesn't see me as Laurel's proper guardian, that's all," he said. "It's a personality thing."

"The hell with that!" M.J. declared. "She has no legal right to decide on the basis of her likes and dislikes if your sister's will..."

"Well, my sister's will is one of the issues." Matt, who was sitting in the front passenger seat next to Allie, rubbed his eyes. "But as I said, it's not your problem. Please, forget it. I had a great time tonight, and so did the rest of you. Let's just go on home."

Allie made no move to start the car. "Is the lawyer questioning your qualifications as a parent, or is she worried you're after the estate money?"

Matt regarded her. No desire showed in his eyes now. Just anger and frustration. "Oh, I'd say both." He looked away. "And, she has some grounds. My past..."

"Is past!" Allie touched his arm. "You're the best guardian in the world for Laurel," she said. "I've rarely seen such an attentive and concerned parent. I'd swear to it in any court of law in the nation. And even more important, Laurel depends on you and loves you. If she lost you, she..."

"She won't." Matt stared out the window. "I don't give a damn about the estate. Not for myself. I'd hate to lose it for her, though. It's her birthright. But if it came to it, I'd..."

"You'd what?" Allie felt hot anger. "Cut and run? Hide with her? No, mister. You stay right here and fight for what's rightfully yours and Laurel's."

"Allie, settle down," Miranda advised. "You can't know what's on Matt's mind."

"I know Jackson," M.J. said. "This woman who doesn't like you has a reputation for being difficult. Maybe I..."

"I don't want to burden you people with this." Matt shook his head. "I'll handle my own problems, thanks."

"Maybe," Allie said, touching him again, "we'd like to be burdened. You need friends if you're really facing a hard time, Matt. Don't shut me... don't shut *us* out." Suddenly, her feelings were as strong as they had been earlier, but now they were different. More grounded. She... *cared.*

No. No... She... loved him?

To hide her confusion and turmoil, Allie reached forward and started the engine. She could not be feeling this! Should not. Not for Matt Glass, a virtual stranger. A man whom she'd only known ten days and who'd be out of her life in a few months at the very latest. But what else could it be? Still soft and tremulous, but real and getting more and more solid and undeniable.

"Look," she said, over the rumble of the motor. "It's late. Almost two in the morning now. We've all had a hard night of partying. There're four of us. I vote we get together tomorrow and talk. But, ultimately, it's up to you, Matt. Do you want our help?"

He was quiet for a long time, his profile etched against the night by the arc lights in the parking lot. "I think I do," he said, finally. "If it were just me, I'd slog it out, in my own way. But Laurel... I'll ask for help because of her. *We* need your help." His voice seemed close to breaking.

M.J. leaned forward and slapped his shoulder. "Don't worry, Matt. There are a fair number of good brains in this car, even if some are a little pickled tonight. We'll combine and conquer. Count on it!"

Allie saw Matt smile, but he said nothing. Just slouched down in the seat and folded his arms across his chest. She started out of the lot, and M.J. and Miranda fell silent also.

By the time she got back to her house, it was clear none of the others were in any shape to drive, and Allie was too tired to taxi them so she offered beds all around.

"I've plenty of room," she said. "Matt and M.J. can sleep downstairs in Sam's room on the twin beds and Miranda can bunk in Sally's queen-size."

"Oh, goodie," Miranda said, with a giggle. "A spend-the-night party."

"Sounds great to me," M.J. echoed her sentiment.

But Matt shook his head. "I can't leave Laurel all night. If she has a nightmare, I . . ."

"Matt, she knows the sitter now. Debbie's steady and reliable. You can't be with her twenty-four hours a day, seven days a week for the rest of your life."

He sighed. "I'm so tired and worried, I guess I can't think straight. You're right. And I did set it up in case I was out all night," he added, looking over at her. His face was expressionless. "Debbie planned to sleep over anyway, since we were getting back so late. And I admit I had some ideas about how I wanted to spend the rest of our date."

Allie smiled. "I'm flattered."

M.J. made some rude noises. "I think this is where I'm supposed to get into the act and be indignantly in defense of my cousin's honor, but frankly, I'd rather go to sleep." He opened the car door. "Coming, dear?" he asked, extending his hand to Miranda. "I'm afraid I have to confess that I don't even have the energy to make a decent pass at you tonight. Forgive me."

Miranda giggled again.

Allie got them all into the house, distributed fresh toothbrushes and showed them to their rooms. She was exhausted herself, and would have fallen right into bed but for the necessity of letting Fred outside for a few minutes. Feeling she needed some fresh air, herself, she went outside with the dog.

The night air was chilly and clear as crystal. While Fred sniffed around, Allie studied the stars, the hills behind the house and the alley that ran in back of her yard...

And the car parked down the alley. In just the right spot to have a clear view of her home. She shivered. Wondered who...?

Fred frisked at her feet, indicating it was time to go inside. Allie shrugged and followed the poodle. If the car was there in the morning, she'd report it. Glancing at the kitchen clock while she got Fred a treat from the pantry, she noted that morning wasn't far away. She pressed her fingers to her temples. Even without drinking, she'd managed to get a headache.

It was undoubtedly due to the cigarette smoke and the noise.

It could not have a thing to do with the crazy notion that she might be in love with Matt Glass. And nothing at all to do with her frustrated lust for him. Not a thing! She checked on the cats, made sure they had enough food and water and shooed Fred into the bedroom. Time to sleep, she instructed herself.

But she did not get much rest, in spite of her exhaustion. Morning came far too soon, bringing with it birdsongs, Fred whining to go out again and the phone ringing. She was tempted to let the machine answer, but it was Sunday, and realizing it might well be her kids, she reached for the receiver.

She listened, and her heart froze. The voice was low, male and gravelly, and the insults and accusations that poured like acid into her ear were words that had never before been leveled at her. Indignation rose, along with bile.

Then, with a shiver of horror, she thought she knew who was talking. At first, she was too stunned to do anything but listen. Then, slowly, she replaced the receiver, the numbness of emotional shock threatening to make her drop it before it cradled. She got it in place, then just lay still.

The bedroom door opened. Fred barked once, then was silent when she saw who it was. Matt stood there, wearing only the pants from the suit he'd had on the night before. His hair was wet and slicked back as if he'd just stepped from the shower. He even looked clean-shaven.

"I heard," he said, his lips twisting in a strange expression. As if he was going to be sick. "Heard it all. I was in the kitchen and grabbed the phone without thinking. Figured it might be the sitter with a problem, and I didn't want to wake anyone else." He moved into the room and shut the door. Fred settled back on the bed, watching him. "Are you all right?"

"No."

"Any idea who?"

She shook her head, tears starting to trickle down the sides of her face. Her breathing became rapid. "It...it sounded like Paul." She gripped the sheet and summer blanket with clenched hands that trembled. "But he's..." Her voice rose to a treble level, almost like a child's cry.

Matt came around and pulled her up to him, embracing her tightly, not even noticing how little separated their bare skin right now. All that he thought of was how to soothe away her fear and horror. "It wasn't your husband, Allie. And it wasn't a ghost with an evil tongue. It was an enemy who's afraid of you. Keep *him* afraid. Don't let the fear turn onto you. You're safe. You're with me."

She tried to cling to the last shred of dignity she possessed, but the sobs came. She collapsed into his arms, and put her head on his shoulder and cried.

And she did feel safe. She felt safer than she ever had before. Safer than she'd felt with Paul, the man she had trusted to be with her for the rest of her life. Fred snuggled in, determined to be part of the moment, and that gesture of companionship from her pet made her cry all the harder.

Matt held her, reveling in the feelings roiling through him. Women had cried in bed with him before, but never had he responded with such tenderness. Her little dog looked up at him with dark brown eyes full of trust and concern. Matt thought he might cry himself in another moment. A quick, hard knock on the bedroom door jarred him out of that, however.

"What the hell's the matter?" The door opened again and M.J. and Miranda entered. Both looked dreadfully hung over and worried. "We heard the phone, then you walking down here and then Allie's crying," M.J. explained.

"The call. Bad news? Is somebody hurt?" Miranda asked.

Allie managed to get hold of her emotions. She wiped her face with the sheet and pushed Matt back a little. "No," she said. "It was..."

"It was a poison-pen phone call," Matt explained. "Some bastard tried to scare her. That's all." He stood up, releasing Allie. Fred placed her front paws on his leg, and he picked her up. "If it happens again, we can get a special gadget that'll trace the caller."

"Scare *you?*" M.J. ran his hand over his face, making the dark bristle of his whiskers rasp. "Allie, you aren't afraid of the devil himself. So who could possibly put such a fright into you?"

"He hinted he was Paul. Back from the grave I'd put him in." She hiccuped, forcing back more sobs. "Said I'd killed him. Said I was... being unfaithful to his memory."

M.J. swore.

"That's the expurgated version?" Miranda asked, folding her arms over her chest. "I take it the real thing was more vitriolic?"

Allie nodded.

M.J cleared his throat. "I need coffee, some aspirin and a shower, and not necessarily in that order. Then, I say we hold a war council. We can deal with Matt's situation first."

"No." Matt stroked the poodle, calming her. "My problems can wait."

Allie reached for her bathrobe and pulled it on. "This may be an isolated incident. It may never happen again and it's no one's problem but mine," she said, getting up. "You all have homes to go to and things you need to do. I'll get some coffee perking, and..."

"My God!" Miranda exclaimed. "I don't know when I've seen two people more stubborn about getting help from willing friends." She put her hands on her head. "If my head didn't hurt so bad, I'd get mad at the both of you."

Allie reached for Fred. "Take a shower, Miranda," she said. "Use my bathroom. Here's a clean robe. You'll feel much better, believe me." She walked out of the bedroom and headed down the hall.

Matt found himself staring at M.J. "She ever have a call like this before?"

The lawyer shook his head. "Not to my knowledge. And I think she'd have told me."

"Take a shower, yourself, M.J.," Miranda said. "We won't let her kick us out so easily. And Matt, if you want to go get your niece and bring her down here so your mind is at ease, do it."

Matt moved his gaze to the woman private investigator. "You think there's any connection between her problem and my situation?"

Miranda shrugged.

"Because if there is, I'll get out of her life. I'll take Laurel and..."

"You'll what?" Allie came back, hurriedly, Fred at her heels. "Leave town? Leave me? Oh, great. That'll be a big help." Her angry expression melted. "M.J., there's a strange car parked just down the alley. It was there last night, too. Gave me a funny feeling. Like someone was watching the house."

Matt looked at M.J. They both left the room at a run. Allie heard the back door slam. "They aren't wearing shoes," she said.

"Hell," Miranda commented. "M.J. doesn't have his pants on. Just underwear."

Their laughter was uneasy, but genuine.

A few minutes later, the two men came back inside to the kitchen. Allie had the coffee going, and Miranda was in the shower.

"We scared 'em off," M.J. announced. "Whoever they were, they saw us both coming and they peeled out fast, backward down the alley."

"I got the license number," Matt added. "But it's an out-of-state plate. Could be a rental, too."

Allie set out mugs, cream and sugar. "What kind of car do you think it was?"

"Toyota," Matt said.

"Land Cruiser," M.J. added.

Allie hesitated, then said "The other night, Matt, when I left your place, I thought someone was following me. It was a squarish kind of car. It could have been a Land Cruiser. I think there were two people inside, but it turned off once I hit the city limits, so I didn't get a chance to really see."

The men glanced at each other. M.J. took a mug and filled it with coffee. "Two people? That how you read it, Matt?"

"Yes." Matt filled another mug. "There were two people in the Toyota. I'd swear to it."

"I'm heading for the shower now," M.J. said, carrying his mug with him. "Don't make any rash moves or important decisions until I return." He left the room as Miranda walked into the kitchen, her hair wrapped in a towel.

"I'm going to get Laurel," Matt said. "All this is making me uneasy. I want her with me." He gulped his coffee. "You'll be all right with M.J. and Miranda here, won't you?" he asked, directing his question to Allie.

Allie stood with her mouth open. Under any other circumstances, she'd have been insulted at the inference that she was unable to care for her own safety. But for now she let it pass. "Yes," she replied. "I'll be all right with them here."

"Good." He nodded solemnly, clearly not seeing the irony in his level of concern for a woman who had managed to take good care of herself and her children for all of her adult life. Then, he went downstairs to get his shoes, shirt and car keys. A minute later, he was back upstairs and out the front door.

"Wow," Miranda whispered. She sipped coffee and studied Allie's expression.

"Yeah," Allie didn't meet her gaze directly. Tears stung her eyes, and she wasn't exactly sure why. "Give 'em an inch." She went over to the pantry to take out pancake mix. As she opened the pantry door, the three cats magically appeared. Sighing, she deposited a fresh scoop of dry cat food in their dishes. Then she took the batter to the counter. "Some men don't know how to stay out of a person's business, so they end up trying to boss everyone around."

"That's not what I mean, and you know it, Allison Ford." Miranda set her coffee mug down on the table and started to towel-dry her hair. "But if you want to play dumb, feel free."

Allie slapped bacon onto a flat iron skillet. "I'm not playing dumb. Just stating facts." She was uncomfortable discussing this with Miranda. They weren't really close friends.

"Right." Miranda got up and gathered one of the cats to her chest, patting the soft fur. "The man is in love with you, Allie. How do you feel about that?" She buried her face in the cat's fur. "Nice kitty," she murmured.

Allie didn't even bother to frame an answer.

IT HIT MATT halfway up the mountain, just as a pickup truck came around a curve in his direction. Last night he'd wanted to make love to Allie. Make love until they both nearly died of the pleasure of it. Today, without that ever happening, he loved her. *Loved* her! He blinked and let out a low whistle.

That changed to a yell of surprise and rage when he saw that the pickup intended either to plow right into him or force him off the side of the road and down the cliff. No mistaking the evil intention. Instinct took over, and he twisted the wheel hard to the left, bluffing the other driver into flinching.

And, instinctively, he glanced up into the rearview mirror to see what happened behind him as he rounded the curve. The sight of the pickup screeching at the edge of the drop was the last thing he saw before he saw the oncoming dump truck and was sent spinning into pain and then oblivion.

WHEN THE PHONE rang again, Allie shrank from it. M.J., clean but wearing the rumpled clothes from the night before, reached over and picked up the receiver. He spoke. His expression twisted, then leveled into unreadablity. "What's his condition, Phil?" he asked finally. His gaze fixed on Allie and didn't leave her.

Allie felt her heartbeat stop. Phil Jacobs was the chief physician in the emergency room at the hospital. "Who's ill?" she cried, grabbing the edge of the kitchen table. "M.J.! Who?"

M.J. hung up. "Matt Glass ran his Jeep into the side of a dump truck coming down the mountain about thirty minutes ago. The Jeep's totaled, and..."

"Matt!" The tears poured down Allie's face, but she had no idea she was crying. "He's dead. It's all happening again. Just like Paul..."

M.J. looked as if she'd cut his heart out. "No, darlin', he's not, and it is not the same. Matt's all right. He's banged up some, bruises and small cuts, but nothing serious. Phil says he's got a mild concussion, that he's mad as hell and raving about some maniac trying to run him off the road, but nothing's broken and…'' He quit talking. Allie had fled from the room.

"Let her go,'' Miranda advised as he tried to follow. "Give her a minute, M.J. I think she's in love with the guy.''

"I know.'' M.J. settled back in his chair. Fred, upset by her mistress's sudden departure, jumped up on the most familiar lap and settled down, as well. M.J. stroked her little head and scratched her ears. "Miranda, how would you like to work for me?'' he asked.

The P.I. smiled. "Investigating things for anyone I happen to know?''

"Uh-huh.'' M.J. nodded. "Two people who are too stubborn and self-reliant to ask for help on their own.''

"You have an employee.'' She held out her hand.

M.J. shook it. Then he turned it over and kissed the palm.

"THE PICKUP CAME right at me,'' Matt stated, speaking to the policeman investigating his case. "It was a deliberate attempt to ram me or force me off the road and over the side of the cliff.'' Anger thrummed in his voice, but he spoke calmly.

Allie sat in a corner of the hospital room, listening and watching. She had raced to him, only to find him full of anger, not seeming to need her attention or comfort at all. Perhaps, not even wanting her there. She wasn't sure yet. She was still trying to read him. Phil and the other physician attending Matt had insisted he stay in the hospital for twenty-four hours observation, but it was clear that Matt Glass had no intention of obeying doctors' or anyone else's orders.

When she had entered the room, the cop was asking questions, so she had only made eye contact with Matt.

It had been like looking into a furnace. The variety of emotions she saw both elated and terrified her. Matt was all right!

But he was killing mad!

"The pickup truck was Teddie Baker's?" The cop looked at his notes. "You're sure about that?"

Matt shook his head, wincing in pain as he did so. "No, I'm not. I only caught a glimpse of it, since I was concentrating on avoiding it and staying alive."

"There was no evidence of a pickup at the scene," the cop said. He was about forty, overweight with thinning sandy hair, and he looked mildly irritated as if this investigation had interrupted his plans for a quiet Sunday. "Just some skid marks on the side of the road, and they could have gotten there at any time. The driver of the dump truck didn't see any other..."

"The driver of the damn dump truck had been partying all night up at a cabin!" Matt put his hand to the sides of his head. His physical pain was obvious. "But you didn't test *his* blood. Just mine."

"You'd been partying, too," the cop commented. "We have witnesses who say you weren't in any shape to drive yourself last night."

"Witnesses?" Allie interrupted, now. "What witnesses? I thought..."

"They're accusing me," Matt said. "Of reckless driving." His eyes shone with a dark, dark gleam. "The dump truck driver says I came out of nowhere and blindsided him. No one else saw the pickup that tried to take me out. And the other guy has lots of friends around here."

Allie stood. "Well, so do you." She looked at the cop. "Mr. Glass's lawyer is outside. I suggest you hold off on any more questions until he is present."

The cop shrugged. "That's his right."

"My right," Matt said, quietly, "is to find Baker and get the truth out of him."

Allie made a decision then and there. "M.J. is going to stay here with you for a while," she said. "I'm going up to get Laurel. And you two are staying with me."

Matt frowned.

"No argument." She softened her expression. "Listen to reason for a change. How can you hope to keep up with her, feeling like you do? You're all bruised up, Matt. And I know your head must be nearly killing you. Let me do this. Please."

He shut his eyes. "If it puts you in danger, I..."

The cop raised his eyebrows, but said nothing. Plainly, he was curious, though.

"We can talk about that later," she said, going over to him and kissing him lightly. "Try to stay still and calm. I'll be back soon. M.J. will be right here." She left, after giving the cop a hard look.

Matt watched her go out the door. The cop was asking more questions, but he didn't hear a word. Something that had happened just before the crash tickled at his mind, but he could not for the life of him remember what it was. Something about Allie. He continued to ignore the cop while he played back the night and the morning right up to the time he'd left her house to go after Laurel. He remembered how much he'd wanted Allie. How his romantic plans hadn't worked out, although that had been acceptable, given the situation. Then, the morning had come all too soon, with the bad things happening. He remembered the horrible phone call she'd received. Remembered holding her and feeling... Feeling... What? Just out of reach, it hovered, teasing him...

"Mr. Glass, are you all right?" The cop was by the bed now. "Should I call a doctor?"

Matt rubbed his aching eyes. "Yeah. I mean, no. Don't call the doc. I'm all right. I had worse headaches from the altitude in the Himalayas."

The officer's eyes widened. "You climbed them mountains?"

Matt regarded the man. "I was on a few expeditions when I was younger. When I could still tolerate the cold conditions. Never made it to the top, though. Why? You climb?"

Pride swelled the older man's face. "I did the Grand up in Jackson Hole once. Greatest time of my life, let me tell you." He glanced down at his notebook. "But I was younger, too. Look. I know you're hurting, so I won't keep at you. For now. But if that truck driver files charges, you..."

"He won't." M.J. came into the room. "Officer, I think we have evidence of a conspiracy here to lay blame for the accident at my client's door, where it clearly does not belong."

Matt blinked. Miraculously, M.J. had managed to transform himself from a Sunday-morning party wreck to a spiffy lawyer, complete with the three-piece suit. Just how much time had he lost, anyway? He tried to follow M.J.'s voice as the lawyer spoke to the cop, but his hearing faded, and he dozed. All he heard for certain was the phrase, "Known acquaintance of one T. Baker."

After that, he only saw darkness and heard the soft sound of Allie's voice echoing in the secret places of his mind and heart.

It was sufficient for him.

CHAPTER NINE

THE FOLLOWING FRIDAY, behind on her carefully planned business and political schedule and in turmoil regarding almost every single aspect of her private life, Allie drove up to Montana to spend the Fourth of July weekend and the following week with her parents and twins. After pulling out of her driveway, she looked back at her three passengers. "Everybody comfy?" she asked.

Matt and Laurel nodded and smiled. Fred didn't smile, but her tiny tail whopped the seat softly. Allie turned her face forward again. The tensions and fears of the last days faded. A sense of pleasure filled her.

She wasn't even worried about being behind. They all needed this trip. She had done the right thing.

The day after his accident, Matt had come home from the hospital to her house and Laurel had been there waiting for him. The child's delight at being reunited with her uncle was matched only by her continued pleasure in Fred's company and the fun though touchy work of getting friendly with the suspicious cats. To Allie and Matt's relief, Laurel did not seem to connect Matt's temporary disappearance with the loss of her parents. Her adjustment to the changes seemed excellent, in fact.

Allie set them both up in Sally's room, thinking that it would be better for Laurel to be as near Matt as possible. While Matt had rested at the hospital, and while M.J. and Miranda had worked on the case, Allie had rallied a few of her friends and had moved most of Laurel's baby equipment down the mountain to her house. If the arrangement had caused anyone moral or social problems, they had kept their opinions to themselves.

Which was undoubtedly wise. Allie would have taken off heads, if anyone had even snickered. She had many reasons to be sensitive about the subject.

Three more phone calls early on during the week from the mysterious "ghost" of Paul Ford had disturbed her deeply, making her even more careful about her behavior. Not that she believed the calls were from Paul, but the nasty, ugly words she heard just before slamming down the phone each time jarred her to her core and made her determined to demonstrate that she could be a friend to Matt without being a lover, as the caller so lasciviously implied. Her relationship with Matt was pure as snow. She was his friend, not his mistress or lover.

But she had enjoyed his company during the week they had lived under the same roof. She glanced back in the rearview mirror once more. He sat, relaxed, one arm around Laurel in her car seat and the other resting on Fred's back. He was watching the passing scenery, a faraway expression on his handsome face. If only he were a different man, she thought, she could watch him watching forever and be perfectly happy. And they hadn't even kissed. Really kissed. She imagined how *that* would be...

"This is incredible country," he said, interrupting her erotic musing. "Just goes on and on forever, doesn't it."

She smiled. "Seems that way. The local joke is you see more antelope and sagebrush than people on this highway." She glanced into the mirror again.

His smile was sad, almost wistful. "Seems that way," he said, repeating her words. Then that faraway look again.

What was he thinking?

All the time they'd been together this last week, he'd been distant. Friendly, of course. Pleasant. But distant, as if she were some stranger he didn't want to bother or offend. If he hadn't still been suffering headaches, she was sure she would have challenged him on his attitude, but it was too soon after his accident to upset him, she felt.

And, frankly, there was really too much going on for her to pursue her relationship or non-relationship with him. She hadn't questioned him on the custody case yet. She hadn't even talked to him about the phone calls. She didn't want him getting upset about the propriety of their living situation. She was sure he knew about the calls. He'd been there when they had come in and she couldn't disguise her disgust. Oh, he knew. But they didn't discuss them.

At Josh's suggestion, she had started doing some door-to-door campaigning. That had taken up the long summer evenings, leaving only time for brief conversation with Matt before she had headed, exhausted, to her solitary bed. Josh had also been working on setting up a public debate for her with Rita, but so far, timing was a problem. Rita's manager, the traitorous Ned, hadn't agreed to a date yet.

Allie had scheduled twice as many meetings with her clients, realizing that, as the fall neared and the campaign heated up, she would have even less time to spend advising them. Matt had stayed out of the way during the day when her clients came and went, but she knew *they* knew she had guests, one of them a handsome, mysterious male and the other a small child. The evidence that others were staying with her was there for anyone who cared to look. Laurel was a normal two-year-old and with her around, it was impossible to keep the house tidy. Toys lay here and there, no matter how well Matt kept after his little charge.

She was, however, according to Matt, less inclined to mess things up deliberately than she had been at her own home. They both found that interesting. Maybe, Allie reasoned, it was because she had the animals and two adults to amuse her and keep her mind off mischief.

And maybe, as M.J. suggested one evening, it was because the little girl felt really secure again. Allie had left that idea alone, afraid to pursue it.

"Think your kids are ready for us?" Matt's question, coming out of his long silence, pulled her back to the present. "Kind of a shock for Mom to be bringing up a guy and a baby. Especially since the guy and kid are living with her."

"They're ready," she assured him, not sure herself. "You two aren't the first stray cats I've adopted. How do you think we got Tom, Dick and Harry?"

Matt chuckled. He hadn't been laughing much recently, and the sound warmed her. "You kept them. Are you keeping us, too?"

Allie gripped the wheel. "Of course not. You don't belong to me, and you have your own homes. T.,D. and H. did not. They simply saw a good thing and settled into it. Smart cats."

Matt didn't respond to that. Silence fell again. He crossed his arms and stared out the window. Allie looked in the mirror and saw his profile. His features were drawn hard, his mouth turned downward. It didn't make him any less handsome.

She wondered if he was thinking about the accident. He hadn't driven himself since it happened, due to the headaches he was still having. They made him moody, which she understood, apparently affected his vision and made him forgetful, he claimed. She wasn't sure what he meant by that, because he seemed sharp enough to her. The doctor hadn't said a word about memory problems, either. Phil had said that, except for the bruises and the lingering headaches, Matt was good as new.

He certainly had followed the orchestration of his defense closely enough to demonstrate mental acuity, Allie thought. He'd kept right up with everything M.J. and Miranda were doing in his behalf.

Miranda had discovered that the witnesses who told the police of Matt's intoxicated state the night before the crash were none other than Rita Morely and David Benning. Apparently, no one else at the dance was willing to say he'd been actually drunk. Of course, there were a number of folk who were in no condition to make such judgments that night, she realized.

The bad part was that there really was no evidence of Teddie Baker's pickup having been on the road. The driver of the dump truck that had actually hit Matt hadn't seen it. And Teddie, according to his cronies, had been down in Colorado that weekend, so he couldn't have been on the mountain road, as Matt claimed. Also, his truck was in the shop. Some kind of trouble with the fuel line. He'd had the engine steam-washed, too.

Matt had muttered something about all evidence being cleaned away by professionals and that Teddie's friends were lying. Miranda had agreed. If they had found the pickup and been able to match dirt on it with the dirt in the tire grooves along the side of the mountain road, they might have a case against Teddie. But now, they had nothing.

M.J., not one to be discouraged easily, had managed to find witnesses to the dump truck driver's revels of the night before. Just the fact that the man, one Gorden Hendry, could come up with no good reason why he'd been driving such a vehicle down the road on a Sunday morning was enough to cast some suspicion on his own sobriety. No criminal charges were laid. The event was simply labeled an accident with no one at fault. Hendry was certainly just an unlucky man who had happened into a collision with Matt.

But, rumors abounded. Gossip slithered. And Allie's reputation was on the line, because Matt was staying at her home. Allie had insisted. For Laurel's sake, if not for his own. They actually had a few hot words on the topic before he'd dropped it.

"Does Josh have you in the rodeo parade next month?" Matt asked, his voice again startling her out of her gloomy reverie. "I just read about it in the paper this morning."

She half turned and looked at him. The bruises on his face were fading, but he still looked as if he'd gone a full ten rounds with the dump truck itself. "What do you mean?"

"You need to ride in the parade. It's a great PR opportunity." Matt sat up. "Allie, I've been moving slow.

Hurting a lot. More than I cared to let on, but I've been watching. Josh Henderson is a lousy campaign manager. You have got to take some initiative yourself, if he doesn't come up with these ideas.''

She frowned, looking straight ahead. "He's all I have, Matt. He'll have to do the job." She felt a hand on her shoulder.

"Well, he isn't." Matt resisted moving his hand to touch her hair. This was a business discussion. If he touched more of her, it was liable to take another turn. And he was too confused to risk that right now. "Isn't doing a good job, anyway. And I owe you more than I can ever repay. I tell you what. Let's go official with my unofficial advice. If you don't think it'll put Josh out too much, I'd like to take over.''

She almost slammed on the brakes. "I can't fire him, Matt."

"Why not? He's not doing squat for you."

She had no response to that. It was almost the truth. But not quite. "I have to live here," she said. "You could be a wonderful help this time around, but there will be other campaigns. You won't always be there. Josh will. He'll learn. As time goes by, he'll pick up the tricks of the trade.''

Silence. Then: "All right. When we get back, I'll ask him if I can work as his assistant at no charge to either of you.''

She gripped the wheel, her emotions twisting and turning. Wanting to stop and confront him with her feelings.

Not daring to. It wouldn't be fair or right.

"Thank you," she said. "I appreciate the offer, and I know Josh will, too.''

Matt said, "Umph." Then nothing at all.

A little later, Laurel woke from her nap, and they didn't talk business for the rest of the long drive. Things were too hectic. Allie had forgotten what it was like to travel a long distance with a very small child. Laurel's job was obviously to remind her of all the details!

THEY REACHED her family's ranch late at night, having decided to drive straight through. Although she yearned to hug them, Allie didn't wake the twins. She just looked in on them. Her parents, Bill and Fran Campbell, were still up to greet her enthusiastically and to welcome Matt. But she could tell they were uncertain about his role in her life.

Well, that made a crowd of them.

Her father helped Matt set up the baby's portable bed in the guest room, while her mom fixed a late snack. The four then spent a pleasant, companionable half hour, talking about nothing in particular, except local gossip. Matt begged off eating too much, saying his head was bothering him, so Allie wolfed down most of the meal alone.

After Matt went on to bed, she spent a little time longer with her folks, explaining about him, his accident and why he was living in her house. She wasn't sure she made all her points clearly, since she was tired and still confused about her feelings, but her folks accepted her explanations and choices without overt criticism. As they always did. Then, they said an affectionate and loving good-night to her.

Allie breathed a sigh of relief, once she was finally alone. Relief and happiness to be at the one place on the planet where she could feel real peace and security. She took Fred to her old, childhood room and fell into bed. She slept like a baby without dreams until sunrise. But with the break of day...

"Mom!"

"Momma!"

The twins burst into her room just as the morning sun turned the air gold. Fred barked in alarm and then started wriggling and giving the little yipping cries that indicated a state of deepest canine joy.

Allie sat up, tears in her eyes as her children flung themselves on her and into her arms and they hugged and kissed, yelled and laughed with happiness.

Sam pulled away first. "Mom," he said, his brown eyes solemn in his tanned face. "Where's the guy and the kid?" His tone indicated he had concerns, and at that moment, he looked older than his mere ten years. Older and uncertain, or maybe, untrusting. As usual.

"Yeah." Sally's eyes were brighter, anticipating rather than worrying. Also, as usual. "Is he cute?" She brushed her soft blond hair back from her little face. "What about the baby? Is the baby cute, too?"

Allie looked up. Matt, Laurel perched on his hip, stood at the open door. The two of them were staring at her and her children. "See for yourself," she said, pointing to the doorway. "Apparently, we've awakened them both."

The twins turned around and stared back, their movements almost mirror images. As usual. While they might be completely different in personality and world outlook, Allie could always count on their bodies moving in harmonious concert.

Matt had on jeans and a T-shirt and his hair was uncombed. Clearly, he was having a hard time adjusting to the sight of the twins. He looked confused. Laurel looked even more so. Her little face screwed up and she cried, "Mmmaaamma."

And she reached for Allie.

IT TOOK a while that morning to sort everything out, but by noon *almost* everyone seemed to accept almost everyone else. It was a tentative sort of acceptance, however, Allie realized. Rather like her little animal family. Each time she had introduced a newcomer to the group, there had been a lot of sniffing and testing and wariness. And so it was with her human family.

She found herself thinking of Matt and Laurel as hers, she also realized. That was dangerous, but she could do nothing to change it. So, she just let it happen.

Sally and Laurel became friends right away. This didn't surprise Allie, since her daughter was much like she was—immediately trusting. Probably too immediately for her own good.

Sam, on the other hand, obviously regarded Matt as an interloper and a threat. That did surprise Allie.

Young as he was, it was clear Sam Ford was a man's man in the making. He liked being around the ranch men. He'd been bitterly disappointed when she had broken off with Mike, the cowboy. Sam was tough, rough and masculine to a surprising degree at times. Never adopting hers or Sally's gentler ways. He doted on his grandfather and on M.J., his uncle.

Though never particularly friendly to strange men, Sam was never actually rude to any of her men friends. Certainly not with the kind of venom he was showing now. Concerned about the boy's attitude, Allie gently suggested they take a walk together and have a chat.

She sent signals to her father, signals Bill Campbell picked up immediately.

"We've jawed enough, don't you think," Bill said, standing up from his seat on the front porch and stretching. "I got some jobs for the lot of you lazy city folk. Sam, while you and your momma go for your walk, why don't you check out the alfalfa field fence for me. Matt, you and Sally and Laurel come on down to the barn." His blue eyes almost disappeared in the smile that crinkled his tanned, lined face. "Got to count this month's litter of barn kittens."

Sally yelled with delight at the prospect.

That brought happy sounds from Laurel, who was more content than Allie had ever seen the child. She had apparently switched loyalties from the now-neglected and abandoned Fred to Sally.

Sam seemed less than thrilled at the prospect of the walk Allie suggested. She could talk if she wanted, he told her, curtly. He would work. He wore dusty overalls, his pockets loaded with fence-mending tools. His hands seemed too big for his skinny arms, and they bore small scars from other working days. Her boy, Allie thought, was growing up.

Maybe that was part of the problem.

They reached the field and started walking the perimeter. "Okay," Allie said, starting right in. "You and I have always been straight with each other, Sam. What's the deal? Talk to me. You've all but spit in Matt Glass's eye. Why?"

"He your boyfriend?" Sam didn't look at her. He ran his hand down a length of wire fence. "Is he staying in your room?" His voice wavered a bit, indicating emotions that did not show on his face.

"No. And no. He's a friend who is a man. And he's sleeping in Sally's room *with* his niece in the portable baby bed beside him. *And* when we get back to Linville Springs, if he's feeling okay, he's going to move back to his own house. I just let him stay with me because he was hurt in an accident." She and Matt had mentioned the crash, but had given no one the gory details. She had not wanted her folks to have any cause to worry. Now she wondered if, in her silence, she had done more damage than good.

"Um." Sam bent down and inspected the wood at the bottom of one of the fence supports.

"Come on." Allie touched his head, feeling the silky blond hair on her palm. "You didn't get so ornery when you thought I was going to marry Mike."

"Mike's a man." Sam stood up and continued walking the fence. "This guy ain't, near as I can see."

"Oh?" Allie kicked at some dust, watched it puff up and settle back down. The summer air was still, and the day was promising to be a hot one. "You figured that out about him in just a few hours?"

Sam didn't reply. He found a split in the wire, raised it up, caught it in a special tool and twisted it so the break was bound together. His small muscles looked like ropes under his soft child's skin. Allie let him work in silence, marveling at her son's skill.

Then, she said, "He runs an adventure-tour business. I don't see why you think he's a sissy."

Sam shrugged. He reached in another pocket and pulled out a crumpled baseball hat. He settled the hat on his head, jerking the bill down on his forehead. "Anybody can run a business, Mom," he said. He stared at her from under the cap. Then, his face twisted. "Mom, he's a jerk. Any guy'd take care of a little baby, carry her around, feed her and talk to her like that's a jerk. He acts like you and Grandma.''

"Oh."

Sam turned away and started walking again. "But I guess if he ain't..."

"Isn't."

"*Isn't* your boyfriend, and he's going to be gone when I get home, it's okay."

"Well, thanks very much." Allie thought a moment and made a decision. Sam's chauvinist attitude bothered her quite a bit. Maybe she hadn't noticed it before because she had sympathized with the fatherless boy. She needed to help Sam see men in a more realistic light.

"Sam, just because a man can take care of a baby, doesn't mean he's a jerk. Laurel has no parents and Matt is trying to help her. He hasn't always run a business or had a little child to care for," she said, casually, as if they were just chatting now, the major part of the discussion already over. "I heard he rescued a bunch of people down in South America a few years ago. They were all so grateful, they've made a movie about it. It'll be on television this fall. He didn't tell me about it. Other people did. He doesn't brag about his life, but it's been extraordinary from what little I know. For sure, about those people, he did something no one else could or would do. He's a hero, Sam. He found them, and he saved them."

Her son stopped and looked at her. "He *found* them?"

"Yes."

"Did you tell him about..."

"About your father?" A chill crept up her back. "Yes."

"Could he find...?" Sam left the question unfinished, and Allie couldn't say a word. If that terrible telephone call had never happened, she could have been able to respond and set Sam's mind at ease as she had done in the past when he'd asked about his real father. But now...

"Find what?" Matt's voice made her jump. Allie turned to see him coming over to them. He was alone.

"Find my father." Sam's voice was clear, the tones ringing a challenge. He took off his cap and stared up at Matt. "My mom says you're a big hero and you rescued some people. Okay. Find my father."

Allie felt caught. Unable to say or do a thing.

Matt stared back at the boy, admiring the strength of will he saw in young Sam Ford. "Why?" he asked. "Why would you want him, Sam?"

Allie smothered a gasp.

But it was exactly what Sam needed to hear. His tough pose softened and he shrugged. "Dunno. Just thought if you were such a big hero and all..." He scuffed the toe of his boot in the dust. "Dunno."

Allie was sure she saw a glint of tears in her son's eyes.

Matt cleared his throat. Looked away from them. "I don't know where my father is, either," he said. "I guess he's probably still alive, but that's about it. I figure, he knows where I am, and if he wants to see me, he can come to me."

Sam digested that, his smooth young face a mask and only his eyes showing emotion.

Allie turned away. There were tears in hers.

But after that, the atmosphere between Sam and Matt began to improve.

THEY STAYED at the ranch until the following Sunday. Everyone thoroughly enjoyed the Independence Day celebration held on Saturday, and she even gave a short patriotic speech at the ranch's barbecue dinner. It was only for practice, since none of the attendants would be voting in the election she was involved in. Matt approved, saying she couldn't get enough practice speech-making if she was truly intent upon a political career.

By then, Matt seemed to feel his old self. He had stopped complaining of headaches and was active and cheerful. He was also willing to discuss some of the problems he was having with the custody case. But mostly, he seemed to be unwinding. He went riding and fishing with Sam and Bill, listened to her mother talk about the best ways to handle two-year-old girls and generally made himself popular with everyone who met him. He spent enough time with Sally for the girl to develop an embarrassing crush on him, and even Mike, Allie's old flame, who dropped by one afternoon, approved of him, saying if he had to lose her, it was good to lose her to a "real impressive kind of guy."

No one seemed to believe she and Matt were just friends.

Allie was no longer sure what the truth was. If she hadn't loved him before, she would have at that special moment when he'd made such deep contact with her son.

But she knew there was no future with this man. Like Paul, he'd be gone from her life eventually. Any anger she had, she hurled at the fate that had sent her two such men. Matt, she would forgive. She knew about and understood his need to leave. Paul, she probably never would forgive, since there had been no warning, no explanation, and therefore, no understanding.

They left around ten in the morning on Sunday, planning to get home the same day. Laurel whimpered when she realized she was leaving her new friends, but when Fred flopped down next to her and put her furry head on Laurel's leg, the little girl smiled and relaxed.

"I have got to get a Fred, I think," Matt said, watching the child. "She's just great with Laurel."

"Years of practice." Allie steered along the straight stretch of open highway. "Remember, she's had the twins to learn on. She's a pro with little kids, Fred is."

"So're you." His hand stroked her shoulder with a touch so light, she almost couldn't feel it. "I have never in my life seen anything so wonderful as that first moment when I saw you with your children in your arms."

Her eyes stung. She blinked. "Well, they're great kids, and I do miss them. But it's important for them to spend time with their grandparents. You could see how good Dad is as a surrogate father."

"Uh-huh."

"You were terrific with Sam, too," she added, unable to help herself. *And I love you for that*, she thought. Along with all the other things about you that ...

"He's a great kid. Going to be a great man. I can see it in his eyes. He's very mature, Allie."

She laughed, feeling things she didn't want to show. "Whereas Sally..."

"Is sweet and gentle, like her mother. Not a softy, though. She's as strong as her brother, in her own way." His hand settled on her shoulder. "She's what you would be, if life hadn't kicked you in the gut so hard. Sweet steel, capable of anything, but first and foremost, capable of great love."

Allie's throat hurt, the tears were so close. "I appreciate..." she started to say.

"I love you, Allie," Matt said.

She looked at him. He stared straight ahead. She returned her gaze to the road. "What?" she asked. "What did you say?"

"I said, I love you. Actually I realized it some time ago, but the accident put it out of my mind," he said, still not looking at her. "It hit me that I loved you just before the dump truck did. But somehow that circuit in my brain got jarred when I concussed. Then, when I saw you with your children..." His hand curled over her shoulder and tightened. He was trembling, just slightly.

"It all came back to me. But I couldn't tell you until now, though. I was afraid or I needed to keep it to myself for a while longer or I just couldn't find the right time. I honestly can't explain it myself. Isn't that odd? You'd think a man'd just have to blurt out a thing like that." He sounded bemused.

She swallowed hard against the tears. "What does it mean to you, Matt?"

She felt him shrug. "I honestly don't know yet." He pointed. "There's a side road. Pull over. I can at least show you, even if I can't tell you yet."

Without thinking about it, she obeyed.

And the moment the brake was set, her seat belt was off and she was in his arms.

CHAPTER TEN

THEY KISSED. Hard, clumsily and roughly at first, full of unfocused energy and wild physical need, but gradually settling into a slow, searching and tasting of each other. Allie lost herself in the wonder of it, and also lost all sense of how much time passed while she held this man, this special man. Desire swept through her, making her dizzy with its sweet power.

Predictably, Fred and Laurel put a halt to their activities. Fred barked, and Laurel said, "Maaa? Daddy? What doing?" The anxiety in her little voice was enough to cut through the sensual fog.

But Matt released Allie only slightly and continued to hold her while he smiled at her and then spoke soothingly to Laurel. "It's okay, sweetheart," he said. "We're kissing. That's all."

Laurel looked puzzled. Fred settled back down.

"Kissing," Allie said, looking at the little girl. "You know." She made exaggerated kissing noises. "Kiss, kiss, kissy."

Laurel giggled and imitated her.

Matt stroked Allie's hair. "What now, my love?" he quipped. "We can't exactly consummate our passion right here on the highway with a child and dog as witnesses."

Allie started to laugh, though she felt more like crying, so intense were her emotions. Until this moment, she'd been able to hide her own deep feelings and feel noble about it. But Matt had confessed his. Should she? Was she a coward to keep quiet?

Or just smart.

"I agree. This is insane," she said, drawing back from him a little more, trying to regain some degree of composure. "Silly, even. Kissing right here with Laurel watching. Now I know how married people must feel when they..." Suddenly realizing what she had been about to say, she blushed.

But Matt touched her cheek, gently. "I know what you meant. To be married, in love and have children together. With all the joys and problems of that condition. You never had that chance, did you?"

She could only shake her head.

"You know I can't promise you any kind of future like that, don't you?"

"Of course, I know that." She found strength to speak. "And I wouldn't ask it. The kind of life I live is so opposite of yours, that it would be foolish to even imagine that we..."

He put his finger on her lips. "Don't say it. It's foolish to predict anything, Allie. Let's just live this from day to day and see what happens."

They kissed again. It was sweet and exciting. But their passion was now blunted by the daunting presence of reality.

Reality in many forms, but mainly in the form of a giggling child who shouted, "Kiss, kiss, kiss, kiss, kiss," for the next hundred miles or so.

But as they drove, they talked.

"I lost out a lot on what it means to grow up with family ties, as you know," he said. "Ties and responsibilities were concepts my father never understood. So, when I say I love you, I'm not sure I can explain what I mean."

"It's okay." Allie glanced at him. "Right now, it means you like being with me, enjoy my company and want to go to bed with me." She smiled. "I can sure relate to that."

"Sometimes," he said, touching her shoulder with a tap of his finger, "you are too plainspoken. How will you ever succeed in politics, if you just give them what's right up front in your mind?"

"Is this politics?"

"No."

"Then don't criticize."

"Point taken."

She drove on. Then: "Tell me how it was, growing up, never knowing what the next day might bring."

He made a soft sound. "It's not a terrific story, believe me."

"But I want to know. See, until I lost... Until Paul disappeared, I was always so sure of everything. That was unwise, I see now. But I still *believed* everything would be all right."

"You still do, Allie."

She shook her head. "I don't think so."

"Yes, you do." Another touch on the shoulder, gentle, brief, as if that was all he dared allow himself for the moment. "At heart, you are a person of faith. A believer. Trusting that things and people won't fail or betray you."

"I do not..."

"That's why you get so angry and upset when they do," he interrupted. "Me? I just shrug and figure the worst is going to happen eventually, anyway, so why get in a twist about it."

She absorbed that truth, somberly. "We are a pair, aren't we?"

"Indeed. Indeed we are." He paused, then began to talk again. Much of the time, he talked about his youth with his father. As she listened, Allie began to realize that Robert Glass was quite a celebrity. He was an explorer and adventurer of long standing and definite renown. He'd done landmark work for the National Geographic Society, among others, and he was praised widely for his bravery and intrepid spirit. This had had the expected influence on his son. Being in the shadow of the great adventurer, Robert Glass, had meant many things to Matt, but mostly had given him the need to excel himself—to do as much or more than his famous father. "It's not uncommon," he added, "for the son of a well-known man to strive to do his old man one better or more."

"Did you?"

"Sometimes."

BY THE TIME she pulled into her driveway many hours later, Allie knew a great deal more about the life of Matt Glass.

Enough to convince her he would leave her eventually. When the call to travel, to adventure became too strong for him to resist, he would simply take Laurel and go.

Just like his father had done with him.

Tom, Dick and Harry greeted their return with studied indifference. M.J. had come by daily to feed and water the three felines, and so their physical needs had been taken care of. Allie carried the sleepy Laurel, and the little one just sighed happily when they walked in the door.

She thinks she's home, Allie thought.

"I know this is about as romantic a pass as you've ever heard, but I have to be with you tonight," Matt said, as he carried the portable crib into Sally's room. "And I don't want to upset Laurel by leaving her alone. Any ideas how we can manage?"

"I do have a plan," Allie confessed. "I gave the logistics of our situation some serious thought on the drive down."

The look in his eyes was warm and admiring. He finished setting up the bed and took Laurel from Allie's arms. The child was half-asleep, calm and limp in his embrace. "But she seems so relaxed, maybe..."

"We let Fred sleep here," Allie said, pointing to Sally's bed. "I'll bring in her special blanket, and she'll stay put with the proper command from me. She sleeps with Sally from time to time, anyway, so it's no big deal. If Laurel wakes, she can see Fred in the glow of the nightlight. Fred represents security to her. Somehow, I think..."

"*I* think that if you run your political life half as sensibly and well as you do your personal one, you'll be president someday." Matt laid Laurel on the clean sheet and pulled a light cover over her. He patted her little head and kissed her good-night.

Allie looked at him. In the soft light of the small bedroom, he looked about as domestic as a man could look, bending over his niece and tucking her in for the night. But he was not domestic. She would be asking for trouble if she ever forgot that.

She was asking for trouble, as it was, anyway. She might be in love with him. That was unavoidable. But, if she let him make love to her, she wondered if she would be able to stand the inevitable loss.

ow was her last chance to back out.

'Get Fred's blanket,'' he said, straightening and gazing at her with a fierce heat in his eyes. "I can't wait much longer to be with you.''

That did it. No chance at all. She ran to grab the blanket.

Matt stood by the door, watching her set things up and order Fred to stay with Laurel. He knew he was making a mistake, that to take her to bed was probably not a good move and would certainly put a spin on their relationship that neither one of them was capable of dealing with well.

But he had no choice. None at all. His desire for her had only increased as time had passed, and he was just too selfish to deny himself the fulfillment of loving her completely. Her face showed her own inner turmoil, her questioning of the wisdom of what they were about to do, but he made himself ignore it. He could see her hesitation now. But, too late. Love for her drove him… Need for her blinded him… Whatever it was, it was too strong for him to resist.

She continued to fuss over the dog and the baby. "Come on, Allie,'' he said, holding out his hand to her. "They'll be fine.''

"I know,'' she said, stepping away from the bed. "But I'm scared.'' She turned out the light.

"Don't be.'' His voice caught in his throat, and he had to clear it. "I won't hurt you, Allie.''

"No.'' She came closer, keeping her voice low. "I'm not afraid of you.''

"What then?''

She didn't answer. They stood in the doorway, and in the diffused light from the living room, he knew he'd never seen a more beautiful woman in his life. She was tired from the long drive and totally devoid of makeup. Her blond hair hung limply, but it glowed with a radiance that came from deep within the woman.

The woman...

He hooked his hand behind her head and tipped her face up to his. *No more waiting. No more denial.*

Allie felt his passion as his mouth covered hers. He was fairly shaking with it, and it fueled her own desire to a white-hot degree. Her mind took one last shot at telling her to stop, but by then it was far too late. Her body and heart took over. She wrapped her arms around him and pushed herself against him. Hard!

"Out of these clothes," he whispered, hoarsely. He pulled at her shirt. "I want you now, Allie."

"Down the hall," she whispered back. "To the bedroom." She grabbed him and led him, both of them stumbling as they tore off clothing on the way.

They fell onto her bed. Pulled off the rest of their clothes. Naked, they touched each other, hands moving with eagerness and need, trembling with passion. Moments later, he was inside her, filling her and bringing her almost immediately to a climax. She forced back her screams of pleasure, remembering just in time the child asleep right down the hall. They had forgotten to shut the door.

Matt watched her, amazed she could be so quiet when he could sense the inferno raging within her. He forced himself to ease back, to give her time to recover.

He was determined to love her as no other man had ever done. Determined with a perverse kind of love-fury to brand her so she'd never want another man. Never need another. Never have another lover but him... Never!

Allie felt the wildness surging in him and welcomed it. Silently, she met his strong passion with strength of her own, matching him, sometimes surpassing him, but always in physical harmony.

The kind of harmony that would make a symphony soar to the highest heaven.

Matt took her through several more climaxes, but eventually, he could no longer control himself and spent his passion in her body. The relief of release was almost overwhelming, and he only managed to stifle his shout of joy by burying his face in the sheet at her neck.

Finally, Matt rolled to one side, his arm over his head, his breath still coming in deep gasps. "I don't know about you," he said, hoarsely. "But I think I might be able to sleep soundly tonight."

Allie laughed and rested her body on her elbows while she looked down at him. "Think I'll let you? Now that you're in my clutches?"

He rolled his eyes. "God, Allie. Have pity. I'm only human."

She traced the line a drop of sweat left on his chest. "You could have fooled me."

"It was all an act." He shut his eyes. "I find you completely undesirable." His smile belied his words.

She regarded him for a long moment. "Let's be serious," she said. Tears filled her eyes. "You know, I love you, too, Matt."

"I wasn't sure until now. Come here," he said, drawing her back down. His body showed that sleep was the last thing on his mind.

THE NEXT MORNING, he woke before she did, and he spent a few minutes looking at her. She was utterly beautiful. Passionate, intelligent, ambitious...nurturing. A mother, a caregiver by her very nature. Look at all the animals she'd taken in, for goodness sake!

Why couldn't he stay with her? Why wouldn't it work? He surely would never find another woman quite like her. One that combined so many delightful qualities...

Maybe, just maybe, he needed to rethink his own life. Was returning to Los Angeles really that vital? Would Laurel be any happier growing up there than she would be right here where she was born?

After all, they could travel. Leave from time to time and go exploring...

But Allie was rooted to the land here. She wouldn't be happy anywhere else. He tried to picture her in L.A. and grimaced.

No way. He'd have to be the one to relocate if...

The phone rang. Laurel cried out, and Fred barked.

Allie sat up, her hair spilling in her face, a feeling that something monumental had happened. Then, she saw Matt, reaching for the receiver.

She felt her heart rate accelerate, wondering if this might be a repetition of the venomous call of two weeks ago, but when Matt shook his head and smiled at her reassuringly, she breathed in relief. The call apparently was for him. She reached for her robe and got out of bed.

Laurel smiled when Allie walked into the bedroom. Smiled and held up her arms. "Momma," she said, clear as a bell.

And Allie lost her heart for the second time.

MATT GRIPPED the receiver tightly, anger growing in him like a living fire. "Can they do this, M.J.?" he asked, wondering if the fury he felt would make his voice shake. Make him sound weak. "Is it legal?"

"So far," the lawyer replied. His tone was unemotional and professional. Almost unfriendly, Matt decided. "They do have some strong arguments going for them. They're a family. Settled. Related to John Essex. The wife kept in frequent touch with your sister and brother-in-law over the years, even though they live out of state while you..."

"While I was off, chasing adventure around the world." Matt swore. "I won't let them have her, M.J. I want to fight this."

"It's your decision, Matt. But I recommend you think about it."

"Who the hell's side are you on?" Matt yelled, finally losing his temper. "Think about it? What do you think I've been doing?"

"Cool down," M.J. said, his voice never changing pitch or attitude. "Talk to Allie about this. See what she says. I'll be in the office in about an hour. Call me there."

Matt slammed down the receiver. "Yeah," he muttered. "I'll call all right." He swore again, softly, heatedly. "The hell I will!"

"What is it?" Allie's voice made him turn. She stood in the doorway, Laurel in her arms, Fred at her feet. Her beauty completely took his breath away. "Matt, what's wrong?" Her expression convinced him she really did love him. That her declaration the night before had not been out of physical satisfaction. Allie Ford loved him!

He felt panic rising now. How could he stand to lose all this? Allie? Laurel? The kind of peace he had found with them?

Simple answer! He couldn't lose it! He'd fight!

"That was M.J.," he said. "Laurel has a second cousin, a Mrs. Turner or somebody, who is going to challenge me on custodial rights. She's married and able to provide a normal home." His lips twisted on the last phrase, making it almost another curse.

Allie regarded him. "And?"

"And what?" He got up, pulling the sheet with him. "There's no question about what." He ran his hand through his hair. "I'm going to take a shower, get dressed, and then I'm going to fight to keep my child." He went into the bathroom and shut the door.

Allie shivered. His expression was exactly like the one she'd seen on his face the night she'd had dinner with him. A dangerous, angry expression. One that boded ill for anyone who opposed him!

Things got worse. After she fed Laurel breakfast, she opened the paper and got another unpleasant shock. One of the letters to the editor questioned Allie's qualification as a political candidate, since, the writer stated, she was obviously living in sin with a man who had a child that wasn't legally his. The latter point was emphasized. The letter was signed, but it was a name she did not recognize. Until she remembered the last name of the woman disputing Matt's claim to Laurel. Turner. One and the same? She reached for the phone, intent on calling the paper and asking to make a statement on her relationship to Matt and Laurel, but thought better of it.

Might stir up waters she wanted left quiet. After all, since last night, she *was* "living in sin." She certainly did not want to cause Matt further problems in his quest to keep Laurel. She cared too much for both of them to do that.

Matt came into the kitchen. "Your cousin sounded less than supportive," he said, his tone near a growl. "I don't know if he's the best lawyer for the job."

Allie bristled. "If M.J. sounded strange to you, then you need to ask him about it. Don't go flying off in a rage just because things have gotten tough. Who is this Turner woman? Do you know her?"

Matt scowled, obviously not happy with her comments. "Never heard of her. Didn't know she existed until now." He poured coffee and sat down at the table.

"Is this her name?" Allie asked, laying the newspaper with the acid letter in front of him. "Turner? If it is, she's playing dirty. Using our private situation to advance her own cause."

Matt read. The veins in his neck and temples stood out. "Son of a bitch," he said, so softly she barely heard him. He looked at her, and all she saw in his eyes was hate and anger. Allie shrank back.

He swallowed the rest of his coffee and stood up, apparently unaware of the effect he was having on her. She could see he was shaking with suppressed rage. His eyes were like steel. She'd never seen a man look quite like that.

He put the mug down and took a deep breath. "I have to go out," he said. "Please watch Laurel. I'll be back." He left the kitchen, not even pausing to touch Laurel, who reached out for him and whimpered when she was ignored.

Frozen, Allie listened as the front door slammed, shaking the house. She heard the grinding of gears and the screeching of tires as he left the driveway in her car.

And then, Matt Glass was gone.

Just like Paul.

She spent the next hour in a fog. She tended to Laurel, readied herself for the working day and set up a play area for the little girl in the basement where Allie could watch her and work at the same time. When the twins had been small, she'd done the same thing. The rules were simple. Keep the kid in view, and don't get too immersed in work to miss any sound of trouble brewing. She even handled a visit from one of her clients with no hitches. Business as usual.

About eleven, Josh called. "We seem to have a little problem," he said. "I think you might want to reconsider your living arrangements, Allie. It's terrible press."

"I understand." She dug her nails into her palms. "I'm working on the problem, Josh. Can you think of any way to do damage control?"

"Kick him out, or marry him."

"Thanks."

"Sorry, Allie. But you know how conservative folks are around here. It just doesn't look good."

"I understand that. But it's a bit more complicated than just my good name."

"What do you mean?"

Allie hesitated. Matt's situation was really not Josh's concern. "Let's just say that the writer of that letter has a personal ax to grind. You might want to look into that."

"Can you be more specific?"

"I'm sorry. I can't tell you any more right now."

"All right." Josh cleared his throat. "Let me see what I can do. By the way, I think I forgot to tell you, I've made arrangements for you to ride in the parade week after next. Keep that Tuesday morning clear."

"I will. Thanks." Feeling a little better, she hung up the phone. At least Josh wasn't the flop Matt claimed he was.

About eleven, M.J. called. "We need to talk," he said, curtly, without even greeting her. "Now."

"I can't, M.J. I'm taking care of Laurel."

"Bring the kid. Come down to the office. Is Matt there?"

"No, he..."

"He's in a pretty scary state of mind right now, Al. If you see him, play it really cool. Promise me."

"What're you saying? Do I need to be afraid of him?"

M.J. hesitated. "I honestly don't know. He's a volcano looking for a place to erupt, and I don't want you or the little girl anywhere near him when he does. Come down to the office."

Allie pushed her chair back from the desk. "I don't have a car. Matt took it. M.J., what happened?"

"Um." Silence. Then: "He was here this morning. I told him he might want to consider giving Laurel up to the other people. They have a home out in Lade, Nebraska. Husband has a good job with a local bank there, a good reputation, and they want several kids. Have one, but the wife can't have any more of their own. They're high on several adoption lists, but now that Laurel needs a home, they want her, instead."

"You met them?"

"No. But Penny Jackson, the lawyer for the Essex estate called and..."

"M.J., she doesn't like Matt. He doesn't know what he did to put her off, but I don't think her opinion is unbiased. What're these people's names?"

M.J. told her. "Frank and Joan Turner."

"Have you read the paper this morning?"

"No, I didn't have time."

"Get it."

"Hold on."

Allie held. She leaned out the door to check on Laurel. The child was banging away on some wooden blocks with a small plastic stick. The three cats observed the action from a respectful distance. Fred sat closer, her tongue hanging out, ready to pounce on a block if it was thrown.

The sound of newspaper rattling. Then: "Oh, damn." More rattling. Then: "I see."

"J.F. Turner? Couldn't be a coincidence."

"No. Most likely it's the same Turner's using some odd idea of putting pressure on you in order to get Matt to cave in." M.J.'s tone was thoughtful. "Now, I begin to understand his anger."

"But it's not going to help, is it?"

"No. Listen, babe. You stay put. I want to make a few phone calls. But tell me one more thing."

"What's that?"

"How do you really feel about the guy? I mean, long-term?"

Allie swiveled her chair around to face a blank wall in her office. "How do I feel? I love him. Long-term? No hope for us." Tears, up to now unshed, rolled down her face.

He sighed. "I guess an explanation would take too long. I'll have to be satisfied with that."

"M.J., for all I know, I still have a husband somewhere. I can't just up and marry again. No matter how I feel."

"Legally, you know you're free, babe."

She shut her eyes. "Legally has nothing to do with it. You should know me well enough to know that. Until I have absolute proof Paul is never coming back, I can't... I just can't, that's all."

"Okay. I guess I understand. Take it easy, Al. I'll get back to you. And, cousin..."

"Yes?"

"I think you're out of your mind."

"How reassuring. Thank you very much." They both laughed, to relieve tension more than anything else. Then Allie said goodbye and hung up. She sat, thinking for a few minutes.

Then, the sound of Laurel's laughter brought her back. The sound of laughter and the cry of joy she gave. "Daddy!" she called out. Allie sat very still, feeling the hairs rise all along her arms and up the back of her neck.

It was Matt. "Come on, honey. We're out of here."

Allie burst from her office. Matt had gathered Laurel up in one arm. He had a duffel bag in his other hand. He wore an outfit similar to the one he'd had on the first time she'd ever seen him—khaki shirt and pants.

But this time, she could tell it was a working outfit. The boots were high, paratrooper style, and laced. A sheathed knife hung from his belt. When he turned, she was sure she saw the shape of a holster tucked in the small of his back at his belt. He was armed and dressed for a fight. He looked like a modern warrior on the way to battle.

"What are you doing?" she cried, not daring to move closer. She was too frightened to think for the moment.

"None of you want to help me," he said, lifting his chin and staring down at her. "So, I'm helping myself. Goodbye, Allie. It's a real damn shame, because I think I could have loved you the rest of my life."

And suddenly, with those words, it all became clear to her. She understood, at long last, what she had to do.

CHAPTER ELEVEN

"YOU'RE A LIAR!" Allie stood her ground, even though a warning surge of fear went through her. She'd slept with this man, made love to him, but she did not really know what he was capable of doing when desperate. Would he use violence to get his way? Was that, ultimately, the only thing he really understood?

Or was love a strong enough force to calm him down and make him listen to her? For now, she knew he loved her, and she knew she loved him. Wasn't that worth the danger? Worth the fight.

You bet, she thought, crossing her arms and glaring at the man in front of her. If it was a fight he wanted, then that was what he was going to get.

"I'm not lying when I say I love you," Matt said, a defensive, vulnerable look appearing in his eyes, contrasting with his belligerent stance. Laurel clung to him, silent and somber, as if somehow she understood how important this moment was for her own future as well as theirs. The very air was charged. Not even the four animals watching the scene dared to move. "No matter what happens or what I do, I meant every word I've said about my feelings for you."

"Sure you did." She sneered, deliberately baiting him. "Just like Paul did."

Matt lost some of his aggressive stature. "That's not a fair assessment of the situation, Allie. And you know it. I'm trying to save what I have. If you really love me, you'll stand aside and let me do it."

"Wrong! You're so wrong. If I really love you, Matt, I won't stand aside. Ever. I'll stand *with* you." She started crying, angry at herself for displaying weakness. "I . . . I don't want to lose you, too."

"Allie." He took a step toward her, longing in his eyes. "Come with me. Or come when I send for you. When I get somewhere safe."

She shook her head. "There is no place on earth that's safe, Matt. Not from what you're running away from. Not from selfishness. Don't you see? If you do this now, one day you'll find yourself running from Laurel. Running from me, if I was stupid enough to go away with you. It's a pattern your father taught you, and if you don't break it now, you probably never will."

He took a partial step back. "Maybe you're right about me, but I can't lose you, Allie," he said, his voice almost a whisper, but fierce and strong. "And I can't lose Laurel. Maybe running is wrong, but I don't know how else to deal with this situation."

She moved toward him. "Then listen to those who do, Matt. Listen to M.J. To Miranda. Listen to me! We know this land and these people, and M.J.'s probably the finest lawyer in the region when it comes to hard legal work and intelligent courtroom maneuvering. If there's a way under the sun to get justice done, he'll do it!"

"But . . ."

"I know." She relaxed a bit. He *was* listening to her. "I know it seems the deck's stacked against you. Against us. But the game's just begun, Matt. The other side has fired their first shots, and all they've done is embarrassed and frightened us. Look." She held up her hands. "Am I bleeding?"

A faint smile turned his lips. A wry smile. "No. You're tough and strong as ever." Matt bent down and put Laurel back on the floor. He kissed the child's head and patted Fred, who moved in to sit close to Laurel. The poodle was trembling. Matt patted the dog, calming her, and then he whispered something to both child and dog. Then, he looked up at Allie.

"I just told them both that we weren't going anywhere," he said, his tone soft. "At least not for the time being. Allie, I can't count the number of times my father and I ran to escape trouble when I was a kid. Sometimes, it was for a good reason. Other times... I suppose it was just because Dad wanted out of an uncomfortable situation. I guess it's just in my bones so deeply that I think only of doing that first. But I'm willing to listen now. If that's what it takes to keep you. I'm making no promises, but I will listen. I will wait."

She felt all the strength go out of her in a wave of relief. "I love you, Matt. And I love Laurel."

"You can't have any more children, can you, Allie." He stated it, rather than asked. No pity in his voice, either. Just a factual tone.

That surprised her. "That's right. When I had the twins, the birth was difficult and damaging to my reproductive system. How did you know...?"

He shrugged. "I didn't know for certain. Just a guess, really."

"I wish I could have your baby, but it isn't possible."

"I know, and it's all right with me. We have three kids between us. That's enough. We have more than enough, Allie. In every way." He straightened and stood up, smiling at her with a truly tender expression on his face. "I realized that last night. Confirmed it this morning when I watched you sleeping."

Her heart nearly burst with emotion. She had never—would never—love anyone else the way she loved him right at this moment. "Matt, don't leave me," she cried. "We'll work it out, somehow. *All* of it!"

He reached for her and embraced her, wrapping her with his strengths and giving her his weaknesses and entrusting her with his future.

And then and there, Allie made a momentous personal decision. Her future and his would fuse. No matter what the cost!

BUT, a few hours later, it seemed the cost was going to be very high. Higher than she had even feared.

After she called M.J. to explain about Matt's change of attitude, her cousin called in the other troops. A hastily convened, informal strategy session with Josh, Miranda, M.J., Matt and herself only emphasized the weakness of their position.

They were all seated in the meeting room at M.J.'s office. The area was small and dominated by a long, polished mahogany table. The walls were lined with law books in wooden bookshelves. Windows in the south wall let in the summer sunlight, giving freshness and life to the somewhat gloomy room.

The lawyer acted as chairman. "I asked Josh to come," M.J. explained, "because as I explore this, I'm beginning to think that there are many strings in the tangled web of the lives we're dealing with here." He rubbed his forehead with his fingers, indicating to Allie that he was deeply troubled. "Ugly strings," he added. "Ones you two don't deserve and certainly a little child like Laurel does not need in her life now or ever."

Matt nodded agreement, saying nothing, but thinking how close he had come to throwing all this away. This . . . comradeship. This opportunity finally to join the human race.

He would have blown it, too, sure as he was now sitting here. His temper had rarely flared hotter than it had this morning in this very place. If it hadn't been for Allie's strength in opposing him . . .

Well, that didn't bear thinking about. It was over and done with as far as he was concerned. He smiled to himself. *The education of Matthew Glass is about to begin,* he thought. How to be a social human, not an isolate like he'd been all his life.

He hoped to hell it would work. Otherwise, he'd be forced to try the old way. And somehow, he'd get Allie to go along.

"First," M.J. said, "we have Allie and her political campaign. She's perceived as a real threat to Rita, the party's candidate. She's a threat despite the fact she's operating on a shoestring budget with an inexperienced manager."

Matt glanced over at Josh, who was avoiding his gaze. Josh reddened slightly, but said nothing. That was a good sign, Matt decided. If he'd gotten defensive, Matt was prepared to chop him into little bits.

Figuratively, of course. The knife was back in his duffel bag along with his gun and his trekking clothes. For this meeting, he'd changed into a suit and tie. There was a time and place for one kind of weapon and a time and place for another. Now, his weaponry was his love for Allie and Laurel.

And, hopefully, his brains and courage.

M.J. held up two fingers. "Second, we have Matt and his desire to take care of Laurel. His legal position as the closest blood relative should be strong. But the problem is, he's a single male with a less than domestic background." The lawyer cleared his throat and looked down at the table. "Then there's the further disadvantage of his morally questionable relationship with Allie."

No one said a word. No one breathed. Most important, Allie realized, no one interrupted. M.J. was playing the devils' advocate and everyone seemed to realize and appreciate that. Especially Matt.

Another finger. "Then, there's the phone call Allie got week before last. Supposedly from her long-vanished husband. A verbal and emotional threat. Devastating in its own horrible way but stopping short of being a physical attack. Clearly, though, it was intended to weaken and frighten her.

"But Matt Glass made a more difficult target. His emotional fears, if he has any, are unknown. So they decided to play hardball. Miranda found out that Teddie Baker, who was humiliated publicly by Matt, worked a few months ago for David Benning, Rita Morely's political mentor. Now, that may seem like coincidence to you, but I wonder. The accident Matt had was no accident and no coincidence, in my estimation and . . ."

"You really think they're interconnected?" Allie was sitting on her edge of her chair. The confrontation with Matt had left her weak and shaky, but she was ready to deal with the devil himself, if she had to. "Could Teddie Baker and Rita and these Turner people have cooked up some kind of conspiracy? It seems far-fetched to me. They're working together? How could that be?"

"We don't know yet, but we've now got an angle that M.J. didn't have this morning when he and Matt tangled," Miranda answered Allie. "It could be all tied into one thing." She smiled. "Or rather, into one person. Little Laurel Essex."

"What about her." Matt spoke. "Is she in danger because of this situation? This complex network of evil?"

His voice was soft, gentle, but at the core of his tone, Allie heard solid steel. She crossed her fingers under the table, praying that Miranda wouldn't say something to set him off again.

But Miranda hastened to reassure him. "No, Laurel's not in immediate danger. At least not physically. She represents a goal, though. It's her money, folks, that's sweetening this hornet's nest. I'll bet good money of my own on it. Old-fashioned greed. Pure and simple." She set some papers down on the table. "Matt, are you aware of the extent of her estate?"

"Yes."

"Then you know what the stakes are in this custody fight you face," M.J. interjected.

Matt frowned. "I didn't think anyone would be able to touch her estate. A guardian would just manage it till Laurel was older. So I can't imagine..." A calculating look came into his eyes. He leaned forward, elbows and forearms resting on the wooden tabletop. "Wait a minute," he said. "What does this Turner guy do?"

Miranda smiled approval. So did M.J. "You got it, baby. Investment advisor at the bank he works for," she said. "Small potatoes, but you know how that can be. Can grate on a guy for years, watching others make big bucks when he's in no position to take any chances..." She let the statement trail off, implying rather than saying what she suspected, Allie realized.

And Matt realized it, too.

"Ah." Matt sat back. "He can't touch Laurel's money directly, nor could I, because it's in a trust. But, there are other possibilities. As administrator, he could use Laurel's money to test investments without risking his own cash. Then, if something proved out, he'd pour in his own money. So, I see. Then we're dealing with something here other than the heartfelt desire on the part of the Turners to have a big happy family, aren't we?" he asked, his tone now edged again, his anger showing only by the tension around his eyes and mouth.

"I'd say so," Miranda said.

"But," Allie added, "there's absolutely no proof of any of this, is there? We're pulling things out of thin air."

"For now," Matt said. "But at least we're aware of the enemy or enemies. And I don't believe they're as good at this kind of thing as they might think they are."

"Excuse me," Josh said, speaking up for the first time. "But I feel really out of my depth with all this. I mean, conspiracy's an ugly word, people. Are you sure you...?"

"Sure enough, Josh," M.J. said. "This is a strange situation, believe me. Don't take it to the bank yet, but there'll likely come a time when you can."

Josh squirmed. "I...I'm not really a very brave man, you know. I..." His voice took on an odd tone.

"Josh, you want out? All the way out?" Matt regarded him. "I'll take over Allie's campaign if you've no stomach for this."

"N-no." Josh shook his head, and the strange expression on his face made Allie wonder what his problem was. "I don't want to quit." He smiled weakly. "But I'd sure like your help, Matt. That is, if it's all right with Allie."

"Fine with me," she said. "In fact, we were planning to talk to you about it even before the crisis. Not that I don't think you're doing a good job. But Matt is..."

"A fighter," Josh finished. "I'm not. And it sure looks to me like you've got a fight on your hands, even if this conspiracy thing is all smoke." He got up. "I expect the rest of this meeting won't directly concern me, so I'm going to go. Allie, give me a call later, please."

She agreed, and Josh left.

"Well." M.J. adjusted the position of some papers in front of him. "Where do you want to go from here. Matt? I think the next move's yours."

"I do want to fight. Take it all the way." He reached in his pocket and took out a written check. "Here's your retainer. Your fee and Miranda's are of no concern to me. I don't need Laurel's money. I'm wealthy enough in my own right. Following my father around the world during my youth did have one advantage—I made business contacts that have paid off in my adult life. My investment portfolio is extensive and more than enough to serve my needs for the rest of my life. I don't need Laurel's money," he repeated, firmly.

"We know that," Miranda said, softly. "We checked."

"Good." Matt nodded approval. "I'd have been disappointed if you hadn't."

Allie sat back and listened as the three outlined legal strategy. They had managed to agree very quickly, and while that was good, she thought, it also made the alliance potentially unstable. She'd had enough political experience to know that. Matt seemed satisfied to play by the rules for now, but she was sure that all it would take to make him jump the traces was one threat to Laurel or herself. He was, in many ways, a very simple man. Out to protect what he loved and cherished, no matter what the cost.

That wasn't all bad.

But it wasn't good, either, when the future depended on his holding back, and trusting people he didn't know. She was going to have to watch him carefully.

She looked away from the three of them. Her eyes clouded. Not with tears but with thought and a hard decision.

Decide, she told herself. And, she did.

It didn't take too long for M.J. to outline his preliminary plan. He intended to file for custody rights on the bases of Matt's financial security, which was more impressive than the Turners' and on Matt's closer blood relationship to Laurel.

Other factors, such as Matt's immediate response to Laurel's need and his avowed declaration to be her adopted father would also weigh in his favor, he said. After that, he warned, the game would depend on the steps the other side took. How ruthless they were willing to be. No one mentioned the problem of Matt and Laurel's continuing to live with Allie, and Allie wasn't about to bring it up. She had no intention of letting them leave.

Also, no one brought up what steps they would take if another act of telephone terrorism or physical violence occurred.

Allie could only hope that the incidents had been one-time shots and that, if indeed there was a conspiracy against her and Matt, the enemy had decided to abandon those methods and move on to a more "civilized" confrontation in a court of law. The thought, put that way, made her glum and unusually quiet. In some ways, Matt's more dramatic, direct approach seemed cleaner. Fight or flight. It was a basic human response to danger, after all.

Matt noticed her silence, but said nothing until they left the law office. "You were awfully quiet in there once you had your say," he said, getting into the driver's seat of her car after opening the passenger door for her. They had agreed he would drive now that his headaches were over. They were sharing the one car until he had a chance to buy himself another. "No other ideas or opinions?"

"Plenty." Allie fastened her seat belt. "But none that are pertinent for now."

"For when, then?" He started the car and pulled out into the street.

"I'll let you know," she said. She slumped a little in the seat. "One thing, though. I do want to apologize to you."

"For what?" He chuckled. "If anyone needs to apologize around here, it's got to be me."

"I accused you of terminal selfishness, when I'm just as guilty."

"You?" Matt laughed. "Not a selfish bone in your lovely body, near as I can tell. And I have had a chance to check," he added.

His tone promised a great deal, and Allie was tempted to reach out and touch his body and let the magic between them start again. But she wasn't willing to drop the issue. "No, Matt. I've lived alone almost all my life. I was an only child. I had things pretty much my way until Paul deserted me. But even after that, I managed to steer my own course."

"But, your children..." He sounded puzzled.

She shrugged. "Are mine. I don't have to deal with a co-parent in the business of raising them. They're terrific kids. I've been able to be quite independent, even though I've taken good care of them in the process. So, as I see it, I have no business casting any stones at you." Then, she gave in to her earlier temptation and she reached over and touched him. "You're just a bit more impressive about getting your way than I am," she said.

"Hmm." He turned a corner. "I think you have a point, though I can't see where it's taking you." He glanced at her. "And I can tell it's taking you somewhere. The wheels are obviously turning, my love."

She looked away, "Like I said. I'll let you know."

BUT SHE DIDN'T. Allie knew that if she told Matt exactly what she had in mind, he'd throw a monkey wrench into her scheme, just as sure as the sun came up in the morning. No, it was better to do what she had to do quietly and without fanfare.

She was right, this time, and she knew it.

But Josh argued, surprising her with his vehemence. "Allie, you cannot throw away everything just because of that man and his problems." He slapped a stack of papers on his desk. "Look at this," he said. "You've really got a chance to make a good race of it. My informal poll indicates you have a better than even chance of beating Rita despite the scandal of. . ."

"Living with Matt," she finished. It was the afternoon of the day following the conference in M.J.'s office. Allie had left Matt at home with Laurel and had gone to confer with Josh.

She was giving up her race for office.

"I don't want to just drop out," she explained. "If I do that, it's likely to affect Matt's situation negatively. Kind of an admission of guilt. What I want to do is slip, lose energy, make it seem that I wasn't a contender, after all." She stared at her manager. "I'll declare my campaign over shortly after the first of September when the polls can show I've no chance at all. Can you do that for me?"

Josh shook his head. "I don't want to, but if you insist, I don't know that I have any choice."

"Thanks." She patted his hand. "After the dust settles, I'll make sure every one knows it wasn't your fault."

Josh shrugged. "I doubt they'll believe you." He put his hand on his desk and slid a piece of paper under a file. Then, he picked up a pencil and tapped it on the file.

"Trust me."

Josh nodded, not meeting her gaze.

She left, thinking of betrayal and what it meant. Why people did it to other people. Wondering if she was doing that herself by dropping out like this, and thinking she wished she was clever enough to think of an alternative that would make everything right for all of them. Josh's position especially bothered her. She was setting him up for yet another failure, and that was unfair.

It wasn't until she had left the office and was driving home that she wondered what had been on that sheet of paper he'd hidden from her sight. By the time she got home, however, she'd put it from her mind. She had far too many other things to think about.

Matt met her at the front door. "I need to use the car," he said. "Mind?"

"No." She lifted her face for a kiss, but he breezed past, grabbing the keys. Allie sighed and went inside. Sharing her car was getting to both of them. Coordinating their plans was a real problem and she wished he'd buy himself a new one. Laurel greeted her with a cheerful, "Momma," that quickly changed to a cranky, whiny tone that demanded she give the child her total attention.

Allie sighed again as she complied. She and Matt might be the cause of gossip, but for all the wild and crazy illicit love they'd had a chance to make in the past forty-eight hours, they might as well just be an old married couple. Laurel did not contribute to an atmosphere of sensual indulgence. Not a bit! "Don' wanna," she whined when Allie tried to interest her in building blocks. "No!"

Sighing again, Allie reached up on the coffee table for a book. Even Fred and the cats had deserted her, undoubtedly the victims of Laurel's bad mood already. "How about a story?" she asked.

Laurel pouted, then nodded and settled into Allie's lap. Her thumb went into her mouth, and she fingered the silky slip that peeked out from under Allie's skirt. Her eyelids got droopy almost immediately.

Ah. "Did Daddy give you a nap?" Allie asked, only realizing after she said it that she had once more referred to Matt as the child's father. She'd been doing that much too frequently. If things didn't work out for them, she was liable to cause more grief for the little girl by imprinting Matt in her mind as the child's father.

Well, Laurel called her momma. So what harm would it do that hadn't already been done?

"No nap." Laurel made the statement emphatically. She scowled as only a sleepy, cranky child can. "No nap," she repeated.

"Yes, I think so," Allie stood up, lifting Laurel in her arms. "I think you need a nap in the worst way, my tiny little dear."

"No nap!"

"Sweetie, I'm afraid so."

"Nooooo!"

And the battle was on.

She hoped if she let Laurel rage for a few minutes, the child would cry her anger and frustration out before she went to sleep. But Laurel had no intention of giving in so easily. This was a big one. Allie had forgotten the extent and determination of toddler fury. Laurel screeched into Allie's ear until Allie was sure she would go deaf. She was also convinced the roof was going to cave in.

And then, in an unexpected way, it did.

Coming in the house as she had, mildly upset about the car situation and Matt's lack of attention to her, she had left the front door open, with only the screen door shut. When she walked past it on the way to the bedroom with the struggling child in her arms, she noted that the front stoop was occupied. Five people, at least, crowded at the door. Allie stopped, startled by the intrusion.

And was even more startled when a bright light hit her.

"See?" A shrill female voice called. "See. What did we tell you? It's child abuse, I say, plain and simple. Horrible, horrible child abuse! Get this. All of it! You have to get this on tape so we can have someone arrest that woman and take that poor, sweet, innocent child to a safe place!"

CHAPTER TWELVE

ALLIE STOOD STILL, dumbfounded by the words and confused by the blinding light. Laurel stopped struggling and crying. She tried to shrink into Allie and her little arms wrapped tightly around her neck. "Momma," she whimpered, burying her face in Allie's bosom. "Daddy? Daaaddyyyy."

Allie held her closer, cuddling her and trying to give comfort. "Who are you people?" she cried out to the group at her door. "Go away. Please. You're frightening this child."

"Mmmaaamma," Laurel wailed, hiding her face against Allie.

But the people didn't leave. Instead, one of the women on the front porch barged straight in, slamming the screen door open. The sight of Allie holding Laurel seemed to enrage her. Laurel's wailing went on, but the stranger yelled over it.

"No, no no! *She's* not your momma, honey. I'm gonna be!" She glared at Allie. "She's mine, you bitch," she snarled, her hands grasping claws. "Give me that child! I want her now, before you can harm her anymore."

Allie continued to stand still, holding her ground with an effort of will. All her instincts shrieked at her to back up, protect Laurel and to retreat in the face of such naked aggression. But she stood firm. "Get out of my house," she said, amazed her tone was so quiet and calm. "Now," she added. "Before something bad happens." Her body was starting to tremble from anger and outrage.

The woman was short, but wide and built with a sort of female heaviness that indicated muscle as well as fat. Her complexion was ruddy with fury. She had black hair cut in a Dutch-boy bob and black eyes that radiated flat hatred. She was also vaguely familiar. Allie was trying to remember where she had seen that face before when the woman lunged. She grabbed for Laurel. "I won't leave without the child!"

Laurel screamed, and Allie swung the child away while striking out at the same time with her foot. She caught the intruder right on a pudgy kneecap with the sharp heel of her dress shoe. The woman went down, howling.

The door banged open again. "Hey now, here." This time it was a thin man addressing her, his finger wagging in the air. "You stop that brutality, woman," he yelled. "My wife's done nothing to you!"

The bright, unnatural light continued to shine on the scene, disorienting Allie almost as much as the unexpected violence. "She's invaded my house," she yelled back. "So have you. All of you! Get out!" Tears started to roll down her face, more from frustration and anger than fear. Fear, though, was a factor. The woman on the floor was now trying to grab at Laurel's dangling, kicking legs. Laurel's cry was one of pure terror. Now, she suddenly remembered where she'd seen the pair—it was the night she and M.J. had had dinner at the Chinese restaurant. They had been spying on her! A sense of nightmare closed in on Allie, pushing her toward actual panic.

Then Fred dashed in and barked, her little teeth showing in a snarl. An amazingly vicious snarl, Allie realized, for an animal as naturally friendly and mild-tempered as Fred. That brought her back to a sense of security and control. Only someone who didn't know dogs would be fooled into believing Fred was really dangerous.

The attack had the desired effect, however. Both strangers screamed and backed away, yodeling about a mad dog. Allie bent down and scooped the poodle up, resting Laurel on one hip and Fred on the other. "Get out of my house!" she shouted. Fred punctuated this with a rapid string of barks, which caused her small, tense body to shake.

Allie waited, every nerve on edge. At first, she thought she was going to be challenged. The woman rose to her feet, but stayed bent in a crouch as if she was readying herself for another launch at Laurel. The man had his fists balled, too. But then, the bright light from the porch went out, and a quiet voice spoke from beyond the screen door. Allie felt her heart leap. It was Matt! She couldn't see him, but his voice was unmistakable.

"I think you should listen to the lady," Matt said. "Because if you don't, I'm going to have to physically remove both of you from her property. And I won't guarantee gentleness."

"Matt!" The cry came from Allie's heart. "They've been spying on me. On us. She tried to hurt Laurel! They're trying to kidnap her!"

"You lying bitch! I . . ."

The short woman's invective was cut off by a dueted shriek and then the sound of breaking glass and metal.

From outside came the cries of another man and a woman, complaining about broken video equipment.

"I asked you to leave," Matt said. "Sorry you stumbled on that first step. You should look where you're going," he added. More crunching of metal and glass.

The man and woman in the house were now looking decidedly apprehensive. Fred, safe in Allie's grasp, continued to bark and snarl at them.

"You had both better go away right now," Allie said. "I don't think he's in any mood to deal reasonably with you, whoever you are."

The screen door banged open. Matt, looking like an avenging angel, stood framed in the afternoon sunlight.

"That was a pair of unlucky and unwise news vultures out there," he said. "They're gone. And these birds are the Turners, Allie." He spoke softly, his tone conversational, a flick of one hand indicating the couple. "Joan and Frank Turner. My sister's husband's second cousin and her husband. Here to challenge my right to Laurel." His lips turned in an expression approximating a sneer of contempt.

No one else said anything. The air seemed to shimmer with tension and hatred. Laurel, silent now, huddled closer to Allie. Even Fred quieted.

Matt gazed at them in a clinical, detached manner and then looked back at Allie. "Now, can't you just see them as the proper parents for Laurel?" he asked, his tone still mild. Only deep in his eyes could the depth of his feelings be seen. "I was warned by Miranda that they might be coming here, so I cut my business meeting with her short and decided to swing by the house and check. Glad I did."

Allie shuddered with combined relief and dread. He was hanging on to self-control by a mere thread. She had already seen what harm he could do to an opponent when he was in control of himself. What would occur if he lost that control? Her heart thudded even harder.

What would happen if he lost it right now?

The Turners seemed unaware of the danger. "You can't keep her," the woman said, her tone much subdued. "We have the law on our side."

"Odd you should say that." Matt regarded her once again, his expression cold and set. "I understand the same thing applies to us. Until a court rules differently, Laurel's ours...mine." He opened the door. "Furthermore, you've violated that law by entering this woman's home. Now, leave before I call the cops."

"You wouldn't dare..." the other woman began. Hatred danced deep in her dark eyes. Her hands curled into claws. It looked as if she was ready to attack both of them.

Allie didn't wait to see what would happen next. Still carrying the child and the dog, she raced for the phone and punched the emergency call for 911.

"WHILE I APPLAUD your quick thinking, cousin," M.J. said a few hours later, "I do believe you might have overreacted a teensy bit. Were fire trucks and ambulances really necessary?"

"Overreacted, hell!" Allie set down her glass of iced tea. She, M.J. and Matt were seated in the kitchen that evening, hours after the Turner episode, sorting out events and discussing possible consequences. One problem was that when she called 911, every emergency agency in the city had responded, drawing unavoidable public attention to the situation.

"Matt had just trashed a video camera with his bare hands and sent two reporters scurrying for the high country," she said. "That Turner amazon was looking for blood to shed. And I'm absolutely sure they were the same people who were listening in on our conversation that night at the Chinese restaurant. They've been plotting and planning this for a long time, I tell you. Matt was ready to fight, too. I wasn't about to wait and see which of them decided to try for the gold first. I figured the sound of sirens would get everyone's attention, and I was right. It did." She paused to catch up with her breath, remembering. The Turners had scurried away like large insects as soon as the police and fire trucks arrived.

"I wouldn't have hurt her or her husband," Matt said. "I just intended to make sure they left, quickly. Before they did any more damage."

Unlike Allie, who couldn't seem to stop talking, he'd been very quiet since the dust had settled. Quiet like a volcano before an eruption or a fault line before an earthquake. The air around him seemed charged with energy and tension.

Negative energy and unhealthy tension.

"I was not looking for trouble," he added.

"I hope not," M.J. said. "I hope you'd have better sense. That would give the woman just the kind of excuse she would need to go to the authorities with a genuine complaint." He shut his eyes and rubbed his face. "As it is, I had to do a lot of smoothing of ruffled feathers to get those reporters to agree not to press charges."

"They were on my front porch," Allie protested, defending Matt again, as she had been doing for the past few hours, first to the police, now to M.J. "Trespassing on my property. Invading my privacy."

M.J. nodded. "They were. That's why they won't do anything about the destroyed equipment." He turned to Matt. "By the way, what did you do to that camera? Run over it with a truck?"

Matt shrugged. Laurel, who was sleeping on his lap, stirred. "I just stomped on it once or twice," he said. "Sometimes, when I'm really angry, I can get a little carried away."

M.J. nodded again. "Just don't let it happen again, okay?"

"I understand." Matt stroked Laurel's head. Leaned his cheek against her hair. "I understand," he repeated, so softly, Allie scarcely heard him. She certainly didn't catch the emotion in his tone.

But M.J did, and the lawyer seemed to read into the words far more than Allie had. "Matt, I mean it," M.J. said. "If you do anything else that smacks of violence, you'll blow your case right out of the water. You'll ruin any chance you have of keeping Laurel. This is no jungle where you can get away with doing as you please. In the eyes of the authorities, a man who uses violence to solve his problems is not a fit parent."

"How can you say that to him when they were the ones who started it?" Allie asked, still feeling defensive about Matt's action. He had, after all, saved her from a dreadful confrontation. Even if he had taken things to extremes by trashing the camera. Matt said nothing.

M.J. looked at them both, his expression sober. "It is their word against yours about that, since the tape in the camera was destroyed. Matt's anger worked against you, because he removed the only sure record of Joan Turner's aggressive behavior. While the two reporters are eye witnesses to her breaking into your home, they are also hostile witnesses. Angry at being run off and upset about the equipment being trashed. I wouldn't look to them for any support."

Matt stood up. "I'm going to put Laurel to bed," he said. "You're right, M.J. I was way out of line, and I'm sorry. I acted out of pure instinct. Gut reaction. I won't do that again."

"I don't think you need to apologize for your behavior," Allie said, folding her arms and glaring at M.J. "There's a time and a place for caution and thought. This afternoon, action was in order."

Matt shifted the sleeping child in his arms. "Yeah, but you were the one who called 911 and pulled the plug," he said, watching her carefully. "You knew the consequences of serious trouble, you could see where things were going, and I was part of the problem."

"Matt, no, you were not...," she protested.

But he had left the room.

Resisting the urge to follow him and continue the conversation, Allie turned to M.J. "What are we facing now?" she asked. "It's clear to any reasonable person that the Turner woman is nuts. Maybe her husband, too. I didn't get much of a chance to hear from him."

M.J. looked worried. "They were revved when they confronted you. Out of control, just like Matt. I think the fact that they were staking out your home with reporters in tow, just watching and waiting for an incident, indicates cleverness, however. I wouldn't put it past them to clean up their act when it comes to a custody hearing. If they can keep a lid on their emotions, they just might look better to a judge than Matt does.''

''How about me?'' She asked the question before she thought.

''What about you, Allie?'' M.J. rested his elbows on the kitchen table. ''Are you really in this, or are you just a bystander?''

She stared at the tabletop, unable to meet M.J.'s steady gaze. ''Good question,'' she conceded finally. ''I thought I was sure, but this incident has really shaken me. I need some time to think about it.''

M.J. nodded. ''I suggest you do that. *Strongly* suggest you do.''

And she knew it was the lawyer, not the cousin, who was speaking to her. Warning her, really.

MATT SAT in the near darkness and watched Laurel settle into deep sleep. She had been more traumatized by the afternoon's events than anyone realized, he thought. She'd had no nightmares in all the time they'd been living with Allie, but tonight, he was taking no chances on not being right by her side if she should wake up with one.

That was the least he could do for her.

There was more, however. Much more, and he needed solitude to think about that. He leaned back on the bed and shut his eyes.

The darkness took him away to a night when he'd been in real trouble for the first time in his life. Trouble that could have brought disaster not only to himself, but also to the one person in the world he knew well enough to love at that time—his father.

It had been a silly thing. A dumb thing. Quixotic. They were in the Middle East then. Nothing modern about the place, especially in social attitudes. Ten years old, nearly eleven, he didn't know yet what girls were all about, but had become interested in one who claimed to be fourteen. As a friend, only. They'd started meeting secretly, whispering to each other through the crack in the wall that ran between her home and the next-door villa his father was renting. Matt smiled, remembering the dry, gritty feel of the rock wall and the sweet smell of the flowers that blossomed along its base.

Then, one evening, she asked him to help her run away. Her father, she said, was going to make her marry an old man she didn't love. Matt believed and aided.

And was very nearly caught. When he ran to his own home with the authorities right on his tail, his father had taken the news with his usual *élan,* packed up their few personal belongings and had fled with his outlaw son into the desert night.

Forget any attempt to explain, he had said. Forget that the girl had lied to Matt. Had been using him to rendezvous with her real lover, with whom she had escaped, leaving Matt to face the music alone. The best thing to do, his father had said, was to run when you were outnumbered, and also when the other side had the cops with them.

"Dad," Matt whispered, "you were almost right." *Almost.* Just close enough to seem correct all the time.

Laurel whimpered in her sleep.

Matt lay very still.

His father was a coward.

He sat up, the realization coming at him like a slap across his face. His father. The great, intrepid Robert Glass, adventurer extraordinare, was a coward.

Not a coward in the sense of being physically afraid of pain, but a moral coward, who wouldn't face up to responsibility. And he'd taught Matt by example to do the same thing. Run. That was the way to handle difficult or dangerous moments in life.

A cold sweat suddenly covered his skin. He looked over at Laurel who now slept peacefully, Allie's daughter's baby blanket drawn over her small body. If Allie hadn't had the courage to stand up to him the other day, he'd be running away, too. Just as his father had. Even now, knowing what he did about himself, the temptation was strong.

Run. Hide. Avoid the danger... Wait out the storm...

He lay back down and thought of old Kelly Mc-Clean and his storm cellar under his shack of a house. Hiding. Waiting out the storm. Other men did that, too. Not just his father. Had Allie's missing husband tried it? Had he succeeded? Or failed? He thought about what McClean had said that day they had been waiting out the storm down in his cellar.

Paul Ford treated some important politician fella.

Hmm.

ALLIE WENT to her bed alone later that night. When she'd looked into Laurel's room, the little girl was sleeping peacefully and Matt had been sound asleep, too. He was curled on his side on top of the covers, still fully clothed, but with one hand hooked into the bars of the crib, as if he wanted to make sure no harm would come to the child. She hadn't wanted to disturb that protective pose, so she shut the door softly and went into her own room with Fred at her heels. The dog seemed unhappy about returning to her old bed, but once the light was off, she settled down.

That was more than her mistress could do. Allie tossed and turned, dealing with the problem of Matt and Laurel in her mind and heart and trying to come to some kind of solution to the dilemma.

M.J had gently and tactfully suggested she and Matt either decide to get married or return the fledgling household to its original status. Matt at his place and Allie at her home, alone. They could still date, of course. Just not live together.

But what if the Turners had gone to Matt's place when he was gone and Debbie was baby-sitting? Would she have been secure enough in her own authority and strong enough to fight them off while safeguarding Laurel?

No. That was too much to ask an outsider.

Well, M.J. had all but said that she, Allie, was essentially an outsider in Matt's situation. Uninvolved, technically.

Was she?

Should she be?

She turned over and lay on her back, staring up at the ceiling. The only way to be involved technically was to be legally tied to him.

Married.

Her stomach rumbled, indicating the onset of nervous indigestion. She tossed around, pulling at the sheet and disturbing the sleeping poodle. Fred sighed and rearranged her position on the bed.

Married. Again. Unimaginable. She couldn't do it. No matter how she felt about Matt or Laurel, she could not do it.

And that was that. She just couldn't live with the sword of uncertainly hanging over her head for the rest of her life. Until the day she knew for an absolute fact that Paul Ford was dead, she just could not take the risk. Tears filled her eyes and poured down the sides of her face. After a while, she fell asleep. Her dreams were fleeting and unpleasant.

In the small hours of the morning, however, a strange low sound woke her. Allie sat up, listening. Fred stirred and woofed softly, indicating that there was indeed something, but nothing dangerous. When Allie got up and reached for her robe, the dog's ears pricked forward. Her tail wagged.

"What is it, Fred?" Allie asked, whispering. "I wish I had keen senses like yours." She moved into the hall and Fred followed, tail awag, still indicating no danger.

The noise sounded again. This time, Allie knew what it was. Matt. He was talking or at least making sounds. A muffled groan. She hurried to Sally's room and opened the door.

Matt was sitting up on the bed, his face in his hands. Laurel still slept quietly. The room was dimly lighted by the glow of the moon coming in the window. The shade had not been closed. He looked up and saw her, standing in the doorway.

"Nightmare," he whispered. "An old familiar one. Nothing at all to worry about. Go back to sleep." His face looked strained and haggard.

"All right, I will," she said. Allie came into the room. She shut the window shade, dimming the room to almost darkness. She went over to the closet and took out a cotton comforter. Pulling it over her, she laid down on the bed next to him. Fred jumped up and arranged herself on top of the comforter. She sighed contentedly and closed her little eyes. Allie sighed, too. She smiled at Matt and patted the other pillow, inviting him.

Matt looked at the two of them for a moment. Then, without saying a word, he eased himself under the comforter, put his arms around Allie and rested his head on the pillow beside her. She could see the smallest gleam of moisture at the edges of his closed eyes, and her heart went out to him.

Soon, they both fell into a dreamless sleep, which lasted until morning. It was a time of peace for everyone.

Morning brought a fresh batch of trouble, however. Over coffee, Allie studied the newspaper, giving Matt a rundown on the essentials while he helped Laurel with breakfast. The little girl was practicing tossing food this morning.

They had made the headlines in the Police Report section. "According to this," she said, "my home was a scene of domestic violence yesterday." She looked up at Matt. "How the heck do they figure that?"

He shrugged. "You called 911, didn't you? They have to give out some reason, I suppose."

"Yeah. But the violence was not domestic. That makes it sound like you and I were in a physical fight." She snapped the newspaper. "That's a lie."

Matt retrieved a slice of pear before it hit the floor. Fred trotted over to sit nearer, looking disappointed at having missed a snack opportunity. "It's the right of the press to print the truth as they see it," Matt said. "You know that. You're also a public figure, having declared for office. That makes a libel suit difficult, if not impossible. Not to say, stupid. Does the editor have a political bias?''

"Oh, yes." Allie slammed a fist down on the offending rag. "She endorsed Rita a while ago."

"Well." Matt stood up and started to towel Cream of Wheat off Laurel's face. "We'll just have to see that the paper is used for carrying out the trash and little else. That it's of no real value when it comes to predicting political winners, won't we."

"Matt, I . . ."

"Don't argue with me this morning," he said, interrupting her. "I'm still in fighting mode, and that nightmare I had last night didn't help my temper. I want to turn my aggressions onto a useful target, such as getting you elected."

"My campaign isn't important . . ."

"It is to me." He tossed the dirty towel in the sink and bent down to help Laurel out of her high chair. "I want you to succeed with your ambitions and dreams."

"But, Matt. You . . ." She ran down, unable to finish.

"I what?" He turned and looked at her. "I'm in your way, aren't I? If I stay here with you, the bad publicity's going to kill you. If I go . . ."

She stood up and went over to the sink. The window above it looked out onto the backyard and the prairie beyond. The high grass was still light green, but it was beginning to fade to summer gold. "If you go," she said, "who will sleep with you when you have nightmares?" She turned around to face him. "Or watch out for Laurel when someone tries to harm her and you aren't there?"

Matt stared at her. He set Laurel down, and she toddled off after Fred. "What are you saying to me, Allie?" he asked.

"I ... I don't know," she replied, hugging herself nervously. "But I do know I don't want you to leave."

"I don't have a choice. Not if I consider what's best for you."

She shook her head. "I'm not sure I know what's best for me anymore." Tears came into her eyes, and this time, she didn't fight them. "Matt, I haven't known you two months yet, but you ..."

"Allie, would you marry me?"

She bent over the sink, crying hard now. "I ... can't. I never will be free. Oh damn!" She hit the counter with her open palm. "Damn, damn, damn."

"You *are* free," he said. "You're just using that as an excuse." He moved nearer, but didn't touch her. "Throw off the past, Allie. Let it go."

"I ... I *want* to, but ..."

He stepped back. "But it's a great excuse, isn't it."

She wiped her eyes. "It's no excuse, Matt. Don't push at me on this."

"Why not?" He folded his arms and frowned. "Do you want to know what my nightmare was about last night?"

"I ... It's your ..."

"No. Listen to me. It was about being lost and alone. Lost from you, from Laurel, from everything I've come to hold precious in my life."

Allie sobbed once more, then began to gain control of her emotions. This was a two-way street, after all, she reasoned. "What you're doing is not fair, Matt," she said. "You're asking me to forget about my past while you keep your future." She glared at him, wanting him to see the need and anger in her heart. "I don't believe you can stay here for the rest of your life, and that's what I need from a man I'll be willing to marry. I need a commitment I can trust."

He jerked his head back as if she'd slapped him. "Don't put it on me. I'm willing to compromise. Are you?"

"How can you compromise? How can you promise me you won't leave me someday, just like Paul"

"Oh, damn it all, Allie! Don't . . ."

"Don't what?" She put her hands on her hips, unreasonably angry now and knowing it, but unable to stop the words. "Don't say what's really in my heart? Oh, forgive me. I forgot for a moment that you . . ."

"Momma?" Laurel came toddling into the kitchen. Fred followed close behind. The little girl looked upset. "Momma crying?" She stared at both of them. "Daddy?" Her question and woeful expression acted like a sharp pin on Allie's puffed up sense of outrage. How could she carry on this way with Matt where Laurel would hear her? It was wrong!

Allie knelt down. "It's okay. Momma's okay, darling," she said, holding out her arms. Laurel giggled and ran to her. Allie embraced her and looked up at Matt. "What are we going to do?" she asked. "This isn't just about you and me anymore, you know." She stroked the child's hair. "Not by a long shot."

"You're right." His wide shoulders slumped. "If it was just you and me, maybe we'd see . . . But . . ." He rubbed a hand over his face. "Damned if I know what we should do," he replied. "Damned if I . . ."

The shrill, chilling sound of screeching brakes interrupted him. Allie straightened up, still holding Laurel. Fred stiffened, her ears perking forward, but her body rigid and trembling. She moved closer to Matt. From their hiding places, the three cats suddenly appeared at Allie's feet, tails atwitch. "What is that. Who...?" she asked.

Matt shook his head. "I don't..." he started to say. Then, he was silent. Listening... Put his hand on her shoulder...

Shouted a warning... Pushed her and Laurel to the floor...

And the world exploded in a series of thunderous roars.

CHAPTER THIRTEEN

SHE COULD HEAR glass shattering, wood splintering with each horrendous blast. Blasts that went on and on. Then, tires squealed again, the sound menacing and evil. Allie struggled against a terror so deep it made her numb. Matt's weight on her body pressed her down, forcing the air out of her lungs just as quickly as she struggled to breathe it in. She began to feel faint. The view at the edges of her sight started to fade to black. From somewhere far away, she heard Laurel crying, Fred howling and the cats yowling all at once. They needed her! She fought to regain her senses.

"Allie! Can you hear me?" His weight lifted. His hands touched her, brought her back from the darkness. "Allie? Say something! Please!"

She blinked, clearing her eyes. Took a deep breath and coughed. The kitchen was full of smoke and dust. A ragged hole gaped in the wall dividing it from the living room. A hole that look like a giant fist had punched it, through wallboard and inner insulation. Electric wire sparked and fizzed and smoked in the ruin. "What happened?" she asked, her tone amazingly normal. "Was it a bomb?"

Matt studied her for a moment, as if satisfying himself she was all right, then he stood, Laurel now in his arms. "No. Close, though. I think we've been shotgunned. Professionally. Get up and see if the phone's still working. Call the cops. 911. This time, we need them all!''

"But, who...?" She got slowly to her feet, her muscles trembling and threatening to give way. Looking around, she saw all her animals, eyes wide with terror, but safe. Fred literally flew into her arms. "Who did it?" Sudden fear and a sense of deep horror at the close call they'd all had made her nauseated. "They tried to kill us! Are they still out there?"

"No." Matt narrowed his eyes against the dust. "I think they ran just as soon as they emptied the gun. I heard tires squealing just after the last shot." He looked at Laurel, at Allie and at the animals. "Listen, forget the cops." He bent down and picked up two cats, holding them securely, even as they struggled to get down. Laurel, silent, watched the two felines, but made no attempt to touch them. "Let's get out of here. Now."

"But..."

"Listen to me, Allie. For once, just do as I say and do it now without asking questions. Get in the car. We're going up the mountain to my place."

"Matt, are you sure?" She shifted Fred and picked up the remaining cat. Tom growled once, then quieted.

"I am." He herded her toward the back door, the one that led from the kitchen directly into the garage. "We've been attacked by someone who doesn't care who they hurt. A pro with a job to do. Well, I'm a pro, too. *This* I know how to deal with."

His words disturbed her, but she was too shocked by the attack to question him.

The few neighbors who were still home at this time of day surrounded the car as they started to pull out of the garage. Questions flew, but Matt dealt with them easily, asking everyone to get back in their own homes and to let the police know what they'd seen and heard. He asked her next-door neighbor to tell the police he was taking them up to the Essex home and could be reached there, but that anyone who wanted to talk to him had better call first, because he was intent on protection. The woman, a retired teacher, nodded.

As soon as possible, they were on their way up the mountain. As they had backed out of the garage, Allie had glimpsed the wreckage of the front of her house and had cried out in anger and horror. The shotgun blasts had destroyed the picture window in the living room and had left large holes in the wall. The window in Sally's room was gone, too. If Laurel had been playing in there... If her own children had been home...

Allie wept, softly, all the way up to the Essex house. She felt sick and weak. More frightened than she'd ever been in her life. Even more so than the day she had finally realized that Paul Ford was not coming back. What was going on? What had she done to have this happen to her? Threats. Harassment and verbal abuse. Now, real violence. A nightmare with no end in sight!

She was, she realized, in a mild state of shock. She let Matt bundle her and the animals and Laurel into the Essex house and let him get things organized. Her four pets seemed just as stunned as she was, content to huddle close to her where she sat with Laurel on the couch in the big living room, staring out at the peaceful mountain scenery. She almost smiled when she realized that the dog and cats weren't squabbling for what was probably the first time in their furry lives.

Almost smiled, but not quite. A smile would mean happiness and there was no joy in her for the moment.

She heard Matt on the phone and thought he must be calling the police. She closed her eyes. Laurel snuggled close, her little face resting on Allie's chest, and her thumb in her mouth. Allie listened to the cats purring, anxiety rather than contentment driving their humming. Listened to Fred panting. Listened to Matt, taking care of their problem . . .

"I don't care how much it costs, man," he said. " I want every damn one of you up here a.s.a.p. And get the weapons on the road yesterday . . ."

Allie's eyes opened wide. *Weapons.*

What about weapons?

"I want trained troops, Chico," Matt said, his tone harsh. "Ones that don't mind trouble. I don't know any around here, that's why I'm relying on you. I want you to get the old team together, my friend. I'm calling in old debts. You guys owe me, and you know it." Pause. "Okay."

She shifted position on the couch and set Laurel to one side. The little girl whimpered until Fred cuddled close. Then, she seemed to fall asleep with the dog nestled next to her. Allie got up. Found her knees shaky, but capable of carrying her up the three stairs into the dining room and kitchen area. Matt was hanging up the phone. He sat down at the kitchen table and made some notes on a pad of paper.

"What are you doing?" Allie asked.

He looked up at her. A new Matt regarded her. One with the hard glint of ruthlessness in his brown eyes. "Taking care of you. Of Laurel. Of . . . things."

She pulled a chair out from the table and sat down. "How?"

"Allie, just let me handle this."

"How?" She put her hands on the wood surface. "How are you planning to handle this? How are you planning on handling me?"

"By protecting you."

She started to reply, but the phone rang. Matt picked it up. His gaze became even more remote and distant. He mumbled a comment, then said, clearly, "Mercs are fine, but no hit men. Try any of the guys who worked with us before. I trust them. I don't want professional killers, understand me?"

Allie froze in place.

Matt replaced the phone after speaking for another few moments in Spanish.

"Who are you?" she asked, more frightened now than she had been when the shotgun was blasting away at her home. She shook her head. "I don't know you."

"Yes, you do."

"Mercs?" She stood up and began pacing around the kitchen. "Mercenaries? Hit men? *Killers?* Matt, I don't know you. I can't imagine..."

"How do you think I pulled off that kidnap rescue in South America?" he asked. "With a troop of Boy Scouts? Come on, Allie. Smell the coffee. I'm the same man you've known since the day Laurel smeared jelly on you. But please remember that I had a different job before becoming her surrogate daddy. I was an adventurer. I know people who have specialized talents. Some of them owe me. I'm just calling in a few markers. To save you..."

"Don't you dare use me as an excuse, Matt Glass." She stopped pacing and pointed her finger at him. "I had no trouble with this kind of horror and violence before I met you and I..."

"You want me to disappear?" He gazed at her with no warmth in his eyes. "I can do that."

"I..." She stopped pacing. Tom, the biggest and oldest of her cats, came into the kitchen and sat down, curling her furry tail around her feet. Watching.

"No," Allie said. "I don't want you to disappear. We've been through that. I love you. That's the problem. Because I'm not sure who it is that I love anymore. Who *you* are."

Matt stood up. "If you don't think you know, I can't tell you. Only show you. Please just trust me for now. Until you do feel you know me again."

"I...I don't know if I can, Matt."

His smile was wry, lopsided. "I guess that's honest enough."

"I'm very frightened." She hugged herself, not daring to go to him yet. He *was* a stranger. A mystery.

"You should be. So am I. I have fears just like anyone else. And, remember, you didn't have a nightmare last night so bad, you woke up crying out. *I* did. And you came to me and comforted me. Made me feel safe and secure." He held out his hand. "What you did for me last night, I can do for you today. Even if you disapprove of my methods. Don't turn from me, now Allie. I love you, too. God help me. I *need* you. And, frankly, you need me, as well."

Still, she hesitated. "I've never needed anyone else before. I...I always made my own way. I don't know how to deal with dependence."

"That makes two of us."

She touched his hand.

And came into his arms. She cried, and he held her close, comforting her. Their embrace was warm, and his kiss burned her doubts away. For now.

IT TOOK the rest of the week to sort out her life as best she could under the circumstances. To rearrange her schedule, canceling those appointments and putting off those clients that she could, to bring many of her belongings up the mountain, and to deal with the new reality of being a target of violence.

Because that's what they were.

After the official investigation, even the police agreed with Matt that they had been attacked by a professional terrorist. Or, at the very least, a local tough who had been instructed by one. She and Matt were advised to be on guard at all times, though no one encouraged Matt to go as far as he actually did.

"The cops can't provide bodyguard service indefinitely," he said, several days later. "We have to deal with this ourselves," he added, his tone indicating he would tolerate no argument.

She had none to give him. The county sheriff, who had jurisdiction on the mountain, was providing only drive-by security in the form of a patrol car passing the house now and then. It was not enough, given the calculated violence of the attack on them, she thought. The city police were conducting an investigation, but were clearly out of their league already.

No one had seen the car, though the neighbors had certainly heard the shots. No evidence, no suspects, no pending arrests. Whoever had done it, whoever was behind it was still free to act against them. So, she had finally agreed to Matt's style and plan of action. It all went against the grain, but for the most part, she kept her opinions to herself.

She had said nothing when some large, mysterious packages had started arriving by private delivery service to the house. Hadn't commented when Matt had installed an elaborate security system around the house, except to make sure he allowed for Fred's bathroom excursions.

Matt had agreed with that. But he had limited Fred to a leash and an adult human companion when she went outside. This made sense, because the property wasn't fenced, so Allie accepted it. Fred was less sanguine about the situation, but seemed prepared to tolerate the conditions for the time being. The three cats weren't allowed out at all and had to be watched closely each time a door was opened. They were not happy with the new rules and spent most of their time looking for messes to make in the new and unfamiliar environment of the Essex house.

Further, Laurel was showing all the signs expected from fear trauma and another change in environment. If there was trouble around that the cats missed, she found it and made it worse. With relish, it seemed to her "Momma" and "Daddy." And, with Matt so concerned with building his electronic fortress for their well-being, most of the supervision of Laurel fell to Allie.

It all made for a full, exhausting day, every day, and when night came, she and Matt fell asleep without even thinking of making love, though they did sleep together. But it was in the same room with Laurel and the four pets. Matt had done an extra-special job on the master bedroom with his security techniques and made certain every living being he cared for was safely inside that system before he finally allowed himself to sleep. A fly would likely set it off, Allie was sure.

But, she did sleep soundly and securely. Even knowing Matt had a loaded gun under his pillow. And though they didn't make love, something special was happening every night as they slumbered, exhausted, in each other's presence.

She was getting used to him, and he to her under far less than romantic conditions. If she'd had time to think about it much, she would have been pleased. Thinking about good things, however, was not a high priority. Too many negatives were still out there, un-accounted for.

On Monday morning, they were on the way out to the airport to pick up Matt's friends. The ones he had phoned a week ago. Until now, Matt hadn't let Allie or Laurel out of his sight for more than a moment or two and insisted on taking then both with him whenever he had to leave the house.

This trip was a small exception: Laurel was staying for the afternoon with Miranda while Allie went to the airport. There wasn't room, Matt had said, for the three of them and the men he was picking up, and he wanted Allie to meet them without having to worry about the child. Allie's patience was wearing thin. But she was still shook up enough to accept having some hired gun watch out for her. Hopefully, Matt's buddy, this Chico person, would help her get on with her life.

When she saw him in the crowd getting off the plane, however, those hopes fell flat to the floor. "Your buddy's actually the Terminator, right?" she asked Matt.

Matt's grin was wide. "Don't joke about it," he said, speaking softly. "He's real sensitive about the scars on his face."

"It wasn't the scars that clued me," she replied. "It was his size." But she was speaking to herself. Matt had run over to the giant and was being caught up in a crushing bear hug, which he was returning with glee. The two looked and sounded like a mismatched pair of professional wrestlers, as they exchanged happy insults. Allie sighed. Male bonding. Who could understand it?

Three other behemoths arranged themselves around the newcomer, and she heard growled greetings in at least two languages besides English. Then Matt summoned her with an imperious wave of his hand. Hating it, she trotted over anyway. She even managed a smile. They were a truly scary bunch.

"This is Mrs. Ford," Matt said, repeating the words in Spanish, then German. "She's the client. She and a two-year-old child you'll meet later on." He paused. "The good news is, the lady will follow orders," he added, not looking at her. "Allie, this is Gunther, Christian and Manuel. And, of course, Chico."

"Hi." Allie managed another smile. *Follow orders?* Well, only if she agreed with them! "Thanks for coming," she added.

This greeting brought no comment from the men. They all just stared at her, as if she was nothing more than an interesting bug. Allie blinked. Pinched herself to see if she was in a bizarre nightmare. But she was wide-awake.

When they picked up the luggage, she could see why Matt had decided to leave Laurel behind. Not only was her Eagle packed to the ceiling, but Matt and Chico strapped baggage onto the roof, as well. As they worked, the men said nothing. They had obviously done this before, Allie realized. They moved and behaved as a team.

A team aimed at what goal? Her safety? Laurel's?

Was Matt actually constructing some sort of private army with the aim of going after whoever was behind the terrorism aimed at them?

And, just what did she, law-abiding citizen that she thought she was, think about that?

She wasn't sure. Yet.

They drove to town, Allie squashed between Matt and Chico. No one said a word until they reached the section of the city that held "car row," the avenue of the automobile dealers. Then Chico pointed to a dealership. Matt slowed and turned in.

"Why are we stopping?" Allie asked, unable to bear silence any longer. "Shouldn't we be getting home? It's near Laurel's nap time. I don't want to impose on Miranda any longer than necessary."

"Be patient," Matt said, scarcely noticing her, she thought. "This is important. We're buying these guys a proper car."

She had to bite her tongue to keep from replying in the manner she felt most suited his attitude and the occasion.

But, they did buy the guys a car. Actually, what they drove out in, after paying the astonished and delighted salesman in cash, was more of a modified tank. It was an off-road, all-terrain vehicle designed for rigorous use, one of the knockoffs of the military Humvee that had captured the American imagination a few years before. Chico's guys seemed happy as clams in sand, Allie though glumly. And Matt had paid for it without counting the cost.

Or asking her to kick in. Somehow, that bothered her more than anything else that had happened that afternoon. It was her neck, too, on the line, wasn't it? She ought to be a contributor to the effort.

Right now, she was angrier at Matt than she was at the person or persons behind their troubles.

In spite of her hidden rage, however, on the way to pick up Laurel at Miranda's house, a strange thing happened. While the other three men had abandoned the crowded back seat of her Eagle for the rarer joy of the ATV, Chico stayed in the front, again wedging her close to Matt. She could feel the play of Matt's muscles pressed against her arm as he drove. Felt his strength and control. Sensed his competence. Her awareness of him expanded.

The physical sensation began to stir her sexually, and by the time they pulled up to Miranda's house-office, she was so aroused, she could hardly get out of the car.

And she was embarrassed beyond belief by the combination.

Laurel greeted the two of them with sublime indifference and paid absolutely no attention to the big stranger with them. She was in the middle of some sort of playtime with two other small girls and clearly did not care to be interrupted. Miranda apologized.

"She's been having great fun," the private detective explained. "I invited my two little nieces over for a few hours, and they've gotten along really well, considering their ages." She stared up at the gigantic Chico. "Hi," she said. "Who're you?"

As Allie watched, the newcomer underwent an astonishing transformation. From a sullen, rather frightening, dark-visaged giant, he became a smiling, charming man. "My name is Chico Roderigez," he said, taking her hand and bowing over it, brushing his lips near the skin. *"Señorita."*

Miranda Stamos actually blushed. And giggled. She looked younger than her thirty-plus years, all of a sudden.

Allie thought briefly of M.J.'s thwarted lust for Miranda and sighed. "Mr. Roderigez is here to help Matt," she said. "They've done stuff together before."

"That South America thing?" Miranda glanced at Matt. Chico still held her hand.

Matt nodded. "Chico was my right arm in that operation." He picked up Laurel, who protested loudly. "Come on, sweetie. Time to go home. Say goodbye to your new friends."

"No home! Want stay 'Randa!"

Matt grinned. "It seems you've made a conquest, Miranda."

"Ah, then that makes two of us," Chico intoned.

Allie glanced heavenward. Laurel yowled. Matt looked embarrassed at his niece's behavior, and Chico and Miranda looked at each other. This was all getting far too complicated for her, Allie decided. She felt a yen for the quiet, simple life she had been leading up until a few short weeks ago.

When she first saw Matt Glass pushing a grocery cart and thought he was so good-looking.

It took some time to extract Laurel from the two other children, but they finally got her into the Eagle and headed up the mountain to the Essex house. The other men had gone on before them with directions from Matt and instructions from Chico. Since they had left the car seat out to make more room, Allie sat in back, holding the child, leaving Chico and Matt up front to talk about security measures.

And countermeasures.

They talked in rapid-fire Spanish, with German on the side, obviously thinking she couldn't understand them. Well, they were almost right. But she could make out enough of the Spanish words to get the general drift. Matt was not content only to protect. He and Chico were plotting an attack strategy. She was sure of it.

And, she found, she approved.

Events in her life were now so far out of her control that she welcomed anything that would start to set things back in order. Even a risky... Her attention was suddenly riveted on the conversation. Her thoughts tumbled, emotions whipping them into a whirlwind.

Matt had mentioned her husband's name.

He'd rolled it along in with a lot of other stuff she didn't catch, but she definitely heard Paul's name. Why? She hesitated to ask. Thought about it, but... What could Paul have to do with the current crisis? She ought to ask, she knew, but...

Then, they were home. And there was no time for questions. Matt and Chico piled out and started unloading equipment and luggage. The three other men were already at work around the grounds, apparently adding extra goodies to Matt's security system. Allie didn't ask about that, either.

Instead, she took Laurel and went inside. The animals were there to greet her, and Laurel came out of her pout when she saw Fred. *Just like home,* Allie thought.

Except, it wasn't home. She had to leash Fred up to take her outside. She had a whiny two-year-old to feed and put down for a late nap. She had virtually no privacy, what with the men coming in and out, ignoring her and going about their business. She had no chance at all to get any serious work done, even with Laurel out of the way for the time being. No one said anything about it, but she was also sure that she was expected to feed the four new faces as well as provide dinner for herself, Matt and Laurel.

Well, why not? Weren't all these guys here to help save her from enemies? Some weird, twisted sickos who'd frightened her and threatened her and destroyed her peace, her future and her home. She went into the kitchen and made coffee. Then, she sat down at the table and started to cry.

Matt found her few minutes later. Without saying anything, he brought over a box of tissues, then poured them both a cup of coffee. Allie sniffed and tried to regain some self-control while she hung her head over the steaming mug. "I don't know..." she started to say. "I just..."

"I'm glad to see you crying, finally," he said softly. "It's a normal reaction to all this."

She looked at him. "Give me a break, Matt. I'm being a wimp, and you know it. Don't patronize me. At least grant me that much."

He didn't seem impressed. "I'll grant you anything you want, Allie. But you are entitled to bawl some. All you want, in fact. Your world's been turned upside down. Anyone'd cry. Or wish they could."

She stretched her arms out on the table and rested her forehead on them. "I feel helpless."

"And you're not used to that, are you?"

"No."

He sat back, folding his arms. "You didn't feel that way when your husband disappeared?"

She shrugged. "Sure, but..."

"But, you took the bull by the horns, so to speak, and did things about your situation."

"Of course, I..."

"You're doing that now. You just don't know it," he said.

She started to reply, but the phone rang.

"I'll get it." Matt stood, went over to the phone and lifted the receiver. He frowned.

Allie tensed.

He glanced over at her and shook his head. "It's nothing. Don't worry," he said. "Just testing the wiretap system, that's all."

"Wire...tap?" She rubbed her sore eyes and took a sip of coffee. "Is that legal?"

Matt spoke in Spanish, then hung up the phone. "No," he said. "It isn't."

"But *we're* doing it anyway."

"That's right. If anyone calls now trying to put a scare into you, we'll be on them like flies on...honey."

She whistled through her teeth. "I'll never get to the governor's mansion by this route, that's for sure."

He threw back his head, finishing the rest of his coffee. "Allie, I'm doing this so you have a chance to stay alive and well enough to run for office."

She regarded him. "Why did you speak to Chico about Paul?"

Matt hesitated.

"Why, Matt? I have a right to know, I believe."

He was silent, but he nodded.

She sighed. "The truth, please. All of it."

"I have to take things one at a time, Allie," he said, looking past her at the wall of the kitchen where his sister's family pictures still hung. "First, I intend to find out who's been harassing us, you in particular, and who's behind it. Then, I..."

"What? What then?"

He paced the room a moment. Rubbed the back of his neck and looked at her. "I want to find out what happened to Paul Ford. I want to know. I want you to be free. I want us to have a chance at happiness together. Whatever we decide about the future, I want that decision to be based on our love for each other. Not fear."

He couldn't succeed, she knew. She had tried for so long and in so many ways herself. It was a rainbow chase. A doomed cause. But he was willing to do it. For her. For them.

Allie thought about that for at least one second. That was all it took for her depression to disappear and for her strong sense of purpose to reestablish itself. She puffed out her cheeks and blew out air and made another decision.

"Matt."

"Yeah?"

"Is there any chance you and I can have a few minutes of privacy any time soon?"

He looked around. "This is private."

She shook her head. "Not private enough. Not for what I have in mind."

He stared, then a smile spread slowly across his face. "I can't make any guarantees."

She stood up. "Well, we're not likely to get them any time soon, are we, so we might as well..."

He moved toward her. "Allie, I'm doing all this because I love you."

She grabbed his belt and pulled him toward her. "Show me, then," she said, passion and need making her voice low and fierce. "Don't talk about it. Show me!"

CHAPTER FOURTEEN

BY THE TIME she dragged him down into the basement to the one room in the house where she was sure they could bolt out the world, she was so intensely aroused, she felt she would scream like a wild thing the moment he touched her. They went into the laundry room, turned on the overhead light and Allie locked the door.

And she did yell, at least, when their clothes came off. Softly, a female howl of primitive need. The passion she had kept buried for so many days and nights came boiling to the surface.

Matt's desire matched hers. He pushed her against the wall, his strong hands moving over her body. When he entered her, they both groaned with a delicious combination of relief and tension. Their mating was fast and furious and satisfying, and when it was over, they were both gasping for breath and damp with sweat, in spite of the cooler air of the underground room.

Allie held him tightly, her arms around his neck. Her body tingled all over from union with him. With this man who had crashed into her life and torn her careful plans for the future into shreds. This man she knew she loved more than any of those plans, now. Not exactly sure what she wanted to say to him, she chose to discuss the immediate and banal. It was silly and cowardly of her, she thought, but she wasn't yet ready to deal with truly serious matters.

"Do...do you want me to fix dinner for the crew tonight?" she asked, panting rapidly between every other word. Making love standing up against a wall was not exactly easy work. She was standing on one leg with the other still hooked around his body, as if she wanted to keep him close as long as possible.

Matt laughed, the sound shaky to his own ears. Their erotic exertions had surprised him with the intensity of feeling that had assailed him. For a second there, he thought he understood what it meant to be an actual extension of another person. He lost sight of the boundaries and differences between them and saw only unity. It was far more than sex, he knew. Even more than love. But just what else, he couldn't say. He, too, wasn't certain enough of himself right at the moment to discuss anything of any depth. So, he went along with her.

"Sure, that would be great," he said. "But you don't have to wait on them. They're here to take care of you, not the other way around." His fingers were still gripping her waist and hips, digging in, tightly, as if he didn't ever want to release her.

She relaxed, putting the other leg down for support. "I know that," she said, running her fingers over his warm, sweaty skin. "I want to help, though. And I can cook, even if I don't get much opportunity to do it for a large group."

He laughed again, his voice firmer. Control and common sense returning. "You're one in a million, Allie. I can't believe I found you."

She moved, gently but deliberately, and his eyes closed in pleasure. "Believe it," she whispered. "*I* do."

And desire overtook them again.

A WHILE LATER, she was back upstairs in the kitchen, humming to herself and working over a steaming kettle of stew. Laurel, rested from her afternoon outing, sat at the kitchen table, copying Allie's moves and banging small saucepans with a big wooden spoon.

"I cooking," she announced, slamming a pan on the table. Her expression was calm and serious.

Allie smiled. "That makes two of us, honey," she said. Fred ambled in and sniffed the air, hopefully. "Forget it," she said, addressing the dog. "This is people food."

"I making Fred food," Laurel said. "Fred, c'mere."

Fred went over and sniffed the little hand, licking the skin and making Laurel giggle. Allie moved over to the sink, wondering how, in the midst of so much turmoil and disaster, she could feel so happy. It had to be temporary, but it was there, nevertheless. She gazed out the window, relishing the breathtaking view of the city down on the plains. This house was ideally suited, she thought, for just living and dreaming and . . .

Loving . . .

Her eyes teared suddenly, thinking of the couple who had built it. Behind her, their little daughter played, chatting with her doggie about dinner, happily oblivious for the moment to the loss of her parents. Oblivious, because someone else had stepped in to take their place and give her the love and security she needed. Matt had done this for his sister's child.

Was he doing the same for her? Allie brushed away the moisture on her face. It wouldn't do to let Laurel see her cry. She moved back to the stove and stirred the stew. A bell dinged, and she opened the oven. She heard the front door open and close. Matt was here. The rolls were ready. Almost time to call in the ...

"Are you out of your mind!"

Allie whirled. M.J. stood in the dining room area, his face red and his expression angry. "M.J.," she said. "What are you doing here?"

"No." He advanced into the kitchen. "What are *you* doing here?" He gestured with both arms. "Look at yourself! You look like a ranch wife preparing dinner for the hired hands. Fixing grub for your man's boys. Matt Glass is really something if he can turn you into a hausfrau just like this! My God, the man has his own personal army out there! Do you know the local TV stations are running this little fortress as prime-time news tonight? Your political career is ..."

"On hold."

"It sure as hell is." M.J. turned redder. "Do you know what that big ape your boyfriend calls his buddy did to me? He searched me, damn it! For weapons, before he'd let me in the house, and I'm your damn cousin!"

"M.J., settle down. You're upset. I'm sure Matt ..."

"Matt was standing right there watching! He's lost it, Allie. Lost it and taken you with him. Allie, I don't think I know you anymore."

"I'm not lost, M.J.," she said, calmly. "Not lost at all."

"Lost!" Laurel said, banging the saucepan on the table. "Lost it. Find it."

"Hi, kid," M.J. said. He sighed, deflated and sat down beside Laurel. "I think I know what you're talking about," he added. "Does your new mommy?" He rested his chin on his hand and regarded Allie. Then, he smiled, letting her know he wasn't really angry at her.

She smiled back, wanly. Went to the refrigerator and got out two beers, cracked them open and handed one to her cousin. "No," she admitted, taking a seat across from him. "Maybe I'm not exactly lost, but I have no idea what I'm doing, what's going on or even where I want it all to end up." She raised her beer can. "Here's to total confusion."

M.J. lifted his beer. "May it also infect our enemies."

"I'll drink to that." She took a sip. "What's this about the newspeople? I can't imagine Matt's allowed them on the grounds."

"He hasn't. They've got a van out there on the highway, and they're filming your commandos at work. Allie, this is the finish of your campaign, your entire political future, if you don't..."

"I don't care about my campaign." She set her beer down. "M.J., I've found a few new priorities recently. Getting shot at in your own house does that to a person."

He nodded. Scratched his head. "I guess I can try to understand. But it seems like such a waste." He put his face in his hands and rubbed it. "I heard about all this when Miranda called to tell me about the storm troopers. She thinks the big guy is cute. Then that woman from the news desk called and..."

"M.J., are you put out because Miranda...?"

"Oh, hell yes. I'm put out, and I'm not happy about it." He lowered his hands and looked at her. "But I'm not cut up because she thinks Godzilla out there is tasty-looking. She's a free agent. I like her, but I don't love her, and that's a fact. Now, you . . ."

"We've had this talk before, remember. I told you, I don't know what I want or expect . . ."

"I know what you said, dear." M.J. leaned forward. "But your actions are shouting otherwise. You've made your choices clear. You're not just Allison Ford anymore. You're Matt Glass's woman. Aren't you?"

Allie looked away. At Laurel. "I'm caught up, M.J. This is bigger than I ever imagined it could be. I never dreamed I'd let myself get swept away from the path I chose. But here I am. Letting the flood take me right along, and I . . ." She stopped, hearing a door slam.

"You what?" Matt came in. He put his hand on her shoulder. "Go on. I think I have a right to know what you mean by being carried along. Are you willing or unwilling?" He pulled out a chair and sat down, giving Laurel's head an affectionate pat in the process. She looked up at him and grinned, then went back to banging her spoon around, in and on her pans.

"I'm willing," Allie said. "If I wasn't, I wouldn't be here." She pushed her beer over to Matt. "Tell the guys that dinner will be ready in a few minutes. M.J., do you want to join us? There's plenty."

Her cousin eyed her. "I wouldn't miss it for the world," he said. "Count me in."

Matt reached over and slapped his shoulder in a comradely manner. "Welcome to the Glass Castle, then, M.J.," he said. "We may look like we'll shatter, but we're strong as steel, believe me."

The Glass Castle? Allie wasn't surprised at the phrase. He was quite serious in using that term, she realized. It reflected his attitude, his fortress mentality. She had no argument with it, either.

At supper, Allie played her role as hostess while the men talked. It was what she wanted to do, and it was extremely instructive.

M.J., who had already met Chico, was introduced to Gunther, Christian and Manuel and his credentials as Allie's relative were established. Matt, sitting at the head of the kitchen table beside an unusually well-behaved Laurel in a high chair, accomplished this task. "He and Mrs. Ford are like brother and sister," Matt concluded. "You may all trust him with your plans."

Gunther frowned. *"Ja,"* he said. "A *bruder* is to be trusted. Usually. But dis one is a lawyer."

"It's all right," Allie interjected. "He's one of the good ones." She smothered the urge to smile. M.J. hated the poor image lawyers had in this day of unlimited and unrestrained litigation.

"Justice is important," Christian said. "But some lawyers..."

"This lawyer believes in the Constitution of the United States," M.J. said, his face reddening. "If any of you guys have a problem with that..."

"Ease up, M.J.," Matt cautioned. "We're just testing water here."

"All right." M.J. sat back. "Test away."

"Let's eat first," Matt said.

Allie served huge bowls of stew. It wasn't her best offering, but it seemed to do. The men ate quickly and with relish. They drank large glasses of lemonade and iced tea. No one drank beer but M.J. Not even Matt.

When the eating slowed, he began to speak, in English, talking slowly. "This is the situation. We have three known sources of trouble. Any one of them could be behind the incidents against Mrs. Ford and myself. They could be acting alone or in concert." He paused here and translated rapidly into German and Spanish, then went on.

"It's unlikely that the Turner couple are the primary villains. I don't see enough intelligence in them, though I may well be wrong. They're certainly full of cunning."

"But their lawyer, Penny Jackson, is the one who's handling Laurel's estate and who dislikes Matt so much," M.J. said. "And Penny's a long-time political supporter of Rita Morely. Don't discount the Turners, Matt."

Chico leaned over to the others, and now he translated while Matt waited. Matt knew they would understand most of what he said but he wanted every detail exquisitely clear. When there was silence again, he went on.

"I'm not discounting the Turners or Penny. I'm just putting them low on the list. For all their eagerness to get hold of Laurel and her money, I don't think they have the capacity for the kind of violence it took to blast Allie's house."

"What about the *hombre* whose arms you nearly broke defending your lady?" Chico asked. "You seen him again? Anywhere?"

Matt shook his head. "Not a hair, Chico. But someone ran me off the road, and I'm sure in my bones it was Baker. Even if I can't prove it."

"Miranda should be here," M.J. said. "She's been tracing Baker's movements over the last month."

"We'll hold a real war council tomorrow," Matt said. "Miranda will have a lot to tell us then." He glanced over at Allie. "She's been doing work for me on a number of projects."

Allie didn't say anything, but she did raise her eyebrows. She continued to remove dirty dishes and then to serve ice cream and cookies while she listened carefully.

And thought about what she was hearing and learning.

Matt outlined the security structure. Chico was assigned to guard her, Gunther to watch out for Laurel with Christian and Manuel as backup and property patrol. The men would sleep outside in tents they had brought, but would take their meals in the house as long as Allie was willing to fix food. This even slight deference to her startled and pleased her, as such consideration was unexpected from such macho men.

"All the people who come to see you must pass through a search routine," Matt said, not looking directly at her. "Every single one, regardless of how long you've known them or how much you trust them. One of the reasons I didn't prevent the TV folks from filming us at work today was to prepare your clients. To prepare the public for the kind of security you'll be under for I don't know how long."

"Wyoming's not used to this sort of situation," she agreed. "It's just as well I don't intend to campaign, then."

Matt didn't respond to that immediately. He looked over at M.J., who shrugged. Then Matt spoke. "You'll continue to campaign, but you'll do it my way," he said. "For instance, when you ride in the parade next week, we'll have you in a bullet-proof vest and..."

"She is a political?" Christian asked. "Dey never listen to orders, Matthew. What you gonna do wit her?"

"She'll listen," Matt responded before Allie could speak. "She's smart, Chris. Not driven just by her ambitions."

"She should drop out of the race altogether," M.J. said, his expression indicating his reluctance to say that. "I think, for her safety, she . . ."

"She will continue to campaign," Matt interrupted, his face stone. "She *will* win."

M.J. cleared his throat. "Allie, you know you don't have to, if you . . ."

"It's okay, M.J.," she said, taking Laurel out of the high chair. "I've made my own decision about things. I'll tell you after I've talked with Matt."

"Well." M.J. shifted position to face Matt. "At least you're right about the television coverage. When I think about it, actually, it's a possible bonus. They had a field day with Allie's house. Now, seeing you enclose her in this place with guards around won't be such a shock. The public *knows* someone's out to hurt her. And that might be a benefit, politically." He turned back to Allie. "Most people hate the thought of violence, so this should get you a lot of sympathy."

"Fine for now." Allie smiled. Strangely, everything was fine with her right then and she was reluctant to spoil the mood. Laurel sat in her lap quietly regarding the strangers. Fred, who was napping by the refrigerator in hopes of a later handout, raised her head for a moment, then relaxed. The smallest cat, Dick, had jumped up on Manuel's lap without an invitation and was being treated to a gentle stroking. Tom and Harry, still unsure, sat by the back door, awaiting a chance to break for outdoor freedom. Allie kept on smiling, wondering at her own feelings.

She was safe, here with these strange, wild men, with *her* man, and her heart was happy for what she was certain was the first time in her life! Her carefully planned future lay in pieces before her, but she was content. And she would tell Matt as soon as she could.

Contentment, however, wouldn't solve Matt's problems. She had plans for tackling that on her own.

They talked into the evening, tossing around ideas about who might have made the phone call pretending to be Paul, who might be the mysterious couple in the Toyota, who was behind the outright violence and if all these matters were connected. At one point, Allie announced that Laurel needed to go to sleep, and Gunther came with her to learn the ropes about dealing with the child. With all the security around, they had decided it was safe to put her back in her old room, and Laurel seemed to be happy about that.

"Matthew chose me," the big blond man said, "because I haf two little daughters." His command of English was halting, but adequate.

"Really?" Allie regarded him more closely. "I thought that you all were...soldiers or something."

"*Ja.* We are soldiers." Gunther said no more on the subject.

But Laurel liked him. She had a short period of testing this new adult in her life, being cranky and fussing over going to bed, but Gunther showed patience. If he was a father, as he said, he'd learned his lessons well. Laurel didn't get a trick past the man without him seeing it coming. He was gentle, but firm, gaining Laurel's trust and respect almost immediately.

And he handled her well, so Allie relaxed. The less she knew about Matt's men, probably, the better, she decided. Better for them, better for her. She went back to the kitchen and announced she was heading for her makeshift office to do a little work before going to bed. The men hardly looked up from their discussion and planning to acknowledge her. Not even M.J., who, she reasoned in a wry way, should know better. Well, these were extraordinary times, weren't they?

They'd better be, she thought, walking slowly back down the hall to her office. There were quite a few lives at stake. She hadn't even considered her own kids, yet. What were they going to think, with their mom a target of some evil, violent intent and guarded by men who seemed almost as dangerous as the person or persons after her and Matt....

Fred followed her as she went into her new office and settled herself at the desk. The dog took up her old place underneath, sighing and seeking the most comfortable position before falling asleep. Oh, to be a poodle, her owner thought. With nothing more vital to worry about than which cat to bother at a given moment. Well, she wasn't a poodle. Nor was she anyone's doormat. This was Matt's fight? Men's business? Not by a long shot. It was hers, too!

Allie spent the next half hour typing up a letter to her children and another one to her folks. She tried to explain things so that they wouldn't worry, but so that if they saw *more* stuff about her on the news, they would be prepared. She had, of course, called them immediately after the shotgunning incident and let them know where she was, that she was safe and that Matt was doing the best possible job of keeping her safe. They had seemed to accept that, but she wrote now to add to their sense of security. In case the news made it look like she was still in jeopardy....

The news. She glanced at her watch. Five of the hour. She probably ought to give it a look, just to see what interpretation the local press was putting on Matt's activities. Spin was everything in the news game. She knew she could expect almost anything, from fear about a private army to sympathy for her situation. She shut down the computer and went across the hall into the den. The television and VCR setup was state-of-the-art, so just for the heck of it, she popped in a fresh tape and recorded the news.

And the special editorial after the regular news.

Too stunned to believe what she had seen and heard, she was removing the tape with hands that trembled when the phone rang. From down the hall, she heard Matt yell that he was getting it. She stayed hunched in front of the television, waiting. In a minute, he was at the door.

"It's Josh," he said. "Did you catch the news?"

She held up the tape. "Better than that. Here it is. I taped it."

Matt whistled, low and admiring. That, and his smile, was all the reward she needed.

They all watched the tape. Allie wanted to view the rerun just to make sure she really believed what she had seen. The presence and reaction of the men helped establish the reality.

"My God," M.J. said. "They're making you out to be some kind of latter-day Western heroine, Al. Cattle Kate, Annie Oakley, Calamity Jane... According to this, you're a darn legend already. Heck, Joan of Arc's got nothing on you, babe."

"It's the victim thing," she replied. "Newsies love that."

Matt said nothing. The newscaster had reported the facts. Allie's house had been shotgunned and her "friend and campaign director, Matthew Glass, was attacked and run off the road a few weeks earlier in a deliberate attempt on his life." Allie and Matt had appealed to the proper authorities for protection and help, but had been forced to resort to their own resources, finally.

It was a positive approach, and one he had not expected. But, there was more. Much more. The woman went on to give an on-the-air editorial. That's what had stunned Allie.

The violence against Allison Ford, the reporter said, is part of a conspiracy against her as an independent, womens'-issue candidate. Rita Morely's backers, particularly David Benning, have too much political capital invested in their pet female candidate to risk allowing a newcomer with no obligations or connections to gain the office. The focus of the report was radically feminist, but also underscored Allie's position as a reformer and a potential ally of the people in the street, male *and* female.

The program also ran clips of Allie's political past to emphasize this last point, showing her working on the school board and the city council, speaking to groups of children and mothers about financial planning and working as a volunteer on a project directed at displaced homemaker-single mothers without the ability to support themselves. She came across as an activist, dedicated not just to women's issues, but to the family and the home. Matt could not believe how well it was done. If he'd tried, he couldn't have put together a more positive campaign advertisement. And since it was presented as an editorial newscast, it had the trappings of real news.

It was the best thing that could possibly have happened for her, politically.

It also gave him another suspect. David Benning. Matt cursed his carelessness in not doing a deeper investigation into the political web in the county and state. If he had, surely he could have turned up this information on his own. The old spider was a bigger factor than he had guessed, and that was important data. He should have had it sooner.

But, it didn't matter. He had it now, and he knew what to do with it. "Josh wants you to call him back," he said. "He's got some ideas on how to capitalize on this immediately, and I want you to..."

"Matt, I need to talk to you about this." Allie looked around the room. Every male was watching her. New respect in the eyes of Chico and his crew. M.J. was just beaming with pride. "In private, please," she added.

Later, when M.J. had gone home and the other men were settled around the grounds, she told him. "I'm not going to run for office," she said, looking up at him from her sitting position on the bed. "I've made a decision. You and Laurel are more important to me than any political campaign. Our staying together is more important than any other dream I've ever had, and I won't give it up."

Matt stared at her. "You're kidding me. After seeing that show?" He frowned. "I mean, I appreciate what you're saying about us and that's great, but..." He rubbed the back of his neck. "Look, I've gone to a hell of a lot of trouble to make sure you can run and win, Allie. I won't accept this."

"Don't. Don't accept it. But *I've* made up my mind."

He sat down on the bed. "Why? Just tell me, unemotionally and logically, why you should give up a dream that was driving your life before you met me. If you can convince me it's the right thing to do, I'll back you all the way."

"Okay. Um. I..." She felt frightened, suddenly. All the convincing words she'd thought of earlier were gone. A cold kind of fear gripped her insides and made chilly sweat trickle down her sides. "Uh..."

"That's what I thought." Matt leaned over and took her hand. "You don't have this worked out in your head yet. Just in your heart. You're reacting and not thinking."

Anger replaced fear. "What does it matter *where* I have it worked out," she replied, jerking her hand away. "I have the right to choose for myself."

Matt shook his head. "Not anymore. Not when your decision will affect at least four other people directly."

She frowned, puzzled, then. "You, Laurel, Sam and Sally?"

He nodded. Took her hand again. "If it's humanly possible to do it," he said, gazing directly into her eyes, "I'm going to see us become a family." He covered her hand with his, encasing and caressing it. "Your kids and mine, you and me, the five of us. A family unit."

"Matt," she said. "When I spoke of giving up the campaign for our relationship, I didn't include marriage in the deal. You know how I feel."

His expression hardened. "I know I can't ask you to consider marriage until you know the truth about Paul.

We've kicked that ball around enough already, and you must know that I..."

"I know that you are beginning to give up a great deal for me, and I don't think you have a corner on that market. If I choose to drop out of the political race in order to concentrate on my relationship and future with you, then I believe you ought to respect that decision, just as I..."

"God, you are stubborn!"

She smiled at him. "No. I'm just in love."

Matt started twice to argue but could find nothing to say in response.

Love, as strong as it was getting to be between them, did change everything. He sighed, temporarily defeated, as she reached over and began to unbutton his shirt. To stroke his chest. And he then reached to unbutton hers.

THE NEXT MORNING, he started in again, however. Laurel slept late, giving them some more private time together. They made love and afterward showered together, then went into the kitchen. There, Matt seemed to think it was all right to talk business. "Your obligation to run isn't just to me or yourself anymore," he said. "You've got voters out there who are counting on you. Call Josh, Allie. At least talk to him."

"I told you last night what I..." She was interrupted by Chico, who came barging into the kitchen where she was preparing breakfast for all of them.

"Many cars outside, Matt," he announced. "Lots of people. They all want to see her." He pointed at Allie.

"Me?" She dried her hands on a dish towel and went over to the dining room area. The road past the house was partly visible through the trees. Cars and pickup trucks were lined along the roadside. She heard some honking and shouting. "Why?"

Chico shrugged. "Don't know. What we gonna do, boss?" He looked genuinely worried for the first time since Allie had seen him trundle his muscled bulk off the plane. "They insisting on seeing your lady. Say they want to hear a speech or something. We can't search all of them."

"No need." Matt controlled his expression, but he wanted to smile broadly. Things were beginning to work out, at long last! The public was taking care of the problem of Allie's stubborn unwillingness to get on with her dreams. *He* would deal later with her problem about marriage. "Just get her a bullet-proof vest, and let's get her out there." He turned to Allie. "It's show time, sugar. Smile!"

CHAPTER FIFTEEN

WHAT COULD she do but go along?

Suitably, safely vested in snug body armor under her shirt and armed only with her wits, a mug of coffee and a smile, Allie sallied forth, Matt on one side of her, Chico on the other. Allie knew both men were armed and ready to protect her. The July morning sunlight was warm, the summer air soft on her face like the caresses Matt had given her when they made love.

And love was the reason Allie was about to betray Matt. Or, at least, to betray his hopes for her political career.

She stood out on the deck, using the microphone setup that Christian had produced from the home entertainment center in the house, and greeted the crowd, acknowledging special friends.

"I really appreciate that all of you came over to see how I was doing. As you can see, I'm doing just fine. I've got terrific people protecting me, and I'm truly grateful for everyone's concern. But, because of what's been happening, I've decided to withdraw from the legislative race. This has gotten too dangerous. It's in the best interest of those I love for me not to run . . ."

That was as far as she got. The first to shout was Walt Resner, the young cop who had warned Matt about Teddie Baker after their confrontation weeks before. "Allie Ford, you can't let us down. We're the people who need you. The ones without a lot of clout. I've got a list of police officers who're willing to help guard you in off-duty hours," he added, holding up a sheet of paper covered with signatures. "We all couldn't come out here this morning," he explained. "But you've got to know folks are really behind you." He rattled the paper. "Look and see, if you don't believe me!"

"Allie, you've got to run," June Watson yelled up at her. The big woman had on a T-shirt that declared Allie's candidacy in bright, bold letters. "We've made up thousands of these!" She pointed to her impressive expanse of chest.

Josh Henderson appeared. "I've got the same number of bumper stickers in boxes in the back of my car," he said. "A whole raft of folks came over last night after the newscast and helped me. Allie, we've got volunteers like you wouldn't believe!"

"But I..."

"But what?" yelled up Tim Swensen, the manager of Safeway. "I've planned a fund-raising barbecue for you day after tomorrow. I'll provide the meat, the volunteer committee will bring side dishes and we'll charge ten bucks a plate. You have to make a speech, Allie."

"I..."

"Give up?" Matt spoke softly so that only she could hear him.

"Someone shot at me," she said, talking into the microphone. "Shot at us, in my house. Friends, I can't go out in public and take the chance they'll hurt some innocent bystander just because I'm there."

"Hell, let 'em," a creaky old voice bellowed from the center of the crowd. Kelly McClean raised a fist.

''If they do, we'll string 'em up like the scum they are. Come on, Miss Allie. You can do it! Fight, girl!''

The crowd roared. A large group from her church loudly informed her they were praying for her and her family, as well.

Allie gave up. "Okay, folks," she said. "You have yourselves a candidate. Good luck!" And then she dropped the mike and embraced the cheering, laughing Matt Glass. He hugged her, made her pick up the mike and told her to give the people a rousing speech.

Which she did.

THE NEXT FEW WEEKS were busy ones for Allie. Having decided to run again, she plunged in with a vengeance. Confidence in Matt and his people, as well as the growing awareness of how much of the community was behind her, gave her the strength and the faith to do this. In the few moments she had to herself to reflect, she realized that her friends and neighbors had always been there for her. She had thought she was on her own. Now, when she needed their help and support, they thronged.

It was good.

And, for a time, it seemed the good would triumph.

Her kids and her parents called a few days after the newscast and after receiving her letters, worried about her and wanting to know what they could do to help. Allie restated her desire that Sam and Sally remain up at the ranch, out of harm's way, until the danger was over, even if it meant going to school there for the first part of the fall. Her parents agreed. Sally thought it was okay. Sam did not.

"I want to be home, Mom," he said. "You need me there, don't you?"

A plaintive note in his voice alerted her immediately. Her son needed to be needed. Allie thought quickly. "Yes," she replied. "I do. But if you two were here, I wouldn't be able to campaign as well, because I'd be too worried about you. That's the fair and honest truth, Sam. If you don't like it, I'm sorry, but that's how it is."

He was silent for a moment. Then: "That Laurel kid's with you."

"She would suffer a lot if she were separated from Matt, Sam. She's too young to know why it would be safer to be up with you all. She has her own bodyguard. I don't have to keep a constant watch over her now. I know if you were here, you wouldn't like having a guy hanging around you all the time. Never being able to get off and do what you wanted, alone. Think about it."

He was quiet for a time. Then he said, "Let me talk to Matt, Mom. Please."

She handed Matt the receiver. "He's feeling left out," she whispered. "From up there, this must seem exciting."

"Well?" Matt smiled at her. "It is exciting, isn't it? You're a celebrity." He took the phone. "Hi, Sam. Listen, your mom is okay, but she doesn't think the same way we do about things. You know and I know you'd be fine and a big help, but all she can see is the trouble and danger. So, give her a break, man. Stay put and take care of your sister, will you?" He listened for a moment. "You have a deal," he said, his tone different. Determined. "I swear it, Sam." He handed the phone back to Allie.

"What he said is okay, Mom," Sam said to her. "You stay out of trouble, you hear me?"

They talked for a little longer about ordinary matters. The horses and cats at the ranch, how Fred and the home cats were doing at Matt's place. Simple, everyday mom-kid talk. After she hung up, she turned to Matt. "What was that last part between you two all about?"

He didn't look directly at her or answer right away. But when he did, it cleared up a few more questions in her mind and answered a few more doubts in her heart.

"I was a twin, remember, Allie," he said. "I had a sister. And I had a mother and father who never lived together. Sam and I talked about that a lot while we were up at the ranch. He just made me promise again that I'd see to it he had some answers about his real dad."

"Matt, I... You don't..."

"And that he won't have to live without a father for much longer," Matt added, pulling her close and kissing her protests away. "I'm not blowing smoke at him, and he knows it," he added, solemnly. "Sam and I are too much alike for me to dare to try that. I made a promise, and I'll turn over every rock between here and hell if I have to in order to keep that vow."

Allie knew she couldn't argue with that kind of resolve. She hoped to high heaven he didn't dash himself to pieces on any of those rocks. Fortunately Allie had enough on her mind to keep her fears about Matt at bay.

THE TURNOUT for the barbecue Tim sponsored was good and the event got terrific media coverage. Allie gave another speech, then invited questions from the audience. In addition to the hundred or so volunteers who provided food, about five hundred curious and hungry voters showed up, and the woman who had done the editorial on Allie's problems made it look like a major political rally.

Which, in turn, inspired more people to get involved and volunteer their help and their resources to her campaign.

"Success breeds success," Matt declared one evening when she expressed wonder at the way things seemed to be snowballing. "Everyone loves an underdog, but they love a winner more." He hugged her. "And, honey, you are a winner."

"Maybe," she conceded. "Maybe I am. But I'll tell you one thing, I've grown a lot politically in the last few days. I have to admit I was pretty naive when I started out, but I'm learning as I go. People seem to agree, too. Support's growing each hour, literally. I wonder what that's doing to Rita's blood pressure these days?"

She spoke jokingly, almost sure, now that her campaign was on the move, that the forces against them had withdrawn their strong-arm tactics. Not even the strident Turners had appeared publicly to continue their pursuit of Laurel and her estate. It was peaceful, Allie believed, because the good guys were winning, finally!

Matt became intent. "It's too damn quiet out there to suit me," he said. "It's like being stranded in shark-infested waters and just waiting for the fins to break the surface."

Allie shuddered, her good mood dimmed slightly. "Maybe the bad guys gave up?" she said.

"Fat chance." He looked at her, put his arm around her and drew her close. "They're just waiting until we let our guard down." He kissed her hair. "Please, promise me you won't forget that."

"I promise." Allie kissed him back, praying that he was only speaking out of an inflated sense of drama.

HER RELUCTANCE to take him seriously controlled her actions on the day of the parade. The event began bright and early on a promising hot July morning. The county fair parade kickoff started at ten o'clock sharp, and Matt had planned for her to ride in the now fully armored ATV he had purchased weeks ago. With the rear section enclosed with bullet-proof Lexan, she knew she would be safe enough, if a little like a goldfish in a bowl.

Chico proudly informed her that the ATV would take a direct hit from a small missile before it would be brought to a halt. The very idea of such an attack made her break into a nervous sweat. The vehicle was air-conditioned, however, so she wouldn't steam-bathe while being driven at three to four miles an hour along the parade route, she was told.

But she could not bring herself to do it. She had made her own set of plans.

"I can't ride the parade route in a thing that looks like a bad science fiction movie prop," she said to Matt. "I appreciate what you've done, all of you, but I won't be the first candidate in history to hide from the people."

"You have to." Matt was tinkering with a video camera he intended to use to film her en route. "It's common sense."

"Matt, even the governor's riding a horse, for crying out loud! I show up in the Batmobile, and I'll be laughed off the ballot."

"No, you won't. People understand your situation."

"They understand that weeks ago someone shot at my house. Nothing's happened since. Matt, the public memory for that sort of thing is short."

He set the camera down. "Mine's not. You're riding in the ATV."

"I'm riding a horse," she said. "Lois Lepo's palomino mare. Lois called M.J. the other day and offered her, saying I'd look terrific on the horse because our manes are the same color." She laughed, hoping to lighten the atmosphere. "Isn't that cute?"

"It could be deadly."

Allie settled in. "Matt, listen to me. I know you're right about a lot of this security stuff. You've been terrific. I haven't even had a hint of trouble since we moved up here and brought in the troops. Everything's gone our way because of what you've done. But this time, I'm asking you to listen to me. The people around here will not be amused at my riding behind Lexan in the parade. It'll be an insult. Like I don't trust them."

Before Matt could reply, Chico came into the den. "Boss," he said, pointing toward the front of the house with his thumb. "There's a guy with a horse trailer waiting out at the gate. Says he's got Mrs. Ford's ride for the parade." His shaggy black eyebrows pulled together, and concern puckered the spiderweb pattern of scars on his left cheek. "I tell him to take a hike?"

Matt looked weary. He rubbed his face. "No, Chico," he said. "Let him in. Allie, I strongly advise you against this, but I won't force you to change your mind. You've proved to me already that you know your

future constituents better than I.'' Worry showed deep
in his eyes, but he managed a small smile.

"Good," she said, standing up and kissing him.
"Because I'm right."

AS HE WATCHED HER later that morning, Matt had to
admit she probably was right. No one else in the parade seemed to give a darn for any kind of security.
Even the governor rode unprotected except for a small
group of nervous sheriff's deputies. This was not a
community used to or likely to be tolerant of candidates who were afraid of the people. Any hopeful who
hid from the voters behind a bullet-proof shield was
probably going to be unnoticed at the polls, as well.

And, damn, but she looked magnificent!

Her horse was a big-muscled mare with a coat of
pure gold and a mane and tail that was silky, long and
white-blond like Allie's hair. She had chosen to wear a
simple costume—plain Western-cut jeans, an oversize
embroidered shirt over the bullet-proof vest, and cowboy boots. Her hair flowed free, unbound by any band
or barrette for a change. And she was showing off like
a little kid, her smile as wide as all outdoors. She wore
no makeup and needed none. In the hot sunlight and
the excitement of the moment, her cheeks glowed with
color and her blue eyes shone like sapphires. If he
hadn't been in love with her before, he would have been
smitten right where he stood, Matt realized. She was a
picture to treasure forever!

The mare was a special animal, trained to perform in
dressage, she had told him. She knew some of the rudiments, she confessed. Rudiments! Matt smiled to
himself as he watched her walk the horse from one side
of the road to the other, letting just the tiniest touch

direct the moment when she would stop and rear back, lifting her front hoofs into the air. Then, Allie would wave and whoop, encouraging the crowd to join in.

And they did. They *loved* her. Matt felt the burn of pride deep in his chest. The people loved his woman!

But not as much as he did. He followed her progress with the camera, intending to use some of the footage for political commercials later on, nearer the November day of reckoning. Beside him and on the other side of the street, Chico and Manuel ranged, watching the crowd for any sign of trouble or danger. Matt relaxed. She was quite safe. This was no time for anyone to strike against her. It would only infuriate the people and bring further support to Allie's cause.

The parade moved through the city streets, which had been cordoned off from traffic for the event. People lined the road, standing or sitting on lawn chairs. Casual and relaxed attitudes were the order of the day. Everyone was out for fun. Simple, old-fashioned good times. Friends greeted old friends. Children frolicked around or sat on the curb, staring in delight and wonder at the passing parade. Marching bands from the city and county schools, elaborate floats put together by local businesses or interest groups, a fleet of vintage automobiles, including an ancient fire truck that sprayed water on the laughing crowd... Matt felt he was experiencing an event from America's more innocent past. It was healthy and good.

And he'd missed it as a kid, because he'd been traveling all over the rest of the world. He stopped, hit by the sudden thought that *this* was what he wanted for Laurel. This life in the slow lane. Growing up in the town and the land that her mother and father had chosen for her.

Standing there, Matt came to a decision. Tomorrow he'd phone his office in L.A. and prepare them for a move of Glass Attacks, Ltd. to Linville Springs, Wyoming. With modems and faxes everywhere these days, he could keep in close touch with the world of adventure travel easily enough from anywhere on the planet. He didn't need an office in the city anymore. He didn't need the city anymore, for that matter.

How could he have dreamed of taking Laurel back to L.A.? She'd be one of millions there. Here, she was one *in* a million. *This* was her home, where she was supposed to be raised. *This* was her home, and that was her mother... He raised the camera to his eye again.

And saw the gun aimed at Allie.

ALLIE WAS READYING her mount for another pass at the left side of the street when the sledgehammers hit her in the back. *Pow! Pow!* Two blows that almost knocked her from the saddle. She slumped forward, striking her solar plexus on the saddle horn, and the breath went out of her. Only the training of a lifetime on horseback and the skills of Lois's grand horse kept her from falling to the pavement. She struggled to get her breath and held on to the animal's heavy mane.

People began to scream. Dizzied from the shocks of being hit and winded, she couldn't understand why they were yelling. She was battered and out of breath, but she wasn't really injured. She tried to sit upright.

And was slammed in the back again. This time, the blow caught her off balance and she lost her seat. As she slipped from the saddle, she heard the sound of a siren yodeling disaster in the distance.

I wonder who's hurt, she thought.

She hit the ground, ready for the impact, and was stunned, but didn't lose consciousness entirely. Strong hands grabbed her and a vaguely familiar voice murmured soothing things. She blinked, trying to get her sight focused. Where was Matt? He wasn't the one talking to her. Where was Chico? Surely, the big man would be right by her side...

But strangers lifted her and carried her along, past the people who stared and screamed. Allie tried to smile and wave and indicate to someone out there that she was all right, but no one seemed to notice her feeble gestures. "Matt? Where's Matt," she called, the sound a soft wail. No one heard.

Then she was set on a stretcher of some kind and lifted into the back of an ambulance. She blinked again, looking for someone in white, someone in charge, someone who would listen to her. Someone was there and turned to her. The doors shut.

And she saw who it was and tried to scream, but the wet cloth covered her face and as she struggled and fought and gasped, the overpowering fumes filled her lungs and Allie knew no more.

MATT DROPPED his camera and ran toward her, but the crowd seemed to close in, preventing him from getting close. Across the street, Chico was also struggling to reach her. When they finally forced passage to the street, Allie's horse was standing there, her head down and her skin shiny with sweat, but Allie was gone. Just the red stains on the pavement marked where she had fallen.

"What the hell happened to her?" Matt grabbed Chico's arm, swinging the man around to face him. "Where is she?"

"I couldn't see, man," Chico replied, his face strained and his muscles bunched. "Somebody took her away." He knelt down on the street and touched the red liquid.

"It was a paramedic," a woman said, pointing up the street. "They're taking the poor girl right to the hospital."

Matt started to move.

"No!" Chico grasped his leg. "Boss, look here." He held up his fingers. Red dripped from them.

Matt fell to one knee. If Chico had something to show him, it paid him to pay attention. He touched the red. Sniffed. "It's paint!"

"Damn straight. Not blood."

"Then what . . . ?" He got no further than that. The sky darkened. Matt looked up. He and Chico were surrounded by men on horseback. Men with drawn guns aimed at them.

The deputies who had been guarding the governor were now covering them. One snarled an order to lay down their guns. At first, it didn't register. Then, Matt realized both he and Chico had their own weapons in their hands. He looked at Chico, who nodded, and very, very slowly, they both lowered their guns and set them on the street.

M.J. FELT LIKE screaming and throwing chairs through windows and beating the hell out of someone. Preferably Matt Glass. Matt and Chico had been arrested immediately after the shooting. He was here to interview his client while his law partner did his level best to get the idiot and his friend released on bail.

"You had to do it your way!" he yelled. "All the macho trappings. Guns and goodies. Did they help?"

Matt said nothing.

"Hell no!" M.J. ran his hand over his hair. "They didn't help her at all!"

Matt stared at the lawyer. His eyes were like dark coals in the hollows of his eyesockets. M.J. relented a bit. The guy was clearly suffering the torments of the damned. "I can get you out of here, Matt, but you..."

"They've got her," Matt said. "She wasn't taken to the hospital. No one knows where she is. She's been kidnapped, M.J., and you know it as well as . . ."

"I don't know that!" The lawyer flung his hands up. "All I know is someone apparently shot Allie with one of those fantasy game pistols that splashes paint on the target. She fell and someone hauled her into a fake ambulance. If I were a cop, it'd look a hell of a lot like a publicity stunt to me, so I don't really blame these guys if that's what they think, too!"

"It's no stunt, and you know it. She couldn't even think of something that twisted."

M.J rubbed his head again. "I know, Matt." He deflated and sat down. "But that's not how the authorities see it. The fact that the governor was just about five yards away when she was 'shot' doesn't help. His boys are livid. They're all sure it was Allie's way of grandstanding. They want to nail you and Chico to the courthouse door by your ears, if not by something far more sensitive."

Matt's smile was grim. "I know. They weren't exactly gentle when they booked us for public disturbance and concealed weapons." His smile faded. "Get me out of here, M.J. I'll find her. I can do it. Just get me some freedom!" His clasped hands strained together, whitening the knuckles.

"I'm working on it." M.J sat back. "Once I get you out, what can I do to help? She's my blood kin, as well as my best friend. I *have* to help."

Matt studied the lawyer for a moment. Then, he told him.

AFTER THEIR RELEASE, hours later and on exorbitant bail, they returned to the Essex house to plan their strategy. Gunther was waiting there, guarding Laurel. And Manuel met them up at the house, as Matt knew he would. When Matt and Chico had been taken, Manuel had stayed low, out of the sight of the cops, waiting for the dust to settle. So had Christian. Then, they'd gone over the scene. Most of the evidence had been trampled by milling people and horses, but Manuel had recovered one special treasure. Something that might provide a clue to Allie's fate.

He had Matt's video camera.

ALLIE STRUGGLED against the chains on her arms and the silver duct tape that covered her mouth. She needed to scream. It might have helped with the overwhelming fear. But all she could do was make strangled, squealing sounds, so she gave up. The drug had nauseated her, too, and she was afraid she would be sick. If she was, with the gag on, she was liable to suffocate. David Benning tapped the syringe he held and smiled at her.

"That's right, Allie, dear, Save your strength. You're going to need it for your long journey," he said. "Long, dark journey."

Allie snarled at him inside her gag.

"Now, now." David set the syringe down on a piece of white gauze. "Must keep that temper under control. What will Paul say, if you swear as you go to meet him?''

Allie screeched, a little sound, but one from deep in her heart.

''Yes, Allison, dear.'' David leaned forward and patted her cheek, his touch gentle, almost fatherly. ''I'm here to see you united with your true love. Your husband, Paul.''

She stared at him.

He smiled, and his grin was a death's-head rictus. ''Yes, I made those calls to you. To remind you how much of an obligation you have to him. How evil you were to let another man into your bed. How wrong you were to think you could change things to make women as well off as men are. Such terrible thinking! Rita could never think like that. Well, that's done with. You have an eternal duty to Paul. It's almost time to fulfill that obligation. Too bad you have to die to do it.'' He chuckled. ''But, that's life, isn't it!'' And then, he threw his head back and laughed and laughed as if he'd made the funniest joke in the whole universe.

Allie shrank inside, closed her eyes and determined to spend her last minutes alive thinking not about the insane man who held her prisoner but rather about her children, about Laurel and about Matt.

About the man who she knew really was the true love of what was left of her life.

It helped her control the fear.

CHAPTER SIXTEEN

MATT SLIPPED the video cassette into the player and turned the machine on. The den had become a conference room. A war room, really. Six men sat stone-still and watched the show. The only movement came from Laurel, who was playing quietly with a coloring set over by the window. Fred slept on the floor near her in the only patch of sunlight. Gunther watched her more than he did the television. She was his job; Allie was theirs.

Allie came on the screen. Matt's heart nearly broke looking at her. So alive and radiant and happy on the palomino mare's back. He pushed fast-forward.

"What we're looking for," he said, "is the face of the guy who blasted her with those rubber pellets. They were like paint pellets, but with more impact capability. That's what knocked her off the horse. I know I got him for at least a moment in my viewfinder, so we ought to be able to pick him out."

"And when we do?" M.J. asked. "What then? How're you going to find a face with nothing else to go on? Sounds like a needle in a haystack to me."

"It is." Matt stopped the fast-forward. The tape was almost at the place he wanted. "But that's what Miranda does best, isn't it? Find that particular needle." The doorbell rang. Matt turned to Chico. "Want to get that, please."

Chico grinned and rose.

M.J. glowered, but said nothing. He'd long since abandoned hope of recovering Miranda's physical affections. They could be friends, he reasoned, but the lover potential was out. Chico was probably more her kind of guy. M.J. harbored no illusions about himself when it came to brains verses brawn. He was definitely not in the latter category.

In a moment, Miranda and Chico came into the room, the private investigator in the lead. Her expression was calm, but deadly serious. "I've got a list of all the properties in the state that Rita Morely or David Benning own," she said, handing a computer printout to Matt. "Since I'd been doing some investigating about their financial activities before this, it was easy to get the data. If they took her, and I really believe they did, it's likely she's stashed somewhere on the land they can control access to. Some place they know well enough to feel secure in or at. At any rate, it's worth checking into."

"Thanks." Matt took the printout. "Have a seat. We're about to see your next quarry."

"'Randa!" Laurel spoke up, startling everyone. She had been so quiet, most of them had forgotten her presence. "'Randa, where my mommy?" She stood up and toddled over to Miranda, holding up her arms for an embrace.

The woman bent down and picked the child up. When she straightened, tears shone in her dark eyes. "Don't you worry, sweetheart," she said, softly. "Your mommy's going to be here soon."

"Mommmaa..." Laurel rubbed her eyes.

Matt tensed, but Laurel seemed content with that answer and didn't start to cry as he had feared she would. She stayed with Miranda, however, sitting on her lap and crooning softly to herself.

He thumbed the remote and the video played on. Soon, the final scene appeared, and he froze the picture. "There he is," Matt said, pointing. Christian came forward with some special camera equipment and took some still pictures. "Any idea who he is?" Matt asked M.J. and Miranda.

M.J. studied the face. He shook his head. "I don't think so," he said. "Just a generic local lowlife, but I've never..."

"Well, *I* recognize him. He's one of Teddie Baker's cronies," Miranda said. "I'll be darned..."

"Get me some still shots," M.J. stood up. "And some depositions and I'll take this right to the governor. He's a fair man, Matt. You just pissed him off with the guns and ruining the parade. I think he was real frightened for a moment, too. Thinking someone was shooting at him."

"An understandable reaction," Matt said, dryly.

"I think we can get some speedy legal action on this." M.J. tapped the television screen. "Even I can see the gun in this guy's hand. With this kind of evidence, I can have a warrant issued..."

"By the time you have that in hand," Matt said, "Allie may be..." He glanced at Laurel. "Well, let's just say we can't wait for the wheels of the regular judicial and legal process to turn. Manuel. Chico. Christian. You know what to do. Gunther, you're still assigned to Laurel. Keep her safe." The men nodded. Gunther picked up Laurel and held her. He would, Matt knew, die for the little girl, if necessary.

As he, Matt, would do for Allie!

Matt stood up. "Let's get going." He turned back to M.J. "Those legal wheels need to be moving at the same time we are, M.J. Get it all going. We're taking down everyone who dared touch her! Understand me?"

M.J. nodded. "I do," he said, firmly. "Yes, I do, indeed!"

SHE WAS SO TERRIFIED, she'd become emotionally numb. Actually, it helped her to think, being numb like that. Fear, worn-out, had receded to the back of her mind. So, she thought, considered and even dared to hope a little. Allie couldn't believe she was still alive. Didn't understand why she could still hear and see and breathe and feel. She ought to be dead, but she wasn't planning on doing anything to bring that condition to a reality. David Benning was just crazy enough to kill her at any moment, once he decided to finish his game.

That "game" had been going on for a day and a half now, as near as she could tell. Maybe longer. Her sleep periods were so disordered, she had lost track of time. David would sit by the rude cot where she lay imprisoned, chained by wrists and ankles to large metal staples in the floor, and he would talk. Talk and talk for an hour or more about his past, his political career. His successes, both real and imagined.

Then, he would ask her questions. Like a professor giving a quiz after a lecture. If she answered correctly, she was allowed a small privilege—a trip to the outhouse, a bite to eat or even an hour or so of blessed sleep.

All privileges delivered, of course, with a loaded gun at her back or head. He gave her some privacy at the outhouse, but not much.

He was as insane as they came, she realized. Completely out of his mind, and dangerous as a rattler or a cornered cougar. She was going to die eventually, she feared. She had no chance with a man like this. He was going to kill her. It was just a matter of when.

And she was determined to grasp at life as long as possible, even if it meant putting up with his mental torture for weeks. She had little hope of being rescued. She wasn't sure where they were, but she did know it was far away from civilization. She'd heard no sounds but those of birds and insects since she'd regained consciousness. No cars or other indication that people were nearby. No, she was alone with David, isolated in a hell of his making. All she could expect was that David would be caught eventually. She knew that Matt and M.J. would see to that.

She only wished she could be around to hug them both and thank them for avenging her. That was, however, most unlikely. She felt tears rising and fought against the weakness of crying. It wouldn't do any good now. She needed to think and rest, not weep!

For the moment, she was alone. David had just finished a grueling session involving his years as chairman of an important Senate committee on Central America, and her answers to his questions had been sufficiently ego-supporting for him to offer her some sleep time. In fact, he'd been downright delighted with her, saying she'd earned a full night's rest. But she wasn't sleepy.

She surmised, from watching the sunlight in the small room, that afternoon had come and gone. The light was gold, not white, so it was late—probably five or six in the evening. David might be needing sleep himself by now, and she could be alone for some time.

Allie leaned over the cot as far as she could and regarded her chains.

They were steel links, a common type he must have bought in a hardware store. New and shiny. No way to break them. The staples were old, though. She jerked an arm. A small puff of dust rose into the air.

Allie felt a jolt of hope so strong she nearly screamed aloud. She might not free the chains, but the staples were another matter entirely. She jerked her arm again.

And again...

"WHERE'S JOSH?" Matt asked. It was less than forty-eight hours since the kidnapping. He heaved the last load of equipment and weaponry into the rear of the stripped-down ATV. "Wasn't he supposed to meet us here an hour ago? He promised to act as backup driver last night. You told him the time, didn't you?"

"I did. He was," M.J. replied. "Don't know about him, though. Josh's no hero. Of course, neither am I, but I have a very personal stake in this...mission. He doesn't, and he knew he wasn't absolutely necessary. Maybe he just got cold feet."

"Maybe." Matt stared out across the city. Dawn was just beginning to pearl the sky to the east, and lights were on here and there in the urbanscape below. Since it was still July, the morning began around four a.m. Early as sin, Matt had complained. He had wanted to strike during the dark, but they had run out of night, getting ready.

He and M.J. and the others were all dressed in battle fatigues and had smeared their faces with black paint. The three blondes, Matt, Gunther and Christian, had tied dark bandanas over their light hair, Vietnam war style. Only M.J. was unarmed. He'd been offered a pistol, but had claimed total unfamiliarity with weapons and declared he'd be more dangerous to his friends than his foes if he carried one. Miranda, who did know how to use a gun, wasn't in the group. She had elected to stay with Laurel, taking over Gunther's job. Her hunting was done.

And done well! She had found where Allie was imprisoned. By sifting through the property locations, she'd come up with the most likely places. And when Matt had looked at a map, he'd picked out Allie's prison as easily as if it were marked by a street sign. Secluded and easy to defend, the spot was perfect—or would have been if Matt and his men were ordinary hunters.

Matt looked down the road to town once more. Josh was supposed to come with them. His absence was troubling. He had called the day before and earnestly begged to be included, his fervor so strong that Matt had been unable to deny him. His absence was not a good sign. Josh knew part of their plans, and had been assigned a role that would now have to be filled by another. Matt looked at M.J. The lawyer looked uncomfortable and nervous.

"You know what you have to do," he said. "It's going to be riskier without Josh."

Now M.J. managed to look grim. "Yeah. I know," he said. "So much for what I learned in law school."

In spite of the deep fear for Allie's safety, Matt had to chuckle. "This is another kind of school," he said. "And I'm a good teacher, so relax."

"I'm so relaxed I might faint," M.J. replied, his painted face twisting in a kind of smile. "Just leave me where I fall, if I do."

"We will." Matt turned away.

And M.J. knew he wasn't kidding.

They drove up the road and over to the back side of Linville Mountain. As the sun began to stain the sky reddish orange, they pulled onto a large, wide meadow and parked under the shelter of a stand of pines. Matt spoke, and they got out and assembled around the hood of the vehicle. He took out a topographic map of the mountain and spread it for all to see.

"Here it is," he said, pointing with the blade of a knife. "Benning's cabin." He traced a pattern on the paper with the knife tip. "Here's how we do it."

M.J. stood back a little, listening. Matt spoke softly, calmly and repeated every sentence in three languages. But it was clear the five trained men had no trouble communicating. They acted, spoke and thought as a unit, now, relying on past experience. They had done this before in another land for another cause when they had rescued the movie crew.

But he had no such experience, and he was scared to death. Not so much for himself, although that was definitely a factor! His true concern was for Allie. If he messed up his part, she could die. Others could die. Hell, *he* could die. Nothing he'd ever done before had prepared him for this moment of truth.

Did he have the stuff to make it?

Matt turned around and looked at him. "You okay, M.J.?"

"Not really."

"Good." Matt folded the map and sheathed his knife. "If you thought you were, I'd be concerned. Stay scared. It'll help keep us all in one piece."

That helped. Some.

They moved out, entering the forest just as the morning sun hit the meadow. M.J. swallowed hard against a rising nausea, fought the urge to stop and go to the bathroom and forced himself to press on behind Matt. The bigger men moved through the forest like they were smoke. M.J. was sure he was stepping on every single dry leaf and crackly branch. He felt like an elephant.

But soon they reached the cabin. M.J. crouched in the shelter of the trees surrounding the clearing while Matt and the other men moved forward, scouting, sensing, preparing. He heard the sound of birds greeting the new day, the chattering fuss of a squirrel disturbed at nut-hunting, the sigh of the slight breeze in the tops of the lodgepole pines, and . . .

The nasty popping sound of a gun being fired inside the cabin. A scream.

Allie!

Another scream, a yell, really. Male. Enraged.

M.J. stood up and started to run toward the cabin. Matt grabbed him and managed to throw him to the ground. "Behind me," Matt snarled at him. "Stay behind me!"

M.J. nodded. His heart felt as if it were going to pound its way out of his chest. He stood and brushed himself off. Then he took a deep breath and prayed. Calm returned.

He followed Matt as the men fanned out, covering all sides of the cabin. Weapons at the ready, black paint jagged across their faces, M.J. thought they all must look like demons from hell.

The view got worse the moment they burst into the cabin. M.J. stayed right on Matt's heels, but crouched down to avoid any gunfire that might come their way. He saw the room clearly. It was a madman's den, full of trash, books, magazines, newspapers and other paper, all strewn around garbage that had piled into stinking heaps. The odor was almost unbearable.

But more horror awaited. From a room in back came an ear-piercing howl like that of a wild, insane animal. Allie's voice sounded, yelling at someone. And a man's voice replied.

Josh Henderson!

Matt checked behind him to make sure M.J. was safely out of the way and then moved quickly to the doorway of the next room. He paused at one side of the door, his back pressed against the hard wood wall, his gun raised and ready to fire. Manuel slipped into the cabin through the front door and signaled to him that there was no window to that back room. He could only guess how many were in the room. Matt nodded.

Then, he stepped from hell into Hell.

The room was tiny. A cot against the far wall. No other door or window. Josh Henderson, his eyes wide with fear, a gun held in both trembling hands, was pressed back against the wall to Matt's right. On the cot...

Allie was on a cot and was chained to the floor. By three chains. The fourth, she had somehow managed to free from the floor, though it still hung from her wrist.

And she had wrapped it around David Benning's neck and appeared to be trying to choke the man to death. They were wrestling on the cot. She had the chain around his throat and her knee in his back and was hauling for all she was worth.

She looked like a Valkyrie or an Angel of Death. But it wasn't the sight of her that froze Matt in his tracks. Josh had his gun on her. Not on Benning.

Allie saw him first. "Matt," she cried. "Watch out for Josh. He's in with them."

Josh whirled, his weapon now aimed at Matt. "Stop!" he yelled. "I'll shoot. I swear it!" He wavered, then steadied. "I know how. You'd better believe me!"

Matt lowered his own gun. Behind him, he heard the sound of stealthy movement, a phrase murmured in German, then Spanish. "I believe you, Josh," he said. "Look. I'm putting my gun down." He set the pistol on the floor and straightened, his hands in the air. "You don't have to be scared of me, Josh."

"I am scared," Josh cried. "Of you, of her, of that madman there. Allie, let him go! Do it, or I swear I'll shoot Matt."

She released the chain. David fell to the floor, coughing and retching and gasping for air. "Don't hurt Matt, Josh. Please," she begged. "Come on. You've got the gun. He's unarmed. You can get out now. Run away from this. We'll let you go."

"I...I can't." Josh was trembling and sweating, gritting his teeth. His demeanor was one of both fear and arrogance, a dangerous, volatile combination. He kicked at Benning's supine form. "He's been my boss all along. Has evidence I was spying on you and reporting to him." He looked at her. "Allie, I was sure you'd lose. Everybody said..."

"You little piece of..." David growled from the floor. "I'll *ruin* you..."

"It's too late for that, David," Josh said, his voice suddenly much more steady. "I guess I know what I have to do now." He glanced at Allie. "I have no choice—I've got to shoot all of you." He paused, thinking, his expression turning sly. "If I burn this place down, no one will ever know what really happened, will they? I'm no killer, myself, understand. Not like David here, but there's no choice, as I see it.'' He wiped sweat from his face. ''It's the only way I . . . ahhhggg!''

His words were cut off suddenly as the back wall of the cabin splintered inward, exploding under an enormous force. As Matt had expected, his troops had taken the initiative and they had chosen to attack right through the wall, punching at it with just enough explosive to cave it in, but not enough to endanger the people inside. Matt had been ready for anything, but this was even better than he had hoped. His men were absolute geniuses with *plastique*. The noise and dust and debris of the small blast distracted Josh just long enough for Matt to move.

But he didn't go for Josh and the gun. There wasn't time, and he wasn't near enough. Instead, Matt flung himself forward toward Allie. He covered her with his body as screams and shouts and gunshots filled the air. He heard Josh snarl a death threat at him and turned to face his fate. . . .

And saw M.J. rise out of the dust and debris and lay a truly inspired roundhouse punch on Josh's astonished face, connecting with the other man's jaw. Josh went down with a sigh and was out for the count. M.J. grabbed the gun and stood over his foe, holding the weapon as if it were a rattlesnake about to strike.

''Good vork!'' Gunther was the first to reach the lawyer. He slapped M.J. on the back and took the gun gingerly from his trembling grasp. ''That vas some punch, *ja!*''

''Thanks,'' M.J. replied in a steady voice. Then, he sat down on the floor, crumpling as his legs gave way.

"It felt great. I think my hand's broken, though."
Gunther, still chuckling congratulations, bent over to
check the injury.

Matt looked down at Allie, who lay under him on the
cot. "You all right?" he asked, examining her quickly
for serious injury. He found nothing wrong that he
could see, but she had been a prisoner for over two
days. "What did they do to you? Are you...?

"I'm okay, but frankly, you look like the very devil
himself," she said, grabbing his neck with her free
hand and dragging his face down to hers. "And am I
glad to see you!" The kiss she gave him told him almost everything he needed to know.

There was one more detail, however. "I can't wait
for this answer," he said, holding her tightly and making her more of a prisoner with his arms than the chains
had. "Will you marry me?"

She smiled. "Let me loose, then..."

"No. Now. Before I unchain you."

Her words went right to his heart. "Matt, yes, I'll
marry you. I decided while I was sure I was going to die
that if I did somehow manage to survive, the past
would have no more hold on me. I don't care what
happened before I met you. Now is all that matters.
Now, and us. I believe we were meant to be, so...
Yes!"

"As soon as possible?"

"Yes!"

He kissed her again, wondering at the miracle that
was their love.

IT TOOK A WHILE to free Allie. While Matt worked the
chains loose, the other men dug the now-babbling

Benning out of the rubble and secured him with stout ropes to a tree in the front section of the clearing.

As they all waited in front of the ruins of the cabin for the sheriff to arrive, Josh talked. Bragged, rather.

"You were a born loser," he sneered at her. "Everyone knew it, and made their plans around it. Rita contacted David who agreed you were the best possible candidate for her to face, since she would undoubtedly trounce you at the polls. She's his creature, you know. I've worked secretly for her for years, and I could tell you stories that would curl your teeth! Would do anything he asked. He needed her in office."

"But it didn't wash that way." M.J. rubbed his hand. "And so the lousy lot of you panicked."

"Not exactly." Josh regarded him balefully. "Taking Allie out permanently was Plan B. Or C. I can't remember. But we did discuss it. When Baker failed to get you both with the shotgun, we had to make fresh plans."

"But David was supposed to kill me right away, not keep me alive to mock and torture me," Allie interjected. "Right?"

"Right." Josh glared at the raving older man. "He lost it a long time ago. We just didn't realize how much until a few days ago. He really got off on pretending to be Paul Ford when he called you." He smiled at Allie. "You know he knew what happened to your husband, don't you?"

Allie felt chilled clear through. "I know from what David said that there's some connection between Paul's death and David's activities on the committee dealing with Central America. I assume from what he said to me that..."

Josh laughed. "You'll never find out now. Too bad. David's mind is mush."

Matt stepped in. "If you know, Henderson, I'd recommend you tell me. Or when the sheriff finally gets here, there might not be as much of you to deliver to him as there is right now."

Another cold smile. "I have no idea," Josh replied.

Matt moved closer. He drew his knife and looked at the tip, speculatively.

"Really! I swear!" Josh shrank back. "M.J., tell him he can't touch me! It's . . . it's illegal!"

"Hey." M.J. turned around to face the trees. "I don't see a thing, Josh. Can't hear you any too well, either. What'd you say?"

After a bit more carefully orchestrated intimidation, Matt finally decided that Josh honestly didn't know the truth.

But David Benning did. The facts were there, somewhere. His mind might be gone, but somewhere, the man must have kept a record of his evil triumphs and of material he could use against his opponents and enemies.

Matt turned to his men, ordering them to clear out all signs of their highly illegal private army action. Gunther, Manuel and Christian melted into the trees, hauling with them the high-powered weapons and the rest of the explosive that had torn down the back of the cabin. Chico stayed, guarding Josh closely, knowing his presence would show the authorities that Matt and M.J. hadn't done the job all by themselves. No one would have believed that. But the full truth would always be their secret. The cops, Matt decided, would just have to work the rest of it out for themselves without his help.

As the sheriff's helicopter sounded overhead, Matt turned to Allie. "I want one quick look through the cabin before the cops take over," he said. "Can you delay them? I hate to ask it of you, but it's important." He touched her wounded wrist. "Maybe make them take care of this, first?"

She looked into his eyes. "I'll try," she said, her tone firm and confident. "I love you," she added.

"I know." Matt touched her face, not trusting himself to do anything more. "But you don't love me as much as I love you. You just can't. It's humanly impossible." He let his hand fall to his side. "I was ready to die for you, Allie. Now, I intend to live for *us*. Get going. They're landing."

Allie felt joy bubbling up inside her and she yearned to forget everything else just to hold him tight, but she turned away from him and faced the clearing where the helicopter was touching down. Branches whipped in the breeze created by the roters, and men spilled out. Clutching her wrist, she ran over to the leader.

And gave the performance of her life.

At first M.J was astounded. The bad guys were wrapped up and tied like Christmas presents, yet here was his cousin, having an apparent case of female hysterics. She'd been brave as a lioness, but now she was weeping and moaning and showing off her hurt wrist and insisting on getting medical treatment immediately before anything else....

Wait. Where was Matt?

M.J. headed back to the cabin. Sure enough, there was Matt ferreting through the mess, that would soon be a police crime scene, off-limits to all but licensed professionals. "Can I help?" he asked, stepping over a stack of old magazines and a pile of dirty dishes.

Matt looked up. "Dig in," he said. "Look for anything that might have to do with Benning's activities regarding Central America ten years ago. His insanity and his treatment of Allie had something to do with that. I know it!"

M.J. rifled through a stack of papers. "How do you figure?"

"Well, let's assume Benning had something to do with her husband's death. He was certainly fixated on it, so I think the assumption's a fair one. Let's say he knows his tracks are fairly well covered—after all, Allie did try to find out the truth years ago and came up empty. I've had Miranda on the case, myself, and she's turned up very little." Matt dropped the stack of books he was searching through and moved over to a small pile of jewelry-type boxes.

"Very little? But something?"

"Right. Seems Benning was the good Dr. Ford's first patient when he opened his office in Linville Springs a decade ago. Brought a bunch of other folks to the doc's door. Made him seem like an important new physician on the scene. Don't you think Ford might believe he had a debt to the great politician?"

"You mean Benning recruited Paul for..."

Matt opened and tossed boxes. All were empty. "It's just a guess. I need proof. But why else would Benning get so hot about Allie's winning the election if he wasn't scared that someday she'd be in a position to discover the truth? Evidence has to exist somewhere."

M.J. whistled low. "Man, you're going too deep for me. I'm just a simple small-town lawyer. This high level stuff's too rich for my..." He stopped talking and stared at the papers in his hands. "My God," he said, whispering the words. "I think you're right. Check these out."

"What have you got?" Matt moved over to him. Took the papers from his grasp. Looked at them....

"Bingo," said Matt Glass, softly. "Home run."

CHAPTER SEVENTEEN

"IN MANY WAYS," Allie said, "it's poetic justice that David's gone around the bend, mentally. Lost touch with the real world, probably for the rest of his life. According to what you've found, in a way the same sort of thing happened to poor Paul, ten years ago. He lost his vision of reality, which was us, his family, and he followed a strange dream of adventure and heroics."

She paused and took a deep breath. "That was his fate and his finish," she added.

Matt nodded. "It could easily have been mine, too," he said, touching her hand. "If you hadn't come into my life, I can't say where I'd be today. Certainly not tomorrow. I know I'd have lost Laurel."

Allie didn't reply, but she squeezed his hand. Words were not needed. Now, it just took a touch to communicate. A touch, a look. Love...

They were all back in his living room three weeks now after the rescue. Allie had delegated her house to the four commandos, who had been required to stay around until the possibility of legal problems arising from the raid on the mountain had been dismissed. Now, finally, the many facets of the case had been resolved or otherwise dealt with. The publicity surrounding the rescue had been incredible. It had been an exhausting and yet invigorating period of time.

Today, Allie had called all the troops together in one place for the first time since that eventful July morning. All being the eight adults who knew everything that had transpired in the case. They had carried out individual assignments and investigations since the day of her rescue, of course, but this meeting she intended to serve as a forum for tying up any loose ends she had not already snipped.

Miranda moved some papers around on the coffee table. "Your husband was duped," she said. "Deluded. Apparently, he had a weakness for heroics that you never realized, and when Benning discovered that, he exploited it. Paul Ford followed Benning's orders to go down to Central America and work with an underground political group that needed a physician. He thought he'd be gone less than a week." She held up an old, yellowed envelope. "He thought he was striking some sort of blow for freedom and democracy. Being a hero, in other words. His letter to you makes that clear."

"A letter that was never delivered," M.J. said, his tone almost a growl. "Entrusted to David Benning and stuck inside an old magazine to be forgotten and never seen again."

"Your husband was a good man," Chico commented. "Whatever his reasons for being down there, he died trying to help people like mine in a small village where the floods had washed away many things and had brought disease."

Allie felt calm. And peaceful. All the tears and regret in the world wouldn't bring Paul back. But the file M.J. had found contained the letter Paul had written to Allie as well as Benning's notes on the coverup he had engineered to keep his role in Paul's death a secret. Now it was time to let go of the past. Allie's heart belonged entirely to the quiet, strong man sitting beside her. But still, it was good to know she hadn't been mistaken in her judgment of her husband. He had intended to come back. He hadn't really ever deliberately deserted her and the kids.

They knew that now, and both Sam and Sally seemed to have a new center of peace, just like she did. Their father would have loved them, if he had known them, and now they could hold that knowledge for the rest of their lives. They knew also he'd been a hero of sorts, saving people, and that made themhappy.

"All of this stays secret, of course," she said. "I'll tell my kids everything in due time, but no one else will know. We just don't have enough concrete proof to bring any charges in the case, and the real villain is paying for his crime by losing his mind. It's a justice I can accept."

Matt made a sound. "You're pretty damn forgiving," he said softly, covering her fingers with his and moving a bit closer. "The bastard was going to pump you full of dope and leave you up there to die of an overdose."

"I know." She put her hand on his thigh. "But it didn't happen. And now Rita's completely discredited personally and politically. The media's seen to it she'll never show her face in politics again. Josh is up on conspiracy-to-murder charges. Teddie Baker's facing criminal charges on the house shooting, and for trying to run you off the road, and attempted murder..."

"Mom. Laurel's awake." Sally appeared on the balcony overlooking the living room. "Debbie says she's asking for you. Can you come?"

"In a second, honey." Allie turned back to her group of special friends. "Duty calls," she said. "Will you all excuse me for a while?" She kissed Matt. "Carry on, darling."

Matt held her hand, then let her go. The house was full with the twins back from Montana. Debbie Preston had taken up the offer of a full-time job as nanny for the three kids. *Their* three kids. Laurel was now Matt's, indisputably. While the Turner's role in the main conspiracy was vague, they had dropped their suit once they realized that Matt was considered a hero by everyone.

ONE WEEK LATER, Matt and Allie stood at the altar. By keeping the wedding trappings and extras to a minimum, Allie had limited the number of "outsider" people in town in the know to six. Including her parents, who drove down from the ranch, that made eight. Of course, there were the four soldiers. Gunther, Chris, Chico and Manuel had insisted on staying on for the wedding. The rest of the wedding party consisted of Miranda, M.J., Debbie, Sam, Sally and Laurel.

Real friends and family. She smiled to herself as she listened to the words of the ceremony. An announcement in the paper tomorrow or the next day would take care of the rest of the world....

The minister spoke on. "...any reason this man and woman should not be..."

She could feel the warmth of Matt's body next to hers. She would be safe and secure with him. She could trust him. He was the real thing—a genuine hero. He had proven that to her the morning he'd saved her life on the mountain.

Listening to the minister's voice, she realized that they were at that one part of the ceremony she had had nightmares about for ten years—she was about to marry again and in the middle wedding ceremony, Paul returned and demanded a stop to it... She relaxed. It would never happen, because the mystery was finally solved.

"...joined together, speak now or..."

"Hold it!"

Allie nearly fainted. A strange male voice rang out, demanding that the wedding halt. She turned around, her muscles almost frozen with fear....

But the handsome elderly man striding down the aisle with a big smile on his face was not the ghost of her late husband. It was...

Someone who looked amazingly like Matt! Matt as he might be thirty years from now.... Silver hair where Matt's was blond. Deeper character lines in the face. The same brown eyes and sturdy build, though the older man's back seemed a little bowed under the weight of those extra years....

"Dad?" Matt tightened his arm around Allie's waist, pulling her closer to his side. "Dad, what are you...? How did you...?" He saw Chico blush and knew how his father had found out.

"Hello, Son." Robert Glass walked all the way up to the altar and threw his arms around Matt, including Allie in the bear hug. "I couldn't just let you go and get yourself married off without showing up to watch, could I?" He grinned at the astonished minister. "Mind starting this over, Rev? I'd like to see the whole show, if you all don't mind?"

After that, the ceremony went off without another hitch.

EPILOGUE

FINALLY, election day arrived. Matt woke up early and found himself alone in bed. The house was dark and cold. Uneasy, he pulled on jeans, moccasins and a sweatshirt and left the bedroom, looking for Allie.

She wasn't in her office. Lately, she'd been spending long hours pouring over charts and poll results, determined to know her fate before the fatal day, though it had done her no good, as far as he could tell. The race was just too unpredictable, given all the dramatic and emotional factors involved in her campaign. She wasn't with the children. The kids were still asleep. He checked each bedroom. But she wasn't in any of them.

Neither was Fred.

Matt hurried down the hall, opened the front door and...

Sighed with relief. She was at the door, ready to come inside.

"Hi," Allie said. She wore a heavy coat and jeans. Fred, on her leash, jumped up on Matt's leg for a pat. "Or rather, good morning. We were just out walking," she said. "I couldn't sleep, so I went into the girls' room, kidnapped Fred and..."

"I love you," Matt declared, taking her face in his hands. Her skin was cold, but her mouth was warm when he kissed her. "You're going to win, darling. Don't let this get to you."

She smiled wanly. "Matt, whatever happens today, I know I'm very lucky. I have you and the children. Is it selfish of me to want more?"

"You, selfish? Never." The indignation and love in Matt's voice brought tears to her eyes. She put her arms around her husband and thought, for at least the hundredth time, how much he'd changed. How different he was from the man she had met at the supermarket months ago. Then, he had been scared of his role as a family man. Now, he was very much at peace with that role. He and his father had both learned the true meaning of home and family. Robert Glass had become a wonderful grandpoppa for all three children. He had moved into her old house when Matt's four compadres had left. And he seemed perfectly content to stay.

"I know. Let's have a party." Matt's voice interrupted her thoughts.

"What?"

"A party. An old-fashioned election-night blast. That way, no matter what happens, you'll have a good time."

"Oh." She looked up at the ceiling and groaned. "I just couldn't. It's too much work, and I don't have any extra energy right now. Too nervous, like I said. I..."

"*You* don't have to," he said. "I'll do all the work. You just enjoy!"

Allie started to protest again, but she couldn't think of a really good reason why he shouldn't do it if he wanted. Besides, she thought, if she was occupied with company all around, maybe she wouldn't stay glued to the television, her nerves screaming at each prediction. "Okay," she said, shrugging. "I suppose it's a good idea. At least it'll take my mind off the whole thing."

She was wrong. By seven o'clock, when the polls closed, their house was jumping with friends and family, company all out to cheer her through the tension of the final hours of vote-counting. But Allie found herself in the kitchen, unable to watch the television. "I'm being ridiculous," she said to Fred, who seemed to have sensed her need for comfort and was curled up on her lap.

M.J. came into the kitchen and tried to hand her a beer. "Drink up, cousin," he advised. "You look like you need it."

She shook her head. "No booze for me. Not tonight."

Miranda took the beer from M.J. "What about the celebration champagne?" she asked, taking a healthy swallow of beer. "When you win, are you going to let us drink it all?"

Allie managed a smile. "If I win, I'll drink."

"Okay." M.J. walked off, his arm around Miranda's waist. Allie smiled again, but to herself. Apparently, now that Chico was gone, Miranda and M.J. were reestablishing their friendship.

A little later, Sally came over and leaned against her, disturbing Fred, who shifted position but did not leave Allie's lap. "Mom," she asked. "What's going to happen if you win? Will you go away?"

"Oh, no, honey." Allie embraced her daughter, spilling Fred to the floor. "I won't leave you all. Ever! What it means is that I'll go down to Cheyenne for a few weeks in the winter to attend legislature. But Matt will be here with you and Sam and Laurel."

Sally considered this. "I'd rather you not go anywhere."

Allie picked Fred back up. "What does your brother think?" she asked.

Sally frowned. "He says you want to be the boss of everyone. So..."

"I see." Allie put her arm around her daughter. "Honey, I didn't realize you still had questions." She stood up. "Where's Sam?" she asked.

A few minutes later, she and Matt were seated at the kitchen table explaining to the twins what Allie's commitment to public service entailed.

"So," Sam said. "Mom'll really be working for *me* if she goes to Cheyenne?"

"That's right," Matt said. "Working for you and Sally and me. Even for your Grandpa Robert. Looking after our rights and our needs. That's what being a boss really means."

"Oh." Sam nodded and seemed satisfied.

Sally was quiet for a few seconds. Then, "I guess it's okay, Mom, if you have to be gone for a little while to help out other people and us. Long as you always come home."

"Honey, I always will come home. No matter where I go. I promise. And I think you have the right idea now. I..." A rising chorus of voices cheering interrupted her.

"Babe!" M.J. rushed into the kitchen. "Allie! You won!"

Miranda was right behind him. "A landslide victory, Allie. Nobody figured that, but you did it. Congratulations!" She opened the refrigerator and took out a bottle of champagne. "Celebration time!" She popped the cork.

But as Allie and Matt looked at each other, Allie realized that an even bigger victory had been the one she had scored right here at the kitchen table a few minutes before. She and her husband and her children had sat down, discussed a problem together and come to an understanding.

Matt took two glasses and filled them. He handed one to his wife. "To you," he said, lifting the glass. "And..."

"No," Allie said. "To *us.*" She included her children. "To our new family... to... us all!"

As she hooked her arm with Matt's and drank, Allie realized that was a toast she could honor for the rest of her life. She and Matt were the real winners. And always would be!

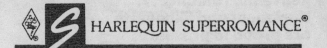
COMING NEXT MONTH

#558 ANOTHER WOMAN • Margot Dalton
Women Who Dare, Book 8
Leah Temple was living a nightmare. Somewhere in her past—
a past she could not recall—was a secret she was terrified of
uncovering. Paul Temple was fighting demons of his own. His
estranged wife was back! Or was she? Gone was the scheming
shrew who'd made his life hell. In her place, a strong, loving
woman he didn't know... and didn't trust.

#559 FLASHFIRE • Judith Arnold
What happened when an old army buddy—a man you considered
family—ripped you off? Matt Calloway figured he had another
battle on his hands. But first he had to get past the thief's sister,
his gorgeous single sister. Linda Villard was enough to make any
man rethink his campaign.

#560 DREAMS OF GLASS • Brenna Todd
Haley Riverton was an actress with a dream, but it was shattered
when she was stalked and shot by a demented fan. Rising star
Keith Garrison tried to teach her how to dream again, but then her
stalker escaped from prison, and the real nightmare began....

#561 HOME AGAIN • Janice Kay Johnson
Rebecca Halstead, divorced mother of a teenage son, had fallen
for his boss—hard. Trouble was, Sam Ballard was the last man
her matchmaking son wanted in the family. Which was just as
well, since Sam had no interest in family. None at all.

AVAILABLE NOW:

#554 THE MARRIAGE TICKET
Sharon Brondos

#555 VALENTINE'S SUMMER
Terri Lynn

#556 MAN, WOMAN AND CHILD
Bobby Hutchinson

#557 BACHELOR FROM BANNACK
Sally Garrett

**Relive the romance...
Harlequin and Silhouette
are proud to present**

by Request

A program of collections of three complete novels by the most requested authors with the most requested themes. Be sure to look for one volume each month with three complete novels by top name authors.

In June: **NINE MONTHS** Penny Jordan
Stella Cameron
Janice Kaiser

Three women pregnant and alone. But a lot can happen in nine months!

In July: **DADDY'S HOME** Kristin James
Naomi Horton
Mary Lynn Baxter

Daddy's Home... and his presence is long overdue!

In August: **FORGOTTEN PAST** Barbara Kaye
Pamela Browning
Nancy Martin

Do you dare to create a future if you've forgotten the past?

Available at your favorite retail outlet.

Where do you find hot Texas nights, smooth Texas charm and dangerously sexy cowboys?

AFTER THE LIGHTS GO OUT
by Barbara Kaye

Trouble's brewin'—Texas style!

Jealousy was the last thing Scott Harris expected to feel. Especially over an employee. But one of the guests at the Hole in the Wall Dude Ranch is showing interest in his ranch manager, Valerie Drayton, and Scott doesn't like it one bit. Trouble is, Val seems determined to stick to Scott's rule—no fraternizing with the boss.

CRYSTAL CREEK reverberates with the exciting rhythm of Texas. Each story features the rugged individuals who live and love in the Lone Star State. And each one ends with the same invitation...

Y'ALL COME BACK...REAL SOON!
Don't miss AFTER THE LIGHTS GO OUT
by Barbara Kaye
Available in August wherever Harlequin books are sold.

THREE UNFORGETTABLE HEROINES
THREE AWARD-WINNING AUTHORS

Untamed

MAVERICK HEARTS

A unique collection of historical short stories that capture the spirit of America's last frontier.

HEATHER GRAHAM POZZESSERE—over 10 million copies of her books in print worldwide
Lonesome Rider—The story of an Eastern widow and the renegade half-breed who becomes her protector.

PATRICIA POTTER—an author whose books are consistently Waldenbooks bestsellers
Against the Wind—Two people, battered by heartache, prove that love can heal all.

JOAN JOHNSTON—award-winning Western historical author with 17 books to her credit
One Simple Wish—A woman with a past discovers that dreams really do come true.

Join us for an exciting journey West with
UNTAMED
Available in July, wherever Harlequin books are sold.

MAV93

HARLEQUIN SUPERROMANCE®

WOMEN WHO DARE DRIVE RACE CARS?!

During 1993, each Harlequin Superromance **WOMEN WHO DARE** title will have a single italicized letter on the Women Who Dare back-page ads. Collect the letters, spell D A R E and you can receive a free copy of **RACE FOR TOMORROW**, written by popular author Elaine Barbieri. This is an exciting novel about a female race-car driver, **WHO DARES ANYTHING . . . FOR LOVE!**

OFFER CERTIFICATE   O86-KAT

To receive your free gift, send us the 4 letters that spell DARE from any Harlequin Superromance Women Who Dare title with the offer certificate properly completed, along with a check or money order of $1.00 for postage and handling (do not send cash) payable to Harlequin Superromance Women Who Dare Offer.

Name: _____

Address: _____

_____

City: _____ State/Prov.: _____

Zip/Postal Code: _____

Mail this certificate, designated letters spelling DARE, and check or money order for postage and handling to: In the U.S.—WOMEN WHO DARE, P.O. Box 9056, Buffalo, NY 14269-9056; In Canada—WOMEN WHO DARE, P.O. Box 621, Fort Erie, Ontario L2A 5X3.

Requests must be received by January 31, 1
Allow 4-6 weeks after receipt of order for de

HARLEQUIN SUPERROMANCE®

HARLEQUIN SUPERROMANCE WANTS TO INTRODUCE YOU TO A DARING NEW CONCEPT IN ROMANCE...

WOMEN WHO DARE!
Bright, bold, beautiful ...
Brave and caring, strong and passionate ...
They're women who know their own minds
and will dare anything ... for love!

One title per month in 1993, written by popular Superromance authors, will highlight our special heroines as they face unusual, challenging and sometimes dangerous situations.

Join us next month for a riveting tale of a wife with her husband's murder on her mind!
#558 ANOTHER WOMAN by Margot Dalton
Available in August wherever Harlequin Superromance novels are sold.

If you missed any of the Women Who Dare titles and would like to order them, send your name, address, zip or postal code along with a check or money order for $3.39 for #533, #537, #541, #545 and #549, or $3.50 for #553 and #554, for each book ordered (do not send cash), plus 75¢ ($1.00 in Canada) for postage and handling, payable to Harlequin Reader Service, to:

In the U.S.
3010 Walden Avenue
P.O. Box 1325
Buffalo, NY 14269-1325

In Canada
P.O. Box 609
Fort Erie, Ontario
L2A 5X3

Please specify book title(s) with your order.
Canadian residents add applicable federal and provincial taxes.

**Collect letters.
See previous page
for details.**

WWD-AGL